AF234813

A Smart Girl's Guide to Second Chances

ALSO BY STEPH VIZARD

The Love Contract

A Smart Girl's Guide to Second Chances

STEPH VIZARD

An Aria Book

First published in Australia in 2025 by HarperCollins Publishers,
Australia Pty Limited

This edition published in the UK in 2026 by Head of Zeus,
part of Bloomsbury Publishing Plc

Copyright © Steph Vizard, 2025

The moral right of Steph Vizard to be identified
as the author of this work has been asserted in accordance with
the Copyright, Designs and Patents Act of 1988.

All rights reserved. No part of this publication may be: i) reproduced or
transmitted in any form, electronic or mechanical, including photocopying,
recording or by means of any information storage or retrieval system without
prior permission in writing from the publishers; or ii) used or reproduced in
any way for the training, development or operation of artificial intelligence (AI)
technologies, including generative AI technologies. The rights holders expressly
reserve this publication from the text and data mining exception as per Article
4(3) of the Digital Single Market Directive (EU) 2019/790.

This is a work of fiction. All characters, organizations, and events
portrayed in this novel are either products of the author's
imagination or are used fictitiously.

9 7 5 3 1 2 4 6 8

A catalogue record for this book is available from the British Library.

ISBN (PB): 9781035925988; ISBN (ePub): 9781035925995

Cover design: Gemma Gorton

Printed and bound in Great Britain by Clays Ltd, Elcograf S.p.A.

Bloomsbury Publishing Plc
50 Bedford Square, London, WC1B 3DP, UK
Bloomsbury Publishing Ireland Limited,
29 Earlsfort Terrace, Dublin 2, D02 AY28, Ireland

HEAD OF ZEUS LTD
5–8 Hardwick Street
London, EC1R 4RG

To find out more about our authors and books
visit www.headofzeus.com
For product safety related questions contact productsafety@bloomsbury.com

To Mum, Dad and Teddy

Prologue

'Love is dangerous,' I said as I attempted to hit a red ball with a wooden mallet through a small white hoop. 'That's the key takeaway from this morning's lecture.'

'Was *that* the professor's thesis?' Alex asked as he watched my ball fly off in the wrong direction. He grinned wolfishly. 'You're going to have to argue your case.'

With a few long strides Alex walked over to his blue ball and carefully lined up his mallet. I could practically see the cogs in his brain whirring as he did some complex calculations involving angles and pressure. I waited to make my first argument. I knew that when he was hyper-focused, the world around him no longer existed. He swung the mallet deftly, his face still creased in concentration, and the ball passed cleanly through the hoop.

Over the past two weeks, Alex and I had developed a routine. We'd roll out of whichever single bed we'd spent the night in, walk to the Oxford Examination Schools and play a game called 'Lecture Lottery' – we'd pick an interesting-sounding lecture and sneak in. Then in the afternoon we'd choose an activity from our 'Salad Days List' and tick it off while we spent hours sparring about what we'd learned that morning. I knew that voluntarily attending random lectures would be most people's idea of hell, but it was the most fun I'd ever had in my life.

That morning we'd crashed a neuroscience lecture – one where a world-class professor with a blunt bob, high-pitched voice and fierce intellect had explained what happened to the brain when a person fell in love. I'd found it revelatory. Now, we were losing our croquet virginity on a perfectly manicured lawn in Alex's college.

'Challenge accepted,' I said. 'Firstly, love is dangerous because when you fall in love your brain shuts down your critical-thinking synapses. Which means that you can't see anything negative about the person you've fallen for.'

Alex, who was kneeling beside his ball as he worked out his next shot, looked up with interest. His eyes, which were the same aquamarine as an English summer sky, met mine. The gentle sun had already turned his skin the same golden colour as the ancient buildings that rose up around us. My stomach did a flip. How was it fair that this Australian guy had the brain of Good Will Hunting as well as the body of a Hemsworth?

I took another swing at my ball and it flew into the garden bed. I glanced around to make sure that none of the college gardeners had seen me assault their navy and yellow pansies, which matched the college's coat of arms.

'You're getting better,' Alex said and almost looked like he meant it.

'I'm really not,' I replied with a smile as I kicked the ball back onto the grass with my bare foot. 'God, another sport I'm terrible at. I once got a PE report at school that said, "Rebecca is good at putting equipment away."'

Alex burst out laughing. 'I feel like you're building a

more persuasive case for "croquet is dangerous". But I'll play along,' he said. I could tell that his mind was searching through the information it had recently and effortlessly absorbed. 'Love is dangerous because ... it's like a drug. The brain has the same chemical reaction to falling in love as it does to taking heroin or gambling.'

'Amazing comparison. Ten points to Ravenclaw,' I said, and Alex laughed again. 'Can I use your mallet? Maybe I have a dodgy one.'

Our fingers brushed as he offered me the wooden handle. I felt a shot of something move through my body. Something that I wanted to feel again and again. Something addictive.

'My turn,' I said quickly. I hit my ball, which moved forwards by about a centimetre, as I worked up my next point in this verbal essay we were writing together. 'So, when you fall in love your brain makes your body feel like you're under attack. Your palms get sweaty and your heart races ...'

I trailed off as Alex walked across the lawn towards me. He gently rested his fingers on the top of my head. I felt every nerve in my body stand on end.

'It's because your brain sends a signal to' – he moved his fingers down the side of my cheek and then placed them just above my stomach – 'a gland here, that creates a burst of adrenaline, which travels through your blood to ...' His fingers gently moved up the left-hand side of my body then stopped. I rested my hand on his much larger one.

'... the heart,' he finished.

I wondered if he could feel mine pounding beneath my thin, white cotton dress through the tips of his fingers.

A few students, black academic gowns flapping off their shoulders, walked past us. I took a step away from Alex. His mallet slipped out of my damp hand.

He picked it up and confidently whacked his ball. It flew squarely into the stake in the middle of the lawn. He'd won, he'd beaten me.

I swallowed so I could speak. 'In conclusion, what I've learned from an Oxford University professor, who knows more about the head than almost anyone else in the world, is that falling in love is a reckless thing to do.'

This was the first time Alex and I had talked about love since we'd agreed to have a summer fling – seven weeks of fun. Which was now five more weeks of fun. Five more weeks of Trinity term, until I had to say goodbye to him forever.

Chapter 1

NOW

'If you say the C word in front of my wedding dress, you're uninvited,' I said, with a bit more edge to my voice than was strictly appropriate in a shop that self-identified as an 'atelier'.

'I didn't say anything, Rebecca!' Mum protested, all faux innocence. 'But even you've got to admit that your wedding planning has been a bit ... What's another word for "disastrous"? I mean, your photographer got cataracts. Your venue burned down. And now ...' She waved her hands towards me.

I re-examined myself in the ornate gold-rimmed mirror. Apparently the seamstress had been having a perimenopausal day when she'd taken my measurements at the previous fitting. (Mum, a GP specialising in women's health, had asked many hormone-focused follow up questions.)

'Though,' Mum continued, 'if they don't finish rebuilding the venue in time we could always use your dress as the marquee.'

I ignored her, wishing again that Dad was here. He'd generously offered to pay for my dress, so I'd invited him to the final appointment. But he'd had to work. In Dad's absence I'd been very happy to do the fitting on my own, but I'd made the mistake of mentioning it to Mum and next thing I knew, she'd cancelled her afternoon clinic. Of course it was thoughtful that Mum had dropped everything for wedding admin. But Dad wouldn't have made the joke that my fiancé, Matt, and I (plus a handful of our guests) could fit into this iteration of my gown.

'They've apologised a million times and said they can take it in,' I said, feeling the knots in my shoulders tighten. Today I was meant to cross 'Wedding dress' off my list.

I wished that my two best friends, Lily and Stella, had been able to come to the fitting to diffuse Mum's energy. But Lily and Stella both had young kids and I knew that for them just getting to the wedding was going to require a military-style operation. In our thirties, weddings had transfigured from 'bacchanal' to 'logistics'.

'Or,' I continued, 'they've got five weeks to make a new one.' I stepped off the pedestal they'd placed me on to pin in my dress.

'So you don't think the wedding is starting to feel a bit …'

I could see Mum casting around for a synonym for 'cursed'. I cut her off before she could find one. 'Do we have to go over the agreed-upon "Rules of Rebecca and Matt's Wedding" again?' I asked. I didn't wait for her to reply. 'Number one: you'll try to get on with Matt's mum.'

Mum pouted. 'But she's just so … nice!' she said. 'I'm convinced she's secretly a serial killer.'

I suppressed a giggle. Matt's mum was unrelentingly lovely. Jane was the kind of woman who'd drive across town to drop off some windfall lemons from her tree.

'Number two: there will be no mentions of the curse. Because there is no family curse. Curses aren't a real thing.'

'I'm just being silly, darling. And of course, "curse" isn't quite the right word.'

'Exactly,' I said.

'Though it *is* interesting that all the women in our family didn't marry their first fiancé.' Mum counted on her fingers. 'There's Grandma Evelyn, her sister, my cousin — and me.'

When I was a teenager, my grandma had sat me down and told me that it was family lore that all the female members of our family were doomed to never marry our first fiancé. But that wasn't all! No, she went on — our engagements would break off and, in a fit of unbridled passion, we would marry another man instead. And that other man would be all wrong for us.

Some teenage girls got a bat mitzvah or a confirmation service. In our family we got a curse.

'Who believes in curses anyway? Apart from Greek yiayias and people in Disney movies?' I asked.

'Many people believe there are things in the world beyond their understanding. That they aren't in control of *everything*.' She gave me a pointed look.

Before I could reply, a woman emerged from a fitting room wearing an ivory silk dress with a corset top and princess skirt. When her mother, who'd been waiting nervously on the edge of a white suede couch, saw her daughter, her hands flew to her mouth and tears began to stream down her face. Though she tried to speak she was clearly overcome. The bride's lips were now wobbling too.

'Do you love it?' the mother finally managed to get out as she pawed at the mascara that had welled under her eyes.

'I do. It's perfect. I just … know this is the one,' the bride said, her own eyes now glistening. 'This. Is. It. I feel it. It's everything I've dreamed of!'

'Oh, my darling girl!' She threw her still-shaking arms around her daughter. Then, entwined like an emotional DNA strand, they both jigged up and down, joy radiating off them.

Mum and I pretended not to watch, but we had both fallen silent, transfixed.

'You do love *your* dress, don't you?' Mum asked.

I pulled my gaze away from the Gilmore Girls.

'Of course they'll alter it. But you love it, right? Because you're meant to wear something that makes you feel like the best version of you on your wedding day, not just something that … you think will do the job. You can't be sensible about your wedding dress – you have to fall madly in love with it,' Mum said, her voice laden with meaning, as she hitched up one of the too-long silk straps that had fallen off my shoulder.

'Did you love your wedding dresses?' I asked. Mum had married Dad in an eighties meringue that would have done Princess Di proud. Then she'd married her second husband, Hamish, at a simple town hall ceremony – a move that was very out of character for a woman who felt the urge to celebrate everything. I hadn't been there but had seen the photos. Mum, whose favourite colour was the rainbow, had worn a simple duck-egg-blue shift dress.

'This isn't about me, darling,' Mum said. 'All I'm saying is that it's never too late to change your mind.'

'This dress ticks everything on my list. One, I can wear a proper bra under it; two, I won't have to go on a juice cleanse to fit into it; and three, I'll be able to sit down.'

'I'm not sure that happiness is as simple as ticking off everything on a list,' she said.

I took a deep yin-yoga breath.

'I am happy, Mum. The dress is great. And in five weeks, I'm going to marry Matt in it. Well, in a version of it that doesn't make me look like an "after" shot in an ad for Ozempic,' I said, as I began to swish towards the dressing room to get changed back into my navy suit.

'Then I'll be the one who breaks the family curse,' I added under my breath. In just over a month, I was marrying my first (and last) fiancé. There were going to be no broken engagements.

'Well, I'm glad you're in love with the dress!' Mum called after me as I yanked the coral velvet curtains shut, wishing my bridal boutique energy was more elegant, chic lady than petulant teenager.

As I shimmied back into my silk camisole and suit skirt, I checked my phone and smiled when I saw that Matt had messaged.

Ready to woo celebrant number two?

Love you.

I made a mental note not to mention to Mum that our original wedding celebrant had cancelled on us.

That evening Matt and I met in Northcote for an appointment with Belinda, our second-choice celebrant. She'd asked us to meet her in a wine bar, which was filled with the type of people who own rescued greyhounds, and clearly doubled as her office.

'Now, I only agree to marry couples when I feel confident about the strength of their relationship,' Belinda said. 'I'm not one of those celebrants who will marry just *anyone*.'

I caught Matt's eyes and swallowed a smile.

'If we decide we want to work together, I like to start each ceremony by telling the guests your love story,' Belinda continued as she scrutinised us. 'So perhaps you could tell me how you met?' She ran her slightly nervy hand through her long, grey hair.

We nodded respectfully; this was Belinda's test.

When we'd set out to book a celebrant, the person who would bind us for life, we'd agreed we wanted someone without a trace of insipidity and ideally with a sense of humour. Now, with just weeks to go until our ceremony, the main quality we were looking for was availability. After many frantic phone calls, we'd found Belinda, who, despite having the aura of someone who'd been repeatedly disappointed by love, met this brief.

The clock was ticking. The law required that our Notice of Intended Marriage be lodged at least a month before our wedding date. And to complete this official document we needed a celebrant. If we didn't submit it soon, we wouldn't be able to get legally married at our wedding ceremony. We needed Belinda more than she needed us.

'We really respect that position,' I said with the pacifying smile that I used when clients made outrageous demands.

I looked at Matt to get the ball rolling. He was a great storyteller. He wasn't gregarious, but because of his gentle yet sharp wit he would find himself holding court at any event we ever attended. And telling stories was his job – he was head of communications for a giant wine company. Plus, older women loved Matt – I think it was the winning combination of the perennial twinkle in his eyes, broad shoulders and a genuine interest in other people.

Matt took a sip of his drink – a blush-pink cocktail. One of Matt's special skills was that no matter what cocktail he ordered at any bar, it turned up in a shade of pink (and was invariably put in front of me). But whether his drink was fuchsia or baby pink he wasn't bothered – he knew what he liked and didn't care what anyone thought. He placed his highball glass back on the table.

'When we met, we were both working in the same building in the city, one that has faux-Grecian columns that hold up the fragile egos of the people who work inside,' Matt began in his typically self-deprecating style, with an easy smile at Belinda. 'Next to the building is a food court, which has a cinema in it. And cinemas are my favourite places in the world. So sometimes when I need to focus at work, I take my laptop and buy a ticket to whatever cinema is empty in the middle of the day. Then I set up in the back row, dim my screen and quietly work away.'

Belinda nodded. Matt had her hooked. I exhaled.

'So, one day I was working in the back row. And I was the only person there until, about twenty minutes into this terrible French film, a woman walked in. She went straight to the front row and fell asleep.'

'In my defence,' I interjected, 'I'd worked through the night but didn't have time to go home before a client presentation. Sometimes when I need a few hours' sleep I go down to the cinema to have a cat nap before I go back to the office.'

Belinda's forehead creased. Evidently exhaustion from overwork didn't have a place in her version of a fairy-tale romance.

'I was meant to be writing an important speech for our CEO,' Matt continued. 'That's the whole reason I was there. But I couldn't focus. All I could think about was the glimpse I'd had of this beautiful woman.'

Belinda's expression softened. Matt turned towards me and smiled. I felt my cheeks warm. Would his smile, the one that lit up the golden specks in his deep-brown eyes and made a small crinkle at the top of his left cheek, always have this effect on me?

'I felt a gentle tap on my shoulder,' I said, picking up the story. 'The movie had finished, even the credits, and the house lights had come on, but I was so tired I'd kept sleeping. A man was standing over me, holding a cup of coffee. That was the first time I saw Matt – a handsome, thoughtful angel, bearing caffeine. If he hadn't woken me up, I would have missed my presentation.'

Matt went on: 'We walked back to our building's lobby together, talking the whole way. And not only was she beautiful, she was smart and funny too. I asked her out, gave her my number. And that was it.'

Had it been that simple for Matt? Had he just seen me – panda rings under my eyes after working for ten days straight, scuffed ballet flats kicked off under the cinema seat, no doubt some dribble – and known I was the one? Or was he such a natural raconteur that he'd turned us into a story?

I watched Belinda closely to see if we'd cleared her hurdle. Another couple, who I assumed were Belinda's next appointment, already hovered awkwardly nearby. They were younger than us, in their late twenties I'd guessed, but looked like they'd been together forever. He held her bag, as she offered him a taste of her white wine, though I could tell they were watching us too. It was a bit like that on the wedding circuit, as you ran into other couples at venue viewings and stationery shops – a performative show of togetherness and adoration was expected.

I leaned into Matt and he put his arm around me. I took a deep breath and felt heady for a moment. How did he always still smell good after a full day's work – an intoxicating mix of the spices and citrus in his aftershave (a present he'd been genuinely happy to receive for his birthday), the wool wash he used on his cloud-soft jumpers and original–flavoured Fisherman's Friends?

Belinda rummaged in her enormous cotton tote and pulled out a stack of documents.

'Over the next week I'll need you to fill out the official paperwork, and I also require my couples to complete a detailed questionnaire to help me write my script,' she said as she handed the forms to Matt.

I exhaled a sigh of relief. We were on! One wedding crisis averted, just the rest of them to solve.

Chapter 2

We finally made it home after battling peak-hour traffic in my old Mazda, arriving at the same time as our takeaway. While Matt, who'd turned over-ordering into an art form, pulled off plastic lid after plastic lid, I opened the package that had been waiting next to the food on our doorstep.

'Our cake toppers have finally arrived!' Matt's mum had offered to make our wedding cake and had insisted that no multi-tiered fruitcake could be complete without bride and groom figurines. I'd decided that this wasn't the hill (or top tier) to die on, so had dutifully ordered custom porcelain figurines.

I lifted out the bride topper. There she was – a brunette in a white dress radiating serenity. I placed her next to the pad thai then reached for the groom. My heart sank. The bottom of the box was filled with shards of china. The figurine didn't have a head.

'What do you think of the likeness?' I asked, holding it up to Matt. He looked up from the coconut rice he was spooning into two bowls.

Before he could reply, I said, 'Mum invoked the curse today.'

'So now would not be a great time to tell you that the venue just emailed to say that they have a new menu, and we need to do another round of food tasting?'

'Seriously? But we've already had the menus printed!' I could feel my heart begin to race as my anxiety ratcheted up.

'Yeah, but we knew we had to redo those anyway,' Matt said gently. The first lot of menus had arrived, announcing that we were serving our guests 'dick liver parfait' as one of the entrees. 'And just ignore Helena when she brings up the curse thing. I think she's only trying to make a joke.'

'But even you have to admit that pretty much *everything* has gone wrong. I mean I'd show you a picture of my trainwreck of a dress but it's … actually, screw superstitions. Maybe doing something that's meant to be bad luck will turn our fortunes around.'

I pulled out my phone and opened the picture Mum had begrudgingly taken at the fitting so I could send it to Dad. I turned the screen towards Matt.

'It's …' He paused for a moment, and I could tell he was digging deep for something upbeat to say. We caught each other's eyes and then both burst out laughing.

'I know!' I managed to squeak out between guffaws. Matt had to put down the tub of red curry he was holding because his eyes had filled with tears.

'Our photographer is now legally blind!' Matt said.

'Our venue doesn't have a roof!' I added, ribs aching.

'Though at the end of the day all that really matters is that we're a photogenic couple,' Matt said, holding up the decapitated figurine next to my phone, which was still displaying the photo of me wearing what looked like a voluminous toga at a student party. We both burst out laughing again.

'Hey, come here,' he said. He pulled me onto the couch next to him and wrapped his strong arms around me. He began to slowly run his fingers up and down my back. I felt both the hysteria and the anxiety begin to recede.

Matt looked straight into my eyes. 'Okay, our wedding is almost certainly going to be a total unmitigated disaster. It'll probably be the Fyre Festival of weddings,' he said. 'But I'm absolutely sure about one thing: it's going to happen and be the best day of our lives. Because it's the day we'll be getting married. It's us. And in the end, that's all that matters.'

'Exactly, that's all I want too,' I said and exhaled. In Matt's embrace it felt like the couch was the entire universe, where nothing bad could happen, and the only noise in the world was Matt's low, calm voice.

'And don't worry about the toppers or setting up the food tasting or the menus. Don't think about them again. They're on my list,' he said. 'I've got it under control.'

'That's an incredibly sexy thing to say,' I said, smiling. His fingers moved down to my thigh where my work skirt met my bare skin. I shivered as I leaned into him.

'I've got it under control,' he repeated, but this time more slowly, his eyes twinkling.

Suddenly I forgot about my low blood sugar and the food on the table. I forgot about our imploding wedding and its endless to-do list.

Mum was totally wrong. We weren't cursed. Every wedding had its hiccups. Sure, maybe we'd had more than the mean. But we were sorting them out – me and Matt – together as a team, as a couple.

My phone pinged and I groaned in a very unsexy way. It was Miranda, my mentor and a senior partner at Stern & Co, the management consultancy firm I worked for.

Good news! You're on my new case. Kicks off tomorrow!

In our business, client teams were often put together at the last minute after the staffing manager triangulated factors like who was available, who had the necessary expertise and who would rather impale themselves than work together.

Client a giant medical company.

Medical? I quickly tapped back, my empty stomach tightening.

I know you'd asked not to work in this sector, but it's a one-off. Adrian and Lucas also on team. I'll email client details / project scope now!

'I've been staffed on a project,' I told Matt. 'The next few weeks will be … a lot.'

'Then tonight should definitely be a last hurrah,' Matt said, his voice still husky.

My phone pinged again as Miranda's email, the one with the background materials on the client, project team and industry, hit my inbox. My thumb automatically moved to open it, but I stopped myself. I dropped my phone on the floor and then turned back to Matt. I stared at his handsome face, my favourite one in the world, then began to unbutton his shirt.

I arrived at work the following morning with my game face on – I couldn't be distracted by any more wedding disasters or non-PG-rated moments with my fiancé. The first few weeks of any project always sat somewhere on the intensity spectrum between 'nervous breakdown' and 'soul destroying'.

'Consultant' was a job title that meant nothing to anyone. Basically, our job was to go into an enormous company and spend a few weeks or months solving the specific problem they'd given us. I'd usually enjoy throwing myself headfirst into a new case, though I'd hoped that this one might be a cruiser project than normal to give me a bit of breathing room in the lead-up to the wedding. At least at this stage my only job was to listen and gather information.

I clacked my way across the marble lobby, which smelled like a Le Labo store, and rode the eerily silent lift to the top of the building. I picked up a temporary company pass from the reception desk, which looked hobbit-sized under the company's enormous name, *ATG*. Even the company's motto, 'Healthcare for the Future', was gargantuan. It wasn't surprising – this company was a global behemoth, a national success story. It was also part of an industry I had no desire to learn about.

'They're waiting for you in "Passion",' the glossy receptionist informed me with a warm smile.

'Sorry?' I asked, confused.

'All our meeting rooms are named after the company's values. It's next to "Integrity Always".'

'Ah, thanks,' I said, trying to conceal any trace of judgement from my face. I had no strong feelings about naming meeting rooms. On my last project I'd spent most of my time in a room called 'Collins Street' (which overlooked Bourke Street). But I did take umbrage with passion as a corporate North Star. Passionate people lacked moderation, rational thought, balance, perspective. These qualities were the stuff that successful businesses were made of.

I wove my way through an open-plan office until I found a room with a plaque embossed with *Passion*.

I began to open the door then paused. There was someone already in the room. A tall man with a mane of blond hair, and wearing a chambray shirt, was bent over the long conference table, furiously scribbling on a piece of paper. I spied the Stern & Co banana-yellow logo in the top left-hand corner of the page.

I knocked softly. The man, evidently annoyed at being interrupted, looked up with a frown. Two bright blue eyes stared at me. I instinctively took a step back and ran my hands down my white silk shirt.

Because sitting at the conference table, in the meeting room I was meant to be in, was Alex Lawson – the only man on earth I truly never wanted to see again.

Chapter 3

Were my eyes playing tricks on me? Had I forgotten to put my contacts in? Had my long black been spiked?

Over the years, I'd occasionally thought I'd seen him. I would be in a cafe and sitting in the corner would be a tall man with fair hair. My heart would begin to thud and my palms would become sticky. But then the man I was staring at would turn his head slightly and I'd realise that it wasn't Alex, that he looked nothing like him. My mind would stop racing and then I'd go back to not thinking about Oxford at all.

'Rebecca.' He said my name in the same deep, slightly gravelly voice I remembered.

'Alex?' I hadn't meant for it to be a question. But how could it not be? Because right then I had nothing but questions. Why was Alex Lawson in Melbourne? Why was he attending the same meeting as me? When had he started wearing shirts with collars?

'Of all the meeting rooms in all the cities in the world,' he said as he stood up. He still looked the same, just sharper. His jawline was stronger, the last traces of the softness of youth gone, his hair looked like it had seen a hairdresser recently, and while his shirt was rumpled and had clearly never been introduced to an iron, it was still more structured than anything he'd voluntarily worn during daylight hours when I'd known him.

My cheeks began to burn. Suddenly I felt like I was in my twenties again. Except not in the Taylor Swift–song sense: that was the good, fun, upbeat version. I was the girl who hadn't yet learned how to blow-wave her hair or that bold jewel colours made her look washed out, and could still not confidently wear heels without feeling like a young girl playing dress-ups. All the armour I'd built as I'd grown up, the tailored clothes in natural fibres and true winter shades, a phone in each hand, had melted away.

'What are you doing here?' I asked, because it was now the only question looping around my brain.

'I work here,' he replied.

'You work here?' I echoed.

'No, I like breaking into office buildings and sitting in meeting rooms wearing company-branded lanyards for fun,' he replied. He'd never had any tolerance for people who took more time to understand something than he did. Which was everyone.

Since we'd broken up, I'd never googled him, not once. I'd never attempted to stalk him on Instagram or connect with him on LinkedIn, and I'd been silently proud of this. I knew people who followed their exes, or the new partners of their exes, on fake accounts. I'd laugh when they confessed this, but secretly felt like I'd taken the higher ground. How were you meant to move on if you were still absorbed by the lives of people from your past? Wasn't it disloyal to current partners if you still cared, even a bit, about flings from yesteryear?

I was the fool. I hadn't kept tabs, which meant that I had no idea what he'd been up to for the previous nine years. Had he been in my city the whole time?

'Ah, I've found "Passion".' We were interrupted by a familiar voice behind us.

No, you've found 'Awkward' or 'Discombobulated' or the 'Seventh Circle of Hell', I silently re-christened the meeting room.

After many years of working together I knew that the brightness of Miranda's outfit was a litmus test for her levels of energy and enthusiasm for a project. Today she was in yellow: she was clearly fired up about this case. She offered her hand to Alex and gave it a vigorous shake.

'Miranda Buchanan.'

'Alex Lawson,' he replied, looking slightly bemused by Miranda's high-octane aura.

'Ah, the great man himself!' Miranda exclaimed. She put her hands together and dipped her head to him. 'We feel honoured to be trusted with your very important work.'

His ego is big enough! It doesn't need any *pumping up*, I wanted to shout. Instead, I gazed at a small stain on the grey carpet.

'And I see you've already met Rebecca,' Miranda said.

I reluctantly looked up from the floor and met his eyes.

'We've met,' he said in a neutral voice. I felt my throat tighten. He could still read me.

'Rebecca is one of our superstars,' Miranda said. 'She'll be your point of contact – the person you can go to if you need *anything* at all. Nothing is too big or small for her to care about.'

My heart sank. Clearly Alex was going to be heavily involved in this project.

A stream of people started converging in the meeting room, including Adrian and Lucas, who I recognised from the office, and others with ATG lanyards like the one Alex was indeed wearing. I checked my watch: it was showtime.

Alex opened the meeting with an introductory presentation. He spoke without slides, which would have made anyone from Stern & Co feel naked. I quickly understood why my firm had been engaged by this medical mega-company: ATG had recently acquired Alex's company, and we'd been hired to advise ATG on a strategy to market the technology they owned but he'd created.

He spoke with the gravitas and experience of a university professor (it turned out he'd actually been a professor before he founded his company) as he gave us the crib-notes version of his research.

I realised, as I watched Alex hold his audience's attention, that I understood more than I'd expected. Everything he'd told me about the embryonic stages of his research that summer nine years ago had stuck in the far recesses of my mind like Blu Tack on a teenager's bedroom walls.

Speaking in a laconic drawl, with only a hint of condescension, he was effortlessly interesting. No one had even surreptitiously turned over their phone since he'd stood up. I knew what held the room's attention: his unbridled enthusiasm for his work was as infectious as the flu, as I well knew – I'd gone down hard and fast before.

While my heart rate still hadn't returned to a normal level, he didn't seem put out by my presence at all. But that had always been his superpower, his ability to be hyper-focused when it came to his work.

I slowly turned over my phone, hiding it with my Moleskine notebook, and typed his name into Google. I clicked the first link, then the second and third and skim-read, while trying to look like I was paying attention.

I pulled together a timeline in my mind based on the few data points I'd gathered. He'd been in Boston pretty much since we'd last seen each other, except for a stint at a university in Switzerland. He'd only been working for ATG for a few months. Somehow this made me feel better – that our orbits hadn't been overlapping for years, that he'd been safely tucked away on the other side of the world.

'Rebecca?'

I jerked my head up from my phone. I'd missed the end of Alex's presentation and Miranda, a vision in citrus, was staring at me expectantly. The wattage of her smile flickered as she clocked that I hadn't been paying attention. My stomach did a flip. Partners often called on us, with no notice, to say something insightful and pithy in front of clients.

I prided myself on my comprehensive notetaking, but as I glanced down at my random scribbles (*Heart disease – good to diagnose* and *Why is he here?*) I realised that it wasn't my best minute-taking work.

'I think this technology will play a crucial role in the transformation of … health,' I ad-libbed. Miranda's eyes narrowed as Alex's lips curled up.

'Powerful words, Rebecca. And it would be great if you could introduce yourself, which is what we're going around the table doing …'

I blurted out my name, cheeks burning with embarrassment. I felt a rush of animosity towards Alex.

The room's attention turned to Lucas, but Alex's eyes stayed on me for a moment longer. And I knew, deep in my gut, that there was only one sensible way forwards. Alex and I could not work together.

After finishing introductions, we shuffled out of the meeting room. Miranda offered to take our team out for a coffee. I'd never worked on a case with Adrian and Lucas, the juniors who'd be doing the heavy lifting, so team building – which mainly manifested in the form of endless (expensed) coffees, dinners and organised 'fun' – was a priority in the first few days. I knew I should go, earn some 'team spirit' brownie points from Miranda. But, instead, I pretended I had something urgent to do. Because there was something urgent I *had* to do.

I waited for a few minutes, until I was sure the team would be safely in a lift, then did a slow loop of the floor until I found the nameplate I was looking for. He saw me through the internal windows before I had a chance to knock or flee.

I opened the door. 'Can I come in?' I asked, in a tone that I hoped was civil.

'Sure,' Alex replied from his chair. His office was sparse – one shelf of an otherwise empty bookcase was filled with what looked like well-thumbed textbooks, a miniature basketball hoop had been suctioned to a bare grey wall and a plastic tray on his desk was overflowing with paper.

I shut the door behind me. I spotted the same battered, black backpack Alex had used at Oxford, sitting on the only spare chair in the room. He didn't offer to move it.

This is not a good idea, was the opening line I'd planned to say as I stormed into his office.

'You weren't surprised to see me today,' I said instead.

'Unlike you, I did my homework,' he said pointedly, picking up a document from the exploding tray. 'Your standards have slipped.' He smirked as he passed the papers to me.

I stared at the back page of the project implementation plan and there we were – the whole project team, including me and Alex, with names, job titles and headshots. I mentally added getting a new, far more flattering photo to my list.

I looked back up at Alex and bristled. But I couldn't throw my company under the bus and say that I'd been staffed on the project at the last minute, or that I'd prioritised date night with Matt over reading the project brief.

'Working together is not a good idea,' I said.

'We're both adults,' he replied, in an irritatingly reasonable voice. He picked up a mini basketball, which had been buried beneath a notebook. He lobbed it towards the basket and it dropped straight through the hoop and bounced on the floor. Alex stood up and caught it.

'You're playing with a toy,' I replied, unable to stem the derision in my voice. 'Look. We ended … not well. We both know there's going to be weird energy between us if we work together.' *Because you're the only person on the planet I never wanted to see again.* 'So …'

'You'd like me to go away?' He reached my point before I had to make it.

'Umm … yes,' I said. 'Please.'

He threw the basketball into the hoop again. Before it could bounce on the floor I stepped forwards and caught it. 'There must be *someone* else in this enormous multinational company that can run this project,' I said.

'No one else has as much skin in the game. If I can help them to "optimise the value of the company's newest asset" over the next few months,' he said, repeating a phrase Miranda had used in our meeting, 'the asset being the diagnostic tool created using my research, then they'll offer me a new contract to fund the next stage of my work. Which I've dedicated my life to.'

'Aren't universities all over the world falling over themselves to throw money at the work of the great Dr Alexander Lawson?' I asked.

'It's the great Associate Professor Alexander Lawson now. And yes,' he said, without a trace of humility. 'But universities are too slow. I'm sick of waiting for grants and writing applications and dealing with a thousand layers of bureaucracy. I need to move quickly. I want the tech to be out there in hospitals, making an impact, saving lives.'

'And of all the companies in all the world, you had to sell your life's research to one headquartered in Melbourne?'

'Someone once told me it was a beautiful city,' he said.

I felt my heart begin to race again. Was he actually here because of me?

'And they happen to be one of the biggest players in the world,' he continued. 'Though the fact that they're Australian *was* the reason I went with them. Patriotism and all. Also, I've had enough of freezing to death during winters. I'm sick of hostile environments.'

There was a cheeky glint in his eye. He was trying to bait me again.

'So there's no chance you'll recuse yourself from this project and let someone else step up to the plate?' I asked as evenly as I could.

'None,' he said. 'Not when there's a research and development pot of gold up for grabs.'

'Fine,' I said. '*I'll* be the sensible one. *I'll* request a transfer to another project.' I threw the orange ball back to him.

'The sensible one? You're going to request a transfer on the grounds you don't want to work with your university ex?' he asked, looking amused. He made it sound so silly, though of course he would. Because then he didn't have to take responsibility for breaking us up, for breaking my heart, for hurting me.

'Of course not,' I said. 'I'll say ... I want more exposure to the heavy industrials sector.'

'What a fascinating life you lead,' he said.

'*You* don't get to minimise the life I've chosen anymore,' I said. A rush of pure irritation, anger even, more than I had felt for years, worked its way through my body.

He threw the ball over my head. It went straight through the net again. He stepped forward, caught it on the bounce then sat down and swivelled his chair towards one of the enormous floor-to-ceiling windows that made up two sides of his office.

'We seem destined to only meet in places with spectacular views,' he said, ignoring me.

'Destiny is just a way for humans to try to make sense of their unconscious thoughts and feelings,' I replied, before I could help myself. *Curses too*, I added silently.

'Discuss,' he said. It had been an in-joke between us, shorthand for 'I don't agree with you – prove me wrong'. I didn't smile, though I did turn towards the window.

It was a gorgeous view – a sweeping one of the best parts of the city. His office overlooked the manicured green gardens of Kings Domain and, beyond them, the bay, which on this perfect midsummer day was the same sparkling blue as his eyes.

He turned back to face me. Had his teeth become whiter in America or did his summer tan just make them gleam more brightly? And had his strong nose always had a tiny kink at the end, like it had been broken, transforming his perfectly symmetrical face into one filled with character, as if he was always on the cusp of telling a wry joke. For the first time all morning he smiled warmly, and it was still as disarming as the first time I saw him.

Chapter 4

THEN

I sat on the roof of my friend Lily's college swigging champagne – well, incredibly cheap, soapy-tasting cava – from a bottle as I watched the sun set over Oxford's dreaming spires. Earlier that day I'd got the call, the one I'd been working towards for the last five years. In a world where jobs were being slashed and entry-level roles were virtually non-existent, I'd managed to snag a rare grad job. All the long hours in the library, the endless 'group' assignments I'd done single-handedly, the countless interviews in my one suit, answering bizarre questions ('How many cats are there in Canada?'), university holidays jammed with internships – they'd all paid off. I waited for a sense of satisfaction or pride or fulfilment to wash over me.

'Are you … okay?' A deep, concerned voice with an Australian accent spoke from somewhere behind me. I spun around and saw a very tall guy walking towards me, with almost exaggerated slowness, down the sloped roof.

'Yeah, I'm fine. I'm … celebrating,' I replied, holding up my bottle.

Visible relief washed over his face. 'Great. I just thought, maybe, you were going to …'

'Oh, no, sorry. The opposite,' I said.

'It's just you looked so sad … and you're on a roof. I've never seen anyone else up here before,' he said. He exhaled and I realised I'd frightened him. 'God, I thought I was about to see the opening of an *Inspector Morse* episode play out in real life.'

'I'm happy. I told you, I'm celebrating,' I said. Though actually I wondered if I *had* looked a bit … morose. 'Though if this was the opening of an *Inspector Morse* episode and I'd … *you know* … you would be the prime suspect.'

'Yeah,' he replied. 'But by the end of the episode they would have worked out that it wasn't me. Your death would have been caused by some strange cult led by a professor who egged on some impressionable students.'

'And the key to the mystery would be hidden in a crossword puzzle. In Greek,' I said.

He laughed. 'I don't think I've met anyone else from our generation who's watched *Inspector Morse*,' he said.

'My grandma Evelyn had a crush on him. We watched it together,' I said. 'You?'

'My mum loved it,' he replied. I noted his use of the past tense but didn't say anything – I got the sense he'd already given away more than he normally would. 'Also, I used to want to be a detective when I grew up.'

'What changed?' I asked.

'I found a new mystery to solve,' he replied with a nonchalant shrug he almost pulled off. 'What did you want to be when you grew up?'

'A ballerina,' I lied.

'So why are you sad on a roof?' he asked. Two piercing blue eyes stared down at me.

'I already said I'm not sad. Why are *you* up here?' I knew I sounded defensive, but I felt exposed. He was really looking at me. And I had the strangest feeling that he could ... read me.

'I like to eat breakfast up here,' he replied, and I now noticed that he was holding a bowl and a spoon.

'Breakfast?' The sun had almost set – the sky was now a darkening swirl of deep pinks and purples over the college walls and towers.

'I have a big deadline, and I often work through the night. I don't like to be interrupted and life's too short to sleep,' he said. He sat down on the grey slate roof, not exactly next to me but close enough that we could easily talk.

'What are you celebrating?' he asked.

'I got a job today,' I said.

'What job?' he asked.

'I'm going to be a management consultant,' I said. I waited for him to be impressed.

'Solving the world's problems one spreadsheet at a time,' he replied, judgement dripping from his voice.

'I think the correct reply is "congratulations",' I said, surprised at myself for saying exactly what I meant. Maybe it was the cava? 'What lofty, noble career are you working towards?'

'I'm going to cure heart disease,' he said. His tone was matter of fact, and there was no arrogance or pride in his voice.

I burst out laughing. 'God, this university is so ridiculous. No one just wants a job, they want a *calling*. Everyone is going to change the world,' I said, feeling uncharacteristically bold.

There was a clang and then another and another, and the roof vibrated lightly. The enormous bells in the clocktower, a few metres from us, pealed and then settled into a rhythm of deep booms that announced that it was now eight o'clock.

We used the enforced silence to surreptitiously check each other out. He looked like he'd just rolled out of bed. He was wearing a crumpled T-shirt and cotton pyjama shorts, and his blond hair stood on end.

As he crunched on a spoonful of cereal, I couldn't help but smile. This situation was bizarre. He grinned back and for the first time I noticed he was, well, gorgeous. His blue eyes were framed by dark lashes, his skin had already picked up a golden sheen despite it still being spring and he had a disarmingly cheeky smile.

I could tell he was, between bites, looking at me too. It was a strange feeling because I wasn't used to being looked at. I'd spent my whole life surrounded by beautiful women. Their hair was blonde or titian and I was a middling brunette, they were vivacious and I was reserved, they were well dressed and I … wasn't. I looked down at my usual uniform of jeans and a navy hoodie.

'So why did you come here if you didn't want to change the world?' he asked after the final peal echoed into the night. He turned to me, looking interested in my reply.

'Because it was as far away as possible from Melbourne.' I began to reel off the checklist I'd put together when organising my exchange. 'My friend was already studying here, so I knew there'd be a familiar face on campus. And it's the most prestigious place I could be a visiting student – good for the CV.'

'I guess those *are* reasons,' he said, unimpressed. He stared at me intently. I'd never met anyone like him. He'd just woken up yet seemed to thrum with a sort of raw energy.

'I better go,' I said, suddenly feeling a bit woozy. Maybe I'd had too much to drink on an empty stomach. 'It's almost dark, my bottle's empty. And you've got to fix broken hearts.'

He laughed, a deep, almost husky one. 'Are you going to keep celebrating?' he asked.

'No,' I said. 'I've been working so hard for so long that I can't really remember how to have fun.'

This time he didn't smile at my answer. He was looking at me again, as if he was trying to solve an equation and I was 'x'.

And because I'd said I was going, I left him alone with his cereal on the almost-dark roof. Except as I carefully crawled through Lily's half-open bedroom window, I realised that I hadn't wanted to leave.

Chapter 5

NOW

After I escaped Alex's office, I convinced Miranda's EA (it helped that I regularly brought in treats from TikTok-approved bakeries) to squeeze me in for a meeting that afternoon. In the name of professionalism, I'd called our appointment 'Catch up' rather than '*HELP – I need to get the hell off the project I've been staffed on!!!*'

Instead of doing any actual work, I'd spent the day working up a speech. I was going to make a compelling case for a transfer. People kicked up a fuss about the type of projects they were assigned to all the time, whereas I'd learned the hard way, early on in my career, that being demanding didn't always end well.

This did mean that I'd been sent to some true holes to do the least sexy type of work and was often thrown on to cases in desperate need of staff. But I'd never complained, not once. Even when I'd been sent to Far North Queensland in the middle of summer to work out the most efficient way to slaughter wild pigs (the answer: don't).

'Rebecca!' Miranda looked up from her laptop with a warm smile when I knocked on her office door. She was the partner who'd mentored me since I joined Stern & Co. If other people had a work wife, I had a work mum – someone to show me what the road ahead should look like. She'd been one of the last people standing on the dance floor at our engagement party, and I'd made *Frozen*-themed cake pops for her youngest daughter's last birthday.

But even after almost a decade, I still found her slightly terrifying. She was many things that I found particularly intimidating in a person: vegan, outdoorsy and naturally blonde. I'd once, at the end of a company Christmas party (featuring unlimited negronis), asked her if there was anything she couldn't do. She'd thought for a moment before replying, 'Relax.'

'I'm so glad you booked in this time. I needed to have a chat with you.'

My stomach froze. A 'chat' with a partner wasn't necessarily a good sign. In fact, it almost never was. Often it was the managing partners, like Miranda, who were tasked with 'difficult' conversations.

'You're going to be up for early promotion in the next round,' Miranda said, with a proud smile.

I stared at her for a moment, absorbing the news. This meant that in a few weeks all the partners would gather, a slide with my name, face and performance ratings would be beamed onto a screen, and they'd collectively decide whether I was ready to be promoted to principal, the step before partner.

But I also knew that the chance for early promotion was a double-edged sword. On the one hand, it was a vote of confidence. On the other, unlike in most businesses, if I didn't make the grade, I wouldn't get another try in a few months. In our industry it was 'up or out'. If I didn't get across the line, I knew that it was only a matter of time before someone from HR would quite strongly suggest that it might be time to start looking for a new job.

'Why?' I couldn't help but ask the only question on my mind.

'First and foremost, you're good at the job,' Miranda said. Then she sighed, an uncharacteristically weary one. 'And also, for your ears only, the firm is struggling to meet its gender target for senior roles. There's been a call-out to push more women forwards for promotions.'

I tried to keep my expression neutral but felt a stab of disappointment.

'You've got to play the hand you're dealt. Life's a series of asymmetric transactions. You've got to jump when the odds are in your favour,' Miranda said, giving me one of her pep talks, which were invariably distilled wisdom from bestselling business books, her daughter's YA novels and lived experience. Evidently, I'd not done a good enough job of hiding the disappointment on my face.

'You know that your new case is crucial,' Miranda continued. 'The partners will be looking at your most recent client feedback and case rating carefully. And the market's tough right now. Not all promotions are going through. It's just not the moment for second chances.'

This was my opening – if I blew it, that was it for me at Stern. Game over. I'd be thrown (though strictly in accordance with prevailing employment law) out of the ivory tower.

'You're on this project for a reason. You've brought new products to market before …' Miranda said.

'Not in this sector. And healthcare is—'

'Look,' Miranda said, 'I know we use a lot of ridiculous terminology and long words around here, but this case is a simple one. The client has bought a fancy new product, and the executive team are paying us to tell them what to do with it.

'It's a short project – only a few weeks. It's a client we haven't worked for before, and now we've got our foot in the door. If we nail it, they've indicated they could buy more work. This could be huge for us, especially in this economy. The partners are watching us on this one. They're watching *you*.'

My heart sank as I processed the news. Miranda was sponsoring my promotion, an early promotion. Which meant that this case would require me to work at the top of my game to prove myself one final crucial time to the partnership.

I thought of Alex, sitting in his glass office, looking smug and infuriating. I couldn't work with him, and I especially couldn't work *for* him.

'Think about it over the weekend,' Miranda said, intuitively knowing when to leave some space in the conversation.

I could see most of the office through Miranda's glass walls. On Fridays there was always a vibe on the floor as my colleagues gravitated back from their clients' offices in time for end-of-week drinks. I could see some of the assistants mixing cocktails on the drinks cart that would be wheeled from desk to desk as soon as the clock struck four – Knock Off O'clock. A group of grads were filling every crevice of a junior partner's office with rainbow balloons for his birthday. When he got back from his meeting it would be hilarious to watch him remove them. Over the last almost-decade, this place had become a home.

I took a deep breath and plastered on a smile. 'Will do. Thanks so much for the heads-up,' I said. 'And for pushing me forwards.'

'You're welcome. We have the ATG offsite on Monday so let me know your answer by Sunday,' Miranda said, smiling warmly. 'Now, I better hit the road. I'm taking the kids camping this weekend.'

Of course she was. Because Miranda never shied away from the hard things. She would finish her eighty-hour work week and then race home to drive, no doubt for hours, to a national park, to spend the weekend with her three school-aged children at a campground lacking any modern conveniences.

I could already picture the out-of-office she was about to write: *After missing two kids' music concerts this week (terrible mother or genius – you tell me!?), I'm taking my gang camping for the weekend. If you need me, please send me a message, though I'll only be checking my phone intermittently at the tops of various mountains. Otherwise, I'll be online Sunday night. Enjoy your weekend!*

She'd chosen to play life at the highest level of difficulty, on every front. How could I turn to her and say, *Actually, in the lead-up to the wedding, I was hoping for an easier project so I can really focus on table arrangements and seating plans. And ideally a job without my awful university boyfriend, who's resurfaced from my past like a swamp monster.*

'Have a great weekend with the kids!' I said instead in my most upbeat voice.

39

By the time I got through the unread emails I'd ignored all day, I found myself completely on edge. Over the next twenty-four hours I would have to decide if, for the next five weeks, I was going to be in regular contact with the only person on earth who made me feel completely dysregulated. Could I play kumbaya with my ex-boyfriend so I didn't miss out on the promotion I'd worked so hard to gain?

And now I had to attend my mum's birthday dinner with my entire extended family while pretending that everything was okay. I swiped on some fuchsia lipstick to offset my navy suit, grabbed her cake out of the office fridge and ordered an Uber.

I called Lily en route. Matt was always the person I'd call when I needed to troubleshoot, but we'd never had the ex conversation. I couldn't exactly call him, tell him I was fifteen minutes away then drop in, *Guess what? This weekend I have to decide whether or not I can work with my uni boyfriend, whom I've never mentioned. He broke my heart … Any thoughts?* Lily, however, had the necessary context.

'I know it's probably bathtime or dinnertime. Or you're doing something hideously cool like drinking orange wine, so hang up on me if you need to,' I said when she answered.

The FaceTime button popped up.

'I need to see you,' she said.

'Why?'

'Because something's clearly wrong.'

I pressed the green tick. Lily's face popped up on the screen. Beneath a razor-sharp fringe, her eyes were framed by heavy square black glasses and her dainty ears supported more earrings than gravity should have allowed. I guessed from her contoured cheeks and the swoops of eyeliner under her frames that she'd just come home from the store – the literal and figurative face of epically cool Lily Li Jewellery.

'Alex Lawson is my new client,' I said. There was a pause down the line.

'Alex-Alex?' she clarified. 'Oxford Alex?'

'Yes,' I confirmed. 'It's really thrown me. The wedding planning lurches from one disaster to the next. Mum keeps wanting to be more involved and it's driving me mad. And now I'm up for promotion in a few weeks, so have to kill myself to impress my bosses. And if I'm going to have a proper shot at getting the job, I have to kiss the arse of the most infuriating man on the planet.'

'Okay, that's a lot,' Lily said. 'Particularly when you have, in fact, kissed his arse in real life.'

'Not helpful,' I said. 'Do you think we could pretend not to know each other? We did today in front of everyone.'

'I'm not sure lying is traditionally a hallmark of professionalism,' she replied.

The phrase 'Integrity Always' floated across my mind. 'It wouldn't be lying so much as making a targeted omission of fact,' I replied firmly.

'Firstly, you're the worst liar on the planet,' Lily said. 'And secondly, even if you were Meryl Streep, I don't think you'd be able to hide the … energy between you two.'

'The energy is currently manifesting in the form of disdain from him and enmity from me,' I said.

'Yeah, well that's thermodynamics: energy never disappears, it always has to become something else,' she said. 'And you guys have always … sparked.'

From the moment we'd met there'd been a zing between us, an instant attraction, even if I hadn't known exactly what it was then.

'Why do I feel so ... on edge?' I asked. 'I never get like this. I never get overly emotional about anything. It's one of the things I like most about myself.'

'I don't know how not to be an emotional train wreck,' Lily said. 'Every week I have Meat-free Mondays followed by Existential Tuesdays.'

I laughed for the first time since seeing Alex and felt a welcome release of tension.

'Maybe the issue is that you never let yourself think about him after you guys ended ... at all,' Lily said. 'You shut away the whole thing, so it's been lurking at the back of your brain's emotional filing cabinet, unresolved, all this time.'

'Yeah, well, I didn't think I'd ever have to see him again. Let alone work with him,' I said, my voice now an octave higher than usual.

'Becs, you've been under a lot of pressure lately,' Lily said in the voice she used to soothe her son, Arlo.

'I know,' I relented. 'I feel like I normally know how to handle pressure and not let it get to me. But lately I can feel the anxiety inside me just ... growing. I mean, Mum keeps banging on about our wedding being cursed. She thinks that I'll be the next victim of our weird family legacy, that Matt and I will break up and then I'll get carried away and marry someone all wrong for me,' I said. 'We're ignoring her, obviously. But then Alex turns up out of the blue ...'

There was silence on the other end of the phone. Lily skewed woo-woo. She believed in astrology and tarot, so I was pretty sure that she believed in curses too.

'Do you think it *is* out of the blue?' Lily finally asked, carefully. 'It *is* a bit weird that your ex-boyfriend has turned up in your city and is working on the same project at the same company as you. Do you think there's any chance he's here because of you? Like, he's doing a nerdy version of Ryan Gosling in *The Notebook*?'

'No. The company he's working for is pretty mega,' I replied firmly. 'And even if I was being Notebooked, I'd know what to do. Rachel McAdams was crazy to pick Ryan. It makes no sense: why would she pick the angry, pushy, moody option when she could have lovely, loves her, stable James Marsden? It's a ridiculous ending.'

There was a squeal from Lily's end of the phone then Arlo's incredibly squeezable face popped up on the screen.

'Ahh … my favourite almost-one year old!' I cooed down the phone.

'He-wo!' Arlo babbled down the phone as he waved, almost taking down one of the many framed canvases that covered every bit of wall space in Lily's house.

'He's a genius,' I said.

'My parents have already labelled him gifted,' Lily said, with more than a hint of darkness in her voice.

'We can undo that! Lots of screen time and processed food,' I said. 'I'm personally convinced enough *Peppa Pig* can lower any IQ.'

The Uber pulled up in front of my brother's house.

'Shit, I'm here,' I said. 'How am I meant to deal with my family right now when I'm feeling so … rattled?'

'Tell them you have a sudden raging case of gastro?'

'Matt's already here, I can't feed him to the wolves,' I said. 'And I made the cake.'

'Valium?' she brainstormed aloud.

'The drinks trolley went around at work. The combination of anxiety meds, alcohol and my brain chemistry isn't famously a good one.'

'Keep drinking!' Lily said firmly. 'And Becs, I know you'll want to repress all thoughts of Alex … but maybe it's healthier to walk down memory lane and actually metabolise what happened nine years ago. Maybe if you remember how obsessed you were with him, it will be the antidote to not thinking about him at all.'

Chapter 6

THEN

Three days after meeting the guy on the roof, I found myself eating dinner in the hall of University College while Lily was in a tute. I pretended to study the portraits that covered the wood-panelled walls as I slowly picked at my food.

I knew no one would be looking at me and wondering why I was eating at Lily's college rather than my own, or, worse, judging me for having dinner alone. But it felt like everyone was. If anyone asked me why I was here, I knew that I would struggle to provide an answer that made sense.

For the last few days all I'd been able to think about was him. I'd manufactured a million reasons to pop into Univ (which is what everyone called University College) – I visited Lily at sunset each day and gazed out of her bedroom window to see if he was on the roof, I checked out a book that only their library had, I visited the (not particularly artistically significant) sculpture of Shelley twice. Finally, I took to wandering around the two medieval quadrangles, looking up at the windows on the top floors, wondering which was his.

I knew the world wouldn't end if I didn't see him. He'd probably forgotten all about our meeting already. But for the first time, in as long as I could remember, I didn't really have anything I needed to do. In the absence of readings to churn through, essays to bang out or exams to cram for, it felt good to have something on my to-do list.

And so I'd found myself turning up to Univ for dinner with Lily's student card to buy food, in the hope that he might be both awake and hungry, and that I'd see him again. Alas, it was a silly plan anyway. Even if he did turn up for his 5.15 pm breakfast, he'd probably be with friends. What was I going to do? Pick up my tray, walk across the room and blurt out, *Sorry for freaking you out on the roof neither of us were meant to be on.*

Except – I swallowed – he'd just entered the hall. Alone.

He looked like he'd just rolled out of bed again, his T-shirt and hair askew, though today he'd at least pulled on a pair of jeans. I'd forgotten how tall he was – he looked like a Viking king or the kind of person they'd happily cast on *Home and Away*. He carried his tray, loaded to the edges with food, and a thick science textbook, as if it weighed nothing. I instantly lost my appetite.

I watched him walk slowly towards the empty end of one of three long wooden tables and put his tray down. He was about to sit when he noticed me in the same spot two tables over. I quickly looked down at my mostly full plate.

He probably didn't even remember me. Or if he did, it wasn't as if I'd made a fantastic first impression – he'd thought I was about to leap off a roof's edge for the first half of our conversation and then spent the rest of the time writing me off as another corporate sell-out.

He smiled. Then he picked up his tray and began to walk towards my table. I felt the same nervous feeling in my stomach that I got just before I was allowed to turn over an exam paper.

He stopped opposite me and cocked his head. 'Is this your college?' he asked.

'If it's not, will you tell the porters?'

'Absolutely. What's the point of having enormous stone walls with fortress-style gates if anyone can just walk in?'

I laughed nervously.

'Can I sit with you?'

'Sure,' I said. 'I'm Rebecca Evans, by the way.'

'Alex Lawson,' he said as he swung his long legs over the bench. 'I've been looking out for you. But when I didn't see you in the hall, the library or on the roof, I came up with two theories.'

He'd been looking for me? I'd convinced myself that even if I did track him down, I'd have to remind him who I was. For a moment I felt a flutter of hope. But I quickly quashed it.

'My first theory is that you're a ghost,' he continued.

'Interesting hypothesis. How are you going to test that assumption?' I asked.

He leaned across the table and rested his hand on mine. I felt a shiver run through me and hoped he hadn't noticed. His hands were enormous and warm, almost hot. No wonder he was only wearing a T-shirt in still-chilly weather. 'My hypothesis has been disproved by the evidence,' he said. 'You're flesh and blood.'

I felt like I was *all* flesh and blood. Which was strange. Until about a minute earlier I'd always felt like a brain that was burdened by a body. Now I felt like my nerve endings had been turned inside out.

'Luckily you have a second theory.' I managed to keep my voice steady.

'My second theory is that you don't go to this college,' he said.

'I'm at Trinity.'

'But eating in Univ?'

'I came to speak to you,' I said quickly. 'I wanted to say that I was sorry about the other night, for the whole freaking-you-out-on-the-edge-of-the-roof situation. I can see why you thought ... not that I would ever ... but I mean, I was feeling weird that day, slightly wobbly.'

'Not an ideal feeling while on the edge of a roof,' he said. I laughed. 'Why were you feeling weird that night?'

'I've been so focused for the past few years. I feel like I've been trying to clear a never-ending series of get-a-job hurdles. I haven't had time to breathe or think. And now I've ticked everything off, and I have time to breathe and think. Maybe that just threw me.' Why was it so easy to open up to him? I hadn't even told Lily how unexpectedly lost I'd felt for the past few days.

'You seem more ... grounded now,' he said.

'I am. I've made a plan,' I said. 'I've written a new list of all the stuff I want to do this term ... All the classic Oxford student experiences you're meant to have except I was too busy studying to do any of them.'

'You've written an actual list?' he asked.

'Yeah, I've called it my "Salad Days List",' I said. 'It's a phrase that Shakespeare made up to describe the period in your life when you're young and it's all meant to be pleasure and fun. And I figured … I'm young. So maybe it's time for the fun part?'

'You like Shakespeare?' he asked.

'I like lists with good names.' I attempted a nonchalant shrug while bracing for a judgemental eyebrow raise or a flat-out laugh.

'Can I see it?' he asked instead.

'Umm … okay,' I said. I reached for my bag under the wooden bench and yanked out my spiral-bound notebook. I flicked through pages I'd furiously covered during lectures and tutorials. He didn't even attempt to pretend not to read my notes over the table. I flicked faster – through weeks of my thoughts and analyses of the assigned readings and feedback from professors. I knew that the way I studied was over-the-top, beyond thorough, but it was how I retained information.

I finally found the list and handed him my notebook. As his eyes darted over the page I was very aware of my neat, schoolgirl lettering. I was equally conscious of the fact that I'd approached my first and last summer of freedom, the few weeks of my academic career when there was nothing left to do, like a graded assignment.

'*Find the witch in the bottle at the Pitt Rivers Museum. Drink Pimm's at Summer Eights. Watch a celebrity speak at the Oxford Union. Play croquet,*' he read aloud. He flipped to the next page where the list continued. 'And there's more. This list is *very* comprehensive.'

If anyone else had made that assessment I would have been sure they were teasing, but he seemed sincere. He looked up at me. 'Can I come with you to May Day morning?'

I stared at him for a moment. While I'd been wandering the college hoping to bump into him, I'd never imagined that he'd suggest we hang out together.

'Yeah, of course. I mean, you're the only person I know who will already be awake,' I said.

His face split into a grin. I smiled back.

Chapter 7

NOW

I plastered a smile on my face and walked into Nick and Stella's house. Mum's birthday party was in full swing, and by that I mean my extended family were all milling around the Nancy Meyers–inspired kitchen. Even though this wasn't the house that my brother, Nick, and I had grown up in, it had a similar energy – it felt like the house was humming with warmth and care because it had absorbed all the energy of a very capable woman.

I put the cake on the bench then picked up my niece Evie, who'd been the first to notice me arrive, because nothing escaped her, ever. I spun her around, her sparkling dress twirling behind her.

'Who invited a fairy?' I asked. Evie was two parts exhausting to one part adorable. A few hours with her was better than any sleeping pill on earth. And yet just one of her twinkly smiles made my ovaries do somersaults.

'I'm not a fairy, I'm Evie,' she replied.

'Oh, am *I* a fairy then?' I asked.

'No, you're my grandma!' she said. I really needed to get on to some preventative Botox. Though at thirty-three, would it still be preventative?

'She's obsessed with your mum, so "grandma" is her highest form of praise,' Stella said, giving me a kiss as she scooped her daughter out of my arms.

'I really need to up the actives in my skincare,' I said.

'One of the mums at Evie's kinder offered me the name of her plastic surgeon for when I'm ready for my postpartum glow-up,' Stella said.

'Is that a thing?'

'Apparently. Honestly, the only thing that has glowed about me recently is my left boob mid-mastitis,' she replied.

I winced. 'How is leftie?'

'Oh, much improved. Praise be for antibiotics. And a husband who's able to source them quickly,' she said.

'It's the small things. Where is said husband?' I asked.

'He got called in,' she said.

'He's on call *tonight*?' I felt a familiar spark of irritation. Nick was an obstetrician, so was often called into the hospital at weird hours. But why hadn't he insisted on taking the night off? Surely his mum's birthday was enough to ring-fence some time in the roster, even if he and his wife, mother to their toddler and baby, weren't hosting the festivities at their house.

'He'll be back soon,' Stella said, as she put Evie down with a small, involuntary groan. We both knew that this was unlikely. Stella had deftly applied concealer, but even heavy-duty cover-up couldn't mask her exhaustion.

'Thanks for having us all.'

'Well, it's easier to have everyone come here than to get our circus out of the house,' she said with a shrug.

I wondered if maybe the binary options shouldn't have been hosting a family dinner party or dragging infant children out at night. Maybe we should have organised a quiet lunch at a time that best suited their nap schedule, or given Mum's non-milestone birthday a miss. A pang of guilt rippled through me for not advocating for Stella.

'And your mum did all the food and looked after Alice this afternoon so I could nap,' she added.

'Are you getting enough sleep?' I asked.

'Yeah,' she said, as if there was no acceptable alternative. 'I mean, she's waking up at night quite a bit …'

I knew that from Stella, who was all stoicism, this invariably meant that Alice was up most of every night. And I also guessed that Stella was doing it solo – that the only thing waking up Nick was the hospital.

'But the finish line is in sight. Only a couple of weeks until Alice and I go to sleep school. So, by the time of your wedding, I'll be a new person!'

'What can I do to help you tonight?' I asked. Matt had sent a load of champagne and wine from work, and I'd put my hand up to make the cake. But I knew that booze and baked goods weren't going to properly lighten Stella's load.

'Could you check on Alice? She's with Matt in there.' Stella jerked her head towards Nick's study, as her arm was yanked in the direction of the kitchen by Evie, who was vigorously campaigning for carte-blanche access to the grown-up cheese platter and bowls of chips and dips.

I popped my head around the study door, holding a flute of champagne and a glass of red wine, and smiled. Matt sat at the end of the leather couch, holding a sleeping Alice in the crook of his arm, a muted movie on the TV.

'Shh.' He held a finger up to his smiling mouth.

I tiptoed towards him, then leaned forwards, kissed him and handed him his drink. I perched on the other end of the couch.

'I'm pretending to be the good guy, but really I'm hiding from your family,' he whispered. 'Alice is my human shield.'

'You are a good guy. But, fair call,' I said. 'I'm planning on drinking my way through it.' I took an enormous gulp of my drink – the bubbles tickled my nose. I felt a temporary hit of warmth and calm as the alcohol made it to my unlined, unsettled stomach.

'Oh, I love drunk Becs,' he said, a hopeful glint appearing behind his glasses.

I smiled back at him, attempting come-hither eyes. Matt looked particularly gorgeous this evening with his shiny brown hair a bit mussed up.

I felt a sense of calm for the first time all day. I was lucky that this was my Friday night. I could smell spices simmering and hear people laughing and talking over each other. I was with my smart, funny fiancé who happily attended my family's gatherings, close enough to my niece to admire her rosebud lips, and drinking champagne that tasted like engagement parties, so was probably expensive – generosity came as naturally to Matt as breathing.

'Is my darling girl in here?' Mum burst into the room, speaking in a mock stage whisper. Alice stirred in Matt's arms.

'I think she's just waking up now,' he said, not ascribing any blame. She swooped forwards to grab Alice, her billowing sparkly kaftan flapping like the wings of a rosella. She tattooed her granddaughter's face with a crimson-lipstick kiss and then held her close, no doubt overpowering Alice's naturally intoxicating baby smell with Shalimar.

I finished my flute of champagne.

'Another drink?' Matt asked, eyeing my empty glass, the hopeful light still in his eyes.

An image of crumpled bedsheets in an ancient stone tower sprang unbidden into my mind.

'Yes, please, keep them coming,' I replied quickly, and he followed Mum out of the room. I shook my head. I didn't need to relive memories from the past, I just needed to let off some steam. I'd drink a little bit too much champagne, help Stella with Evie and Alice as much as possible and then go home for some tipsy sex.

I lingered for a moment in Nick's empty study. Behind the desk was a gallery wall that was clearly Stella's handiwork. In the centre was a family photo that had been taken at my grandma Evelyn's eightieth birthday, sixteen years earlier. Evelyn, Evie's namesake, looked as coiffed as she always did – ash hair curled into submission and lips coated with her signature fairy floss–pink lipstick. In the image she was flanked by Mum and Dad, dressed up and smiling widely at the camera. Mum had her arm around sixteen-year-old me, with my freshly straightened teeth and badly highlighted boofy hair. Nick, who would have been about to finish med school, stood next to Dad. I wondered if this was the last photo taken of our family, unfractured? Had there been clues? I stepped towards the frame as if there might be a clenched jaw or sidewards glare if you really looked hard. I'd always been the kid who noticed everything, then the observant teenager. Except I'd completely missed my parents' marriage imploding.

My memories from the day everything broke, and the rest of that summer, really, were blurry. I'd come home from staying the night at Lily's house and found Mum, as usual, in the kitchen. Except nothing was usual. There was no fresh bread, the flowers in the vase on the bench were wilting, dropping their orange pollen all over the white countertop. Mum sat me down and told me she was leaving.

It was as if she was speaking another language. A really hard one, like Finnish. *I'm leaving* – two words I didn't understand.

She'd fallen in love with another man: Hamish, the father of Caroline, who was in the year below me at school. Dad had found out and they were breaking up. Dad wanted to stay at the house, and given Mum had met someone else, she'd agreed.

Up until that moment, everything in my life had seemed big and important – I was going into my final year of school. Over the summer I had coursework to start, assigned books to read, practice tests to study for ... Now I realised I'd led a life of solipsism and almost no stakes.

Then Dad was home sometimes, which was strange because the house had always felt like mine and Mum's. Nick had moved to Sydney for uni years earlier, and Dad was always coming and going, but mainly going.

A few days after Mum left, Grandma Evelyn arrived. And this I remember clearly, through the fog of that summer. We were in the kitchen, and I was mixing her another Gordon's gin and tonic (a slug of gin and a hint of tonic) when she shook her head and said, 'Well, I suppose it was inevitable. All the women in our family are cursed.'

For the first time since my world had shattered, I felt something that wasn't abject shock, misery or confusion: I was suddenly curious.

'What do you mean "cursed"?' I asked.

'All the women in our family break off their engagements before they finally make it down the aisle. And then we all marry the wrong man: one who makes us miserable!'

'Mum was engaged to someone else before Dad?' I asked.

'Yes. A lovely man,' Grandma said, misty-eyed. 'Then she met your father at the hospital, and called off the wedding. She'd fallen instantly and madly in love with your father. She was intoxicated by him …'

I processed this for a moment.

'And you were engaged to someone else before you married Grandpa?' I'd never met my maternal grandpa; he'd died before I was born. By all accounts he'd been a non-event.

'Yes, I was engaged to a very handsome man. But then he was posted to England during the war and got a bit distracted by a girl there,' she said.

'Distracted?'

'He married her,' Grandma said blithely.

'So you married Grandpa instead?' I asked.

'Yes, I was heartbroken and acted impulsively. He had such a nice moustache,' Grandma said. 'But with hindsight, that probably wasn't enough of a foundation for a marriage.'

It hadn't been. Mum had told me horror stories of the relationship between her parents, fuelled by disdain and whisky, when she'd been growing up.

'My sister did the same thing – when her fiancé died, she married a fool on the hop. Your mum's cousin too. It's the family curse – we're too passionate and make thoughtless decisions that hurt everyone around us.' She daintily emptied her glass, then reached for the bottle of gin.

'I'm a woman in this family. Does that mean I'm cursed?' I asked, following her logic through to its natural conclusion.

'No – of course not! You'll do better than your mum and I did – stay in control of your life and make sensible decisions. Promise me that, darling?'

'I promise,' I said with the sincerity of a teenager who'd been invited to the inner sanctum of adult conversation.

'Or maybe it's no use and we can't fight the curse,' she added.

I must have looked alarmed because she reached out and wrapped her thin arms around me. I snuggled into the powdery nook between her shoulder and neck, which was different from Mum's but similar enough.

'Oh, darling, ignore me. You're much too smart to listen to me,' she whispered in my ear.

By the time we sat down to eat dinner, I'd had more than a few commemorative G & Ts while thinking about Grandma Evelyn. Grandma had died in my second year of uni. She had a heart attack while driving and crashed into a florist (only a display of jonquils had been hurt). It was the way she would have wanted to go. Mum sent the store owner flowers by way of apology, unironically.

After dinner, Mum blew out the handful of symbolic candles on the enormous sponge cake, and I realised everything was slightly blurry around the edges, a touch impressionistic.

Which wasn't totally my fault. Despite being very aware of my nightshade allergy, Mum had cooked a lamb tagine filled with capsicum. All I'd been able to eat was some plain couscous.

'What did you wish for?' Hamish asked, draping his long arms around Mum then giving her a squeeze. She melted into him. Hamish adored Mum, wholly and openly. Soon after they'd met, he'd happily handed over the reins of his family's shoe business to let the next generation have their turn at running the show. Now Mum was his full-time job, one that he didn't seem to mind at all.

Hamish was so easy-going that Stella and I had a secret in-joke for a while where we'd offer him increasingly ridiculous drinks at family gatherings to see if we could find his limit. After he'd accepted a Blue Heaven spider as a pre-dinner drink, we'd given up. Mum, the woman who had an opinion on everything, had found her yang. Hamish was basically a sponge cake in human form: vanilla, dependable and Mum's favourite.

'If you tell us, it won't come true,' Evie said with authority, her finger poking into the cream oozing out of the layers.

'My lips are sealed,' Mum said, though I could have sworn she'd turned to look at me. Then she stuck her finger into the cake next to Evie's. Evie laughed uproariously – she adored her naughty grandma. I watched Hamish give Mum a gentle kiss on the cheek before he began to cut up the cake.

'I'm going to go outside for some fresh air,' I announced. I stood up from the table so quickly my chair fell backwards. I didn't miss the pointed look between Mum and Hamish.

'What's wrong with Auntie Becs?' Evie asked at the top of her voice.

'I think she's had too much party juice,' I heard Nick, who'd rolled in just before cake, still in scrubs, reply as I finally worked out that the backdoor opened outwards.

Stella and Nick's house backed onto a small park, and I let myself into it using their gate. The sun had set, and the park was predictably empty. It had been an oppressively hot day; the air was heavy.

I swung back and forth on the swing a few times then stopped – the world was already spinning.

I pulled out my phone and googled 'Alex Lawson' again. Then I did another search, adding 'Melbourne'. There were a few stories about the sale of his company to ATG. I clicked on his profile on their website. He had a short bio, the type that indicated that he was someone whose reputation preceded him. I stared at the photo. It was a typical corporate head shot, except Alex managed to defy any attempts at uniformity. His blond hair sprang up like he was a farm-based golden retriever. The gaze wasn't the expected one of quiet, reassuring confidence but rather his sky-blue eyes were piercing, like they could X-ray and were searching for fractures and breaks. And his face wasn't centred, as if he'd deliberately resisted the photographer's explicit instructions.

I clicked back to the search-results page and scanned them. I paused, then pressed on the final link. An 'Alex Lawson' in the thirty-five to forty-five age category had

completed the Albert Park Parkrun for the last few weeks.
I swallowed hard.

He'd been a runner when we'd met. He didn't enjoy the
exercise as much as the impact it had on his brain's ability to
function at its peak. But running around a lake that was a
short walk from my house felt very close to my real life. Was
he living around here? Would I run into him as I dashed to the
shops in my tracksuit to buy milk? Maybe it was coincidence,
and it was another Alex Lawson. Surely life wouldn't require
me to be on guard both at work and at home.

There was an enormous bang and then a crack broke
the sky. A chilly breeze swept through the park, picking
up leaves and bits of the day's rubbish. One of the city's
infamous cool changes had arrived. There was another
boom of thunder and thick raindrops started to fall.

I stood and held my palms to the sky as the rain splattered
on my hair. I woke up thirty minutes earlier than usual twice
a week to blast it into submission, so I knew I should run to
shelter – to the picnic area or back to the house. Instead, I
tipped back my head and let the rain fall on my face.

'Are you okay?'

I spun around. Matt was standing behind me. 'Yeah,
fine,' I said. 'I think everything's gone straight to my head.
Mum was trying to kill me with dinner, so I barely ate. She
went to med school ... do you think she's just forgotten
about anaphylaxis?'

'There were heaps of side dishes, but they got stuck at
the other end of the table,' Matt said evenly.

'I mean, this is the lady who filled out the allergy section
of our wedding RSVPs with *Mild intolerance to Chanel
Number Five*.'

'I know these family things can be full-on for you,' he said gently. 'I know it brings up … stuff.'

'Let's practise our wedding dance,' I said. I knew it was a non sequitur, but the words came out before I could stop them. We'd had two classes to learn our first dance, but then the instructor had developed tendonitis. Because, of course.

He took my outstretched hands but didn't move closer. He searched my face. 'Are you sure you're okay?' he asked again.

'Yeah, of course,' I said.

I stared for a moment at the man in front of me – my fiancé. I wasn't a natural writer and every time I'd sat down to draft my wedding vows, I'd ended up staring at a white screen and a blinking cursor for far too long.

But right then, as I stood opposite Matt, who smelled slightly of damp wool and earthy red wine, his kind eyes crinkled with concern and his strong hands wrapped around my mine, I knew the promises I wanted to make. I wanted to promise to honour his best qualities: his easy kindness, his ability to revel in small, everyday pleasures, his instinctive creativity. I'd promise to always be the one to make the microwave popcorn before we curled up together to watch movies. I'd promise to always buy him a novelty pair of socks on a work trip. I'd promise to be with him forever.

Why had it been so hard to get the words down when these commitments felt so clear?

'I can't believe I get to marry you,' I said.

His shirt collar was turning, one splatter at a time, from pale to dark blue. The cotton had begun to stick to his abs, like he was Mr Darcy or Anthony Bridgerton emerging from a lake. Raindrops sat like a spider's web on the top of his hair and his glasses had begun to fog. Even soaking wet, he was handsome.

He pulled me close and spun me like we'd practised. Suddenly I felt incredibly dizzy and out of breath. But while the park turned into a blur of glistening leaves and half-hidden stars, Matt's face stayed totally in focus.

A crack of lightning broke through the sky. We stopped moving and, as the rest of the world became clear again, a wave of panic rushed through me.

I pulled away from Matt, and clung to the back of a park bench for balance. Matt said something but was drowned out by another rumble of thunder and my own whirring thoughts.

I knew exactly what needed to happen. I added a new item to my mental to-do list: 'Negotiate rules of engagement with ex'.

Chapter 8

I woke up on Saturday with a churning stomach – a combination of too much champagne and gin and an undercurrent of anticipation.

I pulled on a navy outfit that had cost an unholy amount at Lululemon as I stared at Matt's sleeping form nestled in the ode to linen that was our bed. He'd been nothing short of heroic last night: helping Stella with Alice, humouring Mum and generally oiling the wheels of familial harmony. No man on earth wanted to spend his Friday night with his partner's extended family, but Matt had turned up with bells on. And I'd got uncharacteristically drunk – instead of taking the edge off the day, I'd gone over the edge.

But, like the lightning bolt that we'd been at risk of being struck by, I'd had a blinding flash of clarity. In exactly five weeks' time, give or take a few hours, I was going to marry Matt. Nothing was going to get in the way of our wedding. Dealing with the reappearance of Alex in my life was just another road bump to get over, like reordering Matt's suit, which had arrived sky instead of navy blue, or reposting the invitations because the last-minute change of lettering meant that the numbers one and seven were indistinguishable. We'd fixed those things; I could fix this.

Miranda had made it very clear that if I wanted to stay at the firm, ATG was the client I needed to impress. If I had to work with Alex, then we needed to lay some ground rules. And given that in two days' time we were going to be thrust together at a team awayday, I needed to speak to him this weekend.

Except I had no way of getting in touch with him. I had his work email, but this wasn't exactly the kind of conversation I wanted to have on a professional platform. I'd rejected his Facebook request a million years ago, and I'd have bet he never checked his social media anyway. I knew he wouldn't sign up for a LinkedIn account even at knifepoint, and I didn't have his mobile number.

My online search had given me an idea. Parkrun took place at 8 am every Saturday at Albert Park Lake. If it was my Alex Lawson – who'd set a ridiculous pace for the last few weeks – then I'd be able to speak with him. And if he was a no-show or the Alex Lawson I'd internet-stalked was another person entirely, well, I'd been meaning to try the community timed fun run for years. I might well have woken up this morning and decided to give it a go anyway. It was a win-win.

I knocked back two Panadol, left Matt happily snoozing in bed and walked through South Melbourne. It was my favourite kind of Melbourne day – crisp and sunny after a summer storm. Surely there was no better smell on earth than steaming asphalt. I checked my watch: 7.45 am. I was early – so far it was mostly volunteers in bright orange vests milling around.

Thanks so much for having us. Hope you got some sleep last night! I messaged Stella.

Are you okay? she wrote back straightaway.

I felt a jolt of shame. Normally I'd have been the one staying back to help clean the house. I was seeing her in the afternoon with Lily; I resolved to give her a decent break.

And what had Matt thought? When we'd got home, I'd just managed to pull off my wet work clothes and roll into bed, wearing one of Matt's old uni T-shirts, before passing out. It hadn't been the striptease I knew he'd had in mind. I pulled my phone back out.

Sorry I got carried away last night. Breakfast at market after my run?

I tucked my phone back into its Lycra pocket and then pulled my hair up into a ponytail, which was a mess of natural curls after the deluge. I wondered if I should get my hair chemically straightened.

The lady in charge of the run, who had the energy of an executive assistant to someone very senior, began to issue instructions through a megaphone. We all – and there were now hundreds of us in activewear – began to shuffle from a wooden pavilion over to the start line.

And there he was. I rubbed my still-blurry eyes just to make sure I wasn't seeing things. No, it was definitely Alex, right up near the front of the pack. And in case I had any doubt, he was wearing a faded blue T-shirt featuring the University College crest in cracked yellow print.

The crowd began to move forwards. I'd been so focused on watching him that I'd missed the starting cue. A few moments too late I began to jog at a slow shuffle. I settled into a pace that was only mildly uncomfortable and watched him stride off. He bounded around the first curve of the lake and out of my line of sight – evidently the part of him that refused to be anything but the best at whatever he decided to do hadn't changed.

He'd never known me as a runner. I'd discovered it in my mid-twenties, and it was now a key part of my 'Stay in Control of My Nervous System Regime'.

I'd had my first run-in with anxiety in my teens, and by trial and error had learned how to keep it in its box. But when I'd started work, and stress became part of my daily life, I'd realised that I needed to up my game. If I was going to last in the corporate world, I needed a pressure valve, and vodka and cocaine were (observationally) less sustainable than cardio. I knew that I'd become a cliché – a woman with a corporate job who meditated often, jogged regularly and had a preferred yoga studio, but given that the combination had fewer side effects than Xanax, I'd never really cared.

With no Alex to fixate on, I soaked in the morning for a few moments – the sense of solidarity that came from doing the same thing at the same time as other people you didn't know.

The lake's black swans guarded the season's cygnets. They all had metal rings around their necks with an engraved number, I guessed so that the park rangers could keep track of them. I glanced down at the tag on my wrist, replete with a barcode, so that Parkrun could record how long it took us to run in a circle. Normally I'd be tempted to analyse this, but today I was too hungover to follow that grim train of thought.

The sound of my feet and the ones around me rhythmically hitting the dusty towpath began to work its magic. Even though last night's alcohol was oozing out of my pores, and my stomach felt like it was filled with battery acid, a rare sense of calm descended on me. This was why I ran – it was like Aerogard for anxiety.

I finished the run in a time I hoped no one would ever see on my Strava app. Then after a volunteer scanned my code (in a moment of wavering willpower I'd likely look up how badly I'd fared compared to other women my age) I went to collect my jumper and water bottle. And talk to Alex.

In my peripheral vision I could see that he was chatting with a group of serious runners (they were lean and wore singlets rather than T-shirts) on the other side of the pavilion. I knew they would be talking about something technical – brands of shoes, interval training, running watches – Alex had never done small talk but would happily chat about the few topics that interested him for hours.

As the crowd thinned out, he spotted me. I crossed the pavilion as he broke away from his conversation.

'I googled you last night and saw that a person with your name had been doing this run,' I said. 'I thought I might be here today.'

'And here I am,' he said warily. Which was fair enough given I'd ambushed him. 'Though I thought our working plan was to never darken each other's doorsteps again.'

'That was Plan A,' I said. 'But it turns out that this project is a pivotal career moment for me, which means not only can I not escape but I have to nail it.'

'I'm sorry the heavy industrials thing didn't work out for you,' he said caustically. I ignored him.

'This project is a five-week sprint. We're both adults, we're both professionals – of course we can work together,' I said.

'I wasn't the one who said we couldn't,' he said.

'So, I pulled together a few ground rules,' I ploughed on, unlocking my phone. I'd drafted these in the middle of the night when I woke up in desperate need of all the water in the world.

'Are they in a PowerPoint presentation?' he asked drily. I ignored him again.

'Number one: we won't hide the fact that we … know each other. But we won't flaunt it either. No in-jokes. No reminiscing, et cetera.' I wished I had a slide deck to hide behind.

'Your love of a numbered list hasn't diminished,' he said.

'Number two: all contact will be strictly work related.'

'Says the woman who's hunted me down on a Saturday morning.'

'For work-related purposes,' I countered.

'How many points are there? I can feel the lactic acid setting in.'

'Three.'

'Okay, what's the last one?'

I read this one from my phone without looking up. 'You meet my fiancé, Matt.'

I waited for a second before I raised my eyes from my screen. Alex was staring at the ring on my left hand. Had he just noticed it? He was the kind of guy who, if stuck on a complex problem, would forget what day of the week it was, or to eat or sleep, so it was entirely possible he had missed it.

'Congratulations,' he said, after another moment.

'Thank you,' I replied.

'When's the wedding?' he asked. Did he really want to know, or had he just got better at small talk?

'Next month, just after the project finishes,' I replied. Did I feel strange telling him about the wedding because he was my ex-boyfriend or because he was my colleague?

'What's with the third rule?' he asked. 'Is he a jealous guy?'

I burst out laughing. Because the notion was so ridiculous. I didn't think it would ever occur to Matt to be jealous of anyone. He saw everyone in the world as a friend he hadn't met yet. Alex seemed a bit disarmed by my reaction.

'No, he's not at all,' I said. 'I just think that it's a good idea.' I knew I hadn't really answered his question. 'So … are you okay with all of that?'

'What happens if I'm not?'

'I have to transfer off this project. And you upend my career,' I said. *Again.* I left that part out, feeling it would be counterproductive in this conversation.

'I accept your terms,' he said, in a voice tinged with false gravitas. He pulled on a faded hoodie.

'It seems that we're going to spend another summer together,' he added. Did I imagine it or did his eyes soften as he spoke? 'It was a pretty amazing summer.' It had been. Until it hadn't. I tried not to think about it.

70

'We're going to *work* together for a summer,' I corrected. 'Not just—'

'Have fun.'

'Don't forget "Rule One",' I said, in a voice that sat somewhere between admonishing and warning.

'I remember,' he said. 'Now, when do I have to meet the guy who gave you that enormous rock?'

'How about now?' It came out before I could stop myself. This hadn't been part of the plan. In the middle of the night when I'd been thinking this through, I'd envisioned a meeting between Matt and Alex at a nice, neutral wine bar after I'd laid the groundwork with Matt first – had the ex chat we'd never got around to having. *This* was why I didn't get drunk very often – I didn't make sensible decisions when I wasn't functioning properly.

'Okay,' he said easily. Then he turned to me and smiled. 'You know what's funny?'

'Nothing at all?' I offered.

He smiled. 'This is just how our summer really began … At least this is a more civilised time than our first date.'

Chapter 9

THEN

I woke up at 4.29 am, one minute before my alarm. It was the first day of May, and I was seeing Alex again. Dressed and under-caffeinated, I walked from my college room to the High Street. I felt like yelling, 'May Day!' in the sinking-ship sense, and running back to bed. An enormous crowd had already amassed and I didn't have Alex's number – how were we going to find each other in this heaving mass of people?

Underneath the doubt and panic, emotions that were old friends, was something else. It was excitement, hope even. The chance of seeing Alex again was propelling me forwards through the crowd like some kind of rocket fuel – stronger than Nescafe Blend 43 or even Jägerbombs. I'd only felt like myself twice since the start of Trinity term – each time I'd been with Alex.

I looked up to see if I could spot any blond heads in the crowd and felt compelled to stop. The city's sky was awash with tinges of blush and tangerine. I rifled through my bag and pulled out my digital camera. I looked at the small screen and took the photo. I hadn't quite managed to capture what had made me stop, but it was still beautiful. To be deeply moved by spires wasn't exactly an original thought, but right then I truly believed that I was the only person who had ever felt that way.

'Hi.' A deep Australian voice spoke behind me. I turned around and there he was in an unbuttoned navy woollen coat with his college jumper beneath it, black backpack slung over one shoulder. He looked exhausted but his bright blue eyes sparkled.

'You haven't slept yet, have you?' I asked.

'No,' he admitted.

'You know you're allowed to shift to the local time zone when you move countries,' I said.

'It's not normal to be jet-lagged for three years?' he asked with mock surprise. I laughed and my nerves settled.

'I'm considering subletting my bed,' he added.

'Don't do that.' The words tripped off my tongue before I realised what it sounded like. He raised an eyebrow, and I knew my cheeks would be flushed. 'I think it's almost time. Should we try to get further down the street?' I asked, keen to move the conversation away from Alex's bed. Whatever effect Alex seemed to have on me couldn't quash my pathological need to be on time.

'Yep,' he said. He offered me his hand as if it was the most natural thing in the world. I took it. It was strong and, just as I remembered, warm.

Together we moved with the tide of people streaming towards Magdalen College. A mix of students, Oxford locals and visitors, who looked like they were at a *Midsummer Night's Dream* costume party had filled the length of High Street, right down to the bridge. Everyone stared up at the college's bell tower, waiting for the show to start.

'I think it's more fun being up on the roof than down here,' he said.

Before I could reply, it began. There were six clangs and immediately the buzz of anticipatory chat died down and the crowd stopped jostling. Out of the silence and stillness, a choir in the bell tower began to sing a hymn in what I assumed was Latin (or was it ancient Greek – neither language seemed dead in this city). It was far too early in the day for choral music hardly anyone could understand, sung from a medieval tower to celebrate the arrival of summer. But it was also magical, the kind of thing that only made sense if you were there in the moment.

I snuck a glance at Alex just as he turned to look at me and we smiled at each other. Who was this guy? And why did it feel as if there had been a surge of electricity through my body from where my fingertips met his.

The choir finished the final hymn, which sounded like it had been composed by someone in a fever dream, and the crowd slowly began to clap. Solemn proceedings completed, a street party sprang up around us. Accordions, banjos, trumpets and many varieties of percussion struck up enthusiastically, and we were part of a jolly, if slightly earnest, street party.

'This country has the most random traditions. I'm obsessed,' I said.

'Australia just can't compete with this level of enthusiastic participation,' he agreed. 'Coffee?'

All the cafes in the centre of town had opened hours earlier than usual. The smell of bacon and coffee seemed to be wafting out of every picturesque pastel shop door. My stomach had a Pavlovian response, either to the smell or suggestion, and rumbled.

'Definitely, yes, and also food,' I replied.

We took the last tiny table in a cafe that was pumping out breakfast sandwiches and ordered two with coffee. We both drank long blacks and somehow this didn't surprise me.

'Do you know what I love about this country?' Alex asked between enormous bites.

'Its unproblematic colonial past,' I guessed. He laughed.

'Its food,' he said. I smiled – I suspected that he held a contrarian opinion on most things.

'No, seriously,' he continued, 'I think the thing I'm going to miss most about this country is cheese and onion crisps.'

'You're moving home?' I asked.

'No. No one's doing work in my research area in Australia. I've applied to Harvard for my post-doc, so I guess I'll have to get used to a whole new world of snackage.'

I felt an unexpected flicker of disappointment. I didn't even know him so why did I care that there would soon be half a world between us?

'So why consulting?' Alex asked. I smiled. I liked that he wanted to have a real conversation.

'Do you want the answer I've given in job interviews?' I asked, though I already knew what he'd say.

'No.'

'I've never told anyone the real answer,' I said. 'Probably because it's not a very interesting story. And it's really nerdy.'

'Luckily you're talking to someone who was in the Australian Science Olympiads team.'

'God, I love this city. It's like Disneyland for geeks. Every college should have a diversity rep for any rogue cool kids that get in.'

'You're changing the subject,' he said, though he looked amused.

'Okay, in my first year of uni I embarked upon "Project Job",' I began. 'I wrote a list—'

'I'm sensing that lists are a thing for you,' he said.

'If you keep interrupting me, I'm going to give you my extremely polished and compelling interview answer,' I said.

He grinned.

'So, I wrote a list of qualities I'd enjoy in a job. I wanted to work with smart people … I wanted to have snappy conversations in hallways like on *The West Wing*—'

Alex laughed, a sound that I was now convinced was causing the release of irregularly large hits of dopamine.

'I wanted to earn enough money to live on. I wanted to … help people. Then when I heard about a career that might fit my criteria, I challenged the assumption. I met people for coffees and asked them a zillion questions about what they did. I did work experience.'

'What jobs did you try?' he asked.

'Investment banking. But everyone was *really* into money,' I said, shrugging dramatically.

'Who would have thought,' he said drily.

'Do I have to remind a scientist that it's important to test a hypothesis,' I countered.

'Actually, if you could remind some of my undergrad

students that would be helpful,' he shot back. I pointedly ignored him.

'I tried law. A think tank. Government policy. Insurance.'

'I've heard that actuaries are wild,' he said.

'There was a high probability of loose Friday night drinks,' I said, and we both laughed. I took a sip of my nuclear-strength coffee.

'The winner of "Project Job" was consultancy: it checked all the boxes. I spent my last few years of uni working my arse off to get a grad job at one of the top firms.'

'It had to be a top firm?'

'Umm, yeah, I guess. None of my family are in the corporate world. I wanted to show them I could pull it off,' I said. I picked up my napkin and wiped a smudge of HP Sauce from the corner of my mouth.

'So why do you want to fix hearts?' I asked.

'Are you changing the subject?'

'Yes,' I admitted. 'So why?'

Alex paused for a moment and pulled off his hoodie. I caught a glimpse of a stomach that seemed far too washboard for someone in STEM. I pulled my eyes back up to his face.

'My mum unexpectedly died of heart disease when I was a teenager,' he said. 'She had a cardiovascular issue that wasn't picked up but could have been treated if it had been. Our early prevention diagnostic tools are expensive and mediocre. I want to make one that's cheaper and better so ...'

'... other people's mums get to live.' I finished his sentence before I even realised what I was doing. But

I'd heard a crack in his voice and wanted to give him a moment to recover. 'I'm really sorry. That must have been … fucked.' I almost never swore but I couldn't think of a better word.

'Maybe that's what I should call my research. "Trying to make something not-fucked out of something fucked",' he said, with a laugh that was different from his other ones. It was darker and from somewhere deep inside him.

'I actually think that's the definition next to the word "innovation" in the *Oxford English Dictionary*,' I said. I could tell he needed me to make a joke, even if it wasn't a great one.

'Do you have time for one more stop?' he asked as he checked the time on his black Swatch watch. We'd both finished eating and people were hawkishly eyeing our table. I sensed that there was more to his story, but he'd hit his capacity for vulnerability.

'Sure,' I said. I had nowhere I needed to be for the next two months. Normally my social battery was quick to run out, but I was as energised and alive as I'd ever been. I wanted to prolong that feeling for as long as possible.

'Thanks.' Without telling me where we were going, he led me out of the narrow sandwich shop and across the street.

I assumed he was taking me back to his college. The image of a bed that hadn't yet been slept in flashed through my mind. It dissolved as he stopped in front of the Examination Schools, a building on the High Street with an imposing stone facade.

Oxford, as a general rule, liked to come up with a weird and specific name for every part of the university. But this building had a self-explanatory name – it was the place where most of the university exams, as well as lectures, were held.

'Is this like one of those bad dreams where a test is sprung upon you with no notice?' I asked. 'Because that is actually my worst nightmare.'

He smiled but still gave nothing away. Even though I was joking, my heart did begin to race as I climbed up the well-worn steps. One of the fun surprises of Oxford (not advertised on its website) was that the university held exams at the beginning of each term to make sure you'd studied over your holidays. I didn't have any this term (due to my professors not really caring about visiting students when their actual students were preparing for their super-serious end-of-year exams) but I'd been filled with epic levels of dread the last time I'd entered this building.

I followed Alex across the mosaic-tiled lobby to a small wooden desk. There was a sign hanging above it: *Submissions*. Alex dumped his backpack on the floor, unzipped it and pulled out three thickly bound documents.

'I'd like to submit my PhD,' he said to the lady manning the desk.

'Fill out this form,' she said, as if he was collecting a parcel from the post office. I watched Alex fill in his name, student number and what must have been the title of his thesis. She checked his student details, took his trio of documents and then stamped the form with the date and time.

'Congratulations,' the lady said in the tone of someone who saw milestone moments all day, every day.

I managed to wait until we were a few metres away from the desk.

'Did you just … hand in your doctoral thesis?' I asked.

'I did,' he replied. 'That's what I've been working on around the clock for the last three years. Last night I finished it and had it printed. Hence the no-sleep thing.'

'That's huge, congratulations!' I squealed. 'Wait, I have to take a photo. This is one of those big moments. You need to record it.'

He smiled, but I saw a flicker of something pass over his face, a shadow.

Before I knew what I was doing I stepped forwards and wrapped my arms around him. I felt him tense up and then after a moment exhale. Then slowly he circled his arms around me.

We were so close that I could feel the beat of his heart. And I'd lost control of mine. I'd experienced a lot of panic attacks and this felt similar, like my body was responding to a crisis. Except the feeling wasn't really the same at all.

Chapter 10

NOW

I stood in the corner of the Parkrun pavilion staring at the message I'd drafted to Matt.

Hey! On my way to meet you! I bumped into someone on my run. He's just moved to Melbourne! We knew each other at Oxford. We dated actually haha! Can't wait to see you!

No, I couldn't send it. No one sane used that many exclamation marks. But mainly because I couldn't announce the existence of an ex-boyfriend over a text. Not having the ex chat always seemed like I was taking the high road – very Michelle Obama. It was a massive oversight. I pressed delete.

I was overthinking it. It would be fine. We'd have one coffee together, and Matt would see that Alex and I working together on a case was nothing to worry about. There would be no hiding and no secrets.

I put my phone away.

'Let's go!' I said.

'Yes, ma'am,' Alex replied, and he clicked his heels together.

'Wow, I'm not old enough to be a ma'am,' I said.

'You're about to be married. And you live in a land filled with nuclear families, wearing pale shades of linen,' he said. I wanted to take offence, but it wasn't a totally unfair observation. The area we were walking through, which wasn't far from our house, was dominated by young couples who all seemed to be out and about, walking their one to two children – dressed in Purebaby or Seed – in American or Danish prams. Matt and I called them the 'Beautiful Families', and though it was easy to laugh off the Steiner kinders and the yummiest of mummies, Matt and I hoped that soon we would be their people.

'Congratulations on working out how to fix hearts,' I said, changing the subject. And although I was teasing him, the praise was sincere.

'God, I can't believe I used to say stuff like that!' he said with a laugh. 'I had so much bravado back then. I think I was compensating for a complete lack of confidence.'

I turned to him to see if he was being facetious. He'd seemed nothing but confident back then. The idea that it wasn't how he saw it, that he might have changed and become more self-aware was somehow unsettling.

'Well, you did the thing. The tool you made sounds incredible. Seriously,' I said. Alex had created a diagnostic tool that was able to use AI to review chest scans and determine the probability of future heart disease. Once it was in the market it would be able to prevent a lot of the issues that were missed, particularly in women, whose heart conditions were often overlooked because their cardiac episodes didn't look like the ones men had on TV. His work would save lives.

'I think I got lucky with timing,' he said. 'A lot of the

technology went from theoretical to scalable while my team was researching.'

'I bet your mum would have been really proud,' I said, feeling compelled to meet his humility with genuine praise.

'There's still a lot of work to do,' he said finally. He kept his gaze straight ahead.

'Yeah. I guess there're always broken hearts to fix,' I said, and then instantly regretted it.

'Rebecca … we should talk about what happened that night—'

'Hey, we don't get nostalgic, remember?' I knew I was being unfair, but I wanted to get through coffee, not excavate the past.

By the time we reached the market, it was already pumping. I led him past the fruit and vegetable stands around the market's perimeter, where shoppers were piling produce into trolleys.

I checked my phone and saw that Matt had messaged me: *Got our usual table.*

My stomach tightened.

I led Alex past the row of butchers' stalls, trying not to think about all the mornings we'd spent in Oxford's Covered Market, drinking strong coffee in a small cafe we'd discovered hidden away in the market's rafters.

'Do you eat meat now?' I asked.

'Still no,' he replied. I wasn't surprised. He wasn't a man of moderation, I knew he'd either eat no meat or eat it like a caveman. He didn't live life in liminal spaces.

We turned the corner and walked until we reached Padre Coffee, my favourite cafe, in the centre of the market. Matt was already perched out the front. As usual, he was wearing an outfit that could take him anywhere – an inky blue jumper and brown cotton shorts. He had his AirPods in, and I guessed he was listening to one of the many podcasts he churned through every week.

He saw me walking towards him and smiled broadly, pulling out his headphones.

'This is Alex,' I said, before we were close enough to warrant an introduction. 'We knew each other at Oxford. We were together for a bit. Like dated, you know!' I laughed as if I'd made a joke.

'Hi, Alex. I'm Matt.' He stuck out his hand with a friendly smile. I exhaled.

'I bumped into Alex on my run,' I said, slightly glossing over the stalker element as they shook hands. 'He's been living in the States and is new to Melbourne, so I thought I'd show him where to get a decent coffee.'

'We're coffee snobs here,' Matt said as we all sat around the table that was slightly too small for the three of us. 'What can I get you?'

'He drinks a long black,' I said quickly. Though that could have changed in the intervening years – maybe he was a Starbucks Gingerbread Latte guy.

'That would be great, thanks mate,' Alex said. Mate? Where had that come from?

'I can grab them,' I offered, but Matt had already jumped up. I exhaled – I was glad I didn't have to leave Matt and Alex alone.

'He seems nice,' Alex said.

'He is. He's the best,' I said. 'But you don't like "nice" people. You always said that nice people were compensating for something.'

'I've since learned that everyone is compensating for something.'

'What are you compensating for?'

'You already know the answer to that,' he said.

Before I could reply, Matt returned to the table, holding a plate filled with what looked like one of every pastry they sold.

'In case your run didn't knock the hangover on the head,' Matt explained. 'We had Rebecca's mum's birthday dinner last night.'

'Ahh – no wonder you drank,' Alex said.

'Thanks, Matt – these looks delicious,' I said, ignoring Alex.

I reached forwards and grabbed a croissant and began to tear it into chunks.

'Alex is the client on my new project. ATG bought his research, and they've hired us to work out the best way to sell it,' I said in one big gush of words. I stuffed a piece of flaky pastry into my mouth. It should've tasted like a buttery cloud, but felt like chewing cardboard.

'Congratulations, mate,' Matt said to Alex. Where were all these 'mate's coming from? I could see the recognition on Matt's face as he realised that this wasn't the first time I'd run into Alex. He gave me a sideways look. I could see him replay the previous night in his mind, with the overlay of this new information.

I picked up another piece of croissant.

'If you're new to town, we'll have to show you around. Do you know anyone here?' Matt asked. I scanned his voice for any traces of wariness or annoyance. But no, he sounded like his usual friendly, upbeat self.

'Not really,' he said. 'I grew up in Adelaide, so I know a few friends of friends who have moved here. But no one close.'

'I'm in Sydney for work a lot – I know what it's like to be at a loose end in a city,' Matt said with a warm smile. 'I'm going to the tennis with a few mates this afternoon if you want to come along?'

'If you're sure, that'd be great,' Alex replied without hesitation.

My stomach dropped. It didn't surprise me that Matt had made the offer – he was the guy who was chair of our street's Christmas party and led his company's social committee. But I hadn't expected Alex to accept the invitation.

'You want to watch sport?' I asked incredulously. Unlike Matt, who'd yet to find a sport he wasn't happy to tune in to, Alex thought that exercise was for doing and couldn't understand why anyone would want to sit still and watch other people doing it.

'Yeah, I do,' he said. 'Thanks, Matt.'

Matt offered him the plate of pastries and Alex selected a cinnamon swirl with a smile.

What was happening? I'd thought introducing Alex to Matt was the right thing to do. If I was going to be spending time with my ex-boyfriend, it made sense that my fiancé had the full picture. But the purpose of the exercise was to reassure Matt that there were clear boundaries in place. This breakfast was meant to restore my temporarily displaced sanity and contain Alex – not *You, Me and Dupree* him.

Chapter 11

'Any of these the one?' Lily asked. I stared at Evie's pudgy fingers, which were each decorated with a different gold or silver ring. I hadn't meant for our Saturday afternoon catch-up at Stella's house to be *all* about the wedding. But Lily was making our wedding bands, and between work and Arlo's nap schedule we'd struggled to find time to meet in person to make a final decision.

'Umm ...' My eyes flicked from one band of metal to another.

'I cried when Nick showed me the ring he'd picked,' Stella said as she burped Alice.

'Of course you did,' Lily replied as I laughed. Nick could have given her the ring from a can of Diet Coke, and she would have been in floods.

'If there's something you've seen that you like, I can make a version of it,' Lily prompted.

Matt had asked for a simple gold band, and I'd assumed that I'd want the same. I looked at the array of rings in front of me. I was going to wear this ring for the rest of my life. Did I want gold or platinum? Thin or thick? Encrusted with diamonds, or some kind of symbolic stone, or plain? Normally I knew exactly what I wanted, but I was confused. I felt like I was trying to get somewhere without Google Maps.

'This is the one I made with you in mind.' Lily pointed at a thin band, which Evie was trying to shove on her doll's wrist. 'It looks like it's one solid band but it's actually three thin pieces of metal, each a different type of gold, woven around each other.'

Her tone was nonchalant, but I knew how much skill, how much work, how many stolen hours had gone into making that ring. Lily's custom pieces, particularly ones like this, weren't just jewellery – they were art.

'It's called a trinity ring,' Lily said. 'The three pieces of metal represent the past, present and future.'

I felt my throat tighten. The notion of the past and present intertwining felt too real this afternoon.

'Do you like it?' Lily asked.

'I do!' I said, and swallowed. 'You're an absolute genius, Lil.'

Lily snorted. Stella and I glanced at each other. Lily was many things, but derisive of her talents wasn't one of them.

Stella plucked the ring off Evie's doll's arm and handed it to me. 'Wear it for a bit this afternoon and see how it feels,' she suggested.

I slipped it onto my finger, where it sat snug against my engagement ring. It was strange that in a few weeks I'd be a wife and Matt would be my husband and because of a band of metal, everyone in the world would know it. Nick had chosen not to wear a wedding ring ('I'd just have to take it on and off to scrub in!') and Lily wasn't married to Aaron (she thought it would be funny to call him her 'current boyfriend' when they were in their seventies), but for Matt it hadn't been a question – he couldn't wait to wear a ring.

'Seriously, why don't you go have a nap?' I suggested to Stella as she tried to cover a yawn. Nick was on call all weekend, so she had no backup.

'No, it's okay,' Stella protested.

'Please go!' I said and reached out my arms for my niece. With only one backwards glance at her baby, Stella stumbled towards her bedroom.

'Do you think Alex is one of Matt's groomsmen yet?' Lily asked with a cheeky smile, as she started to pack up the rejected rings. In an emergency phone call, I'd told Lily about the Matt-and-Alex-together-this-afternoon situation.

'Oh god, don't,' I said. Matt's portion of the bridal party was already coming in at six to my two (though Holly and Ivy, his twin sisters, were going to stand next to me for symmetry purposes). What was a scarier notion: Matt having seven groomspeople or Matt and Alex becoming friends?

'What are they even talking about?' I asked.

'Matt can talk to anyone about anything, you know that,' Lily said.

'Yeah, I know.' I had to leave buffers of time wherever we went because he invariably ended up chatting with every barista, retail assistant and dog owner we encountered.

'Anyway, it's happening, so try not to freak out,' Lily added.

We were interrupted by a knock on the door. I jogged down the hallway, jiggling Alice, to answer it before Stella was disturbed.

'Darling!'

'Dad!' I rushed into his arms.

'Group hug!' Evie, who'd followed me down the hallway, flung her short arms around the trunks of our legs.

'What are you doing here?' I asked, once we'd all disentangled.

'I thought I'd drop in on my way home from the hospital,' he said.

'Oh, great,' I said. I felt a sting of irritation – I knew the feeling well after two recent encounters with Alex. I'd asked Dad ages ago if he'd be free to help pick out the watch I wanted to give Matt as a wedding present, but he'd told me he had plans all weekend. Except the scheduling conflict had been work.

Dad squatted down in front of Evie. 'I brought something for you!'

He pulled an ice cream in a lurid wrapper from behind his back. Evie squealed with delight. I felt a tug of discomfort. Stella was pretty careful when it came to what Evie ate – I didn't want her to regret having some downtime when she returned to find her high-energy preschooler jacked up on sugar. But Dad didn't respond well to feedback. And what was I meant to do – yank the rainbow Paddle Pop out of the tight fist of a thrilled child? I decided I'd cut up some carrots to counteract its effect.

'Hi, John,' Lily said when he reached the kitchen.

'Lily! What a nice surprise,' he replied. He gave her a kiss on the cheek and then lowered himself onto a couch. 'Business booming? Do what you love, and you'll never work a day in your life! What are you girls up to?'

'Trying on wedding rings,' I said, holding up my finger.

'Oh, that reminds me, I have some bad news,' Dad said. I braced.

'My colleague who was going to lend us his Bentley now needs it that day.'

I exhaled. This I could troubleshoot. I'd thought for a moment that Dad was about to tell me that he'd been given the keynote at some important international conference on our wedding date and wouldn't be able to make it.

'That's okay. We can ... Uber or something,' I said quickly, adding 'wedding car' back onto the to-do list, with a sub-item not to mention to Mum that the one task Dad had taken on had fallen through.

'The curse strikes again!' Lily said with a wry smile.

'What curse?' Dad asked, turning towards her, an eyebrow raised.

Lily helpfully filled him in. 'The one where every woman in Helena's family gets engaged to a man before the person they marry.' I shook my head at her behind Dad, but she missed it. 'Because Becs is marrying her first fiancé, Helena thinks the whole wedding is doomed.'

A rare belly laugh exploded from Dad.

'Sometimes I miss her dramatic flair,' he said, wiping his eyes. 'She was never going to marry ... I can't even remember his name. He had less personality than Hamish does.'

'Dad,' I said, jerking my head towards Evie. Brown and pink ice cream was dripping down her face onto the dove-grey couch, and she was was looking more interested in our conversation than she normally did watching *Gabby's Dollhouse*. I ran to the bench to grab a roll of paper towel.

'It happened to Grandma Evelyn too,' I said as I dabbed at the pale fabric.

'Evelyn probably forgot she said yes to two men,' he said. He'd always loved Grandma and had been grateful for how much time she'd spent with me as a kid, but he'd always treated her like a child he found adorable but occasionally exasperating.

'Maybe,' I said, but Dad's attention was already on Evie who was campaigning heavily for access to his phone.

A few minutes later I retreated to the bathroom, Alice strapped to me in her carrier. I stared at myself in the mirror and smiled. The reflection was reassuring. A thirty-something face and a baby on my chest. This is who I wanted to be. I was no longer a confused teenager or a girl in her early twenties, unsure of everything. Now I knew exactly what I wanted. I held my left hand up next to my face. Matt and I had a plan. I just needed to get through the next month. I just needed to get through today.

In a few hours, Matt would come home, and we would order something fried and watch a movie. I'd apologise for throwing him in the deep end and thank him for being so welcoming and explain what I'd been trying to achieve.

I heard a car crunching across the gravel driveway – it was probably Nick, home after being called in to see a patient. I looked out the window and was surprised to see the car was Matt's. We'd planned to meet back at home.

I quickly washed the residue of Evie's ice cream off my hands and raced out to greet him. I was dying to know how the afternoon had gone, to make sure that everything was okay, preferably away from my dad, best friends and assorted children.

But I stopped in my tracks as I reached the front step. Not only were Dad, Lily, Evie and Arlo already in the front garden, but Alex was standing next to Matt looking relaxed in a faded T-shirt and a new Australian Open cap. Matt was wearing a matching one. How did the same cap look entirely different on each of them? Alex, in his oversized sunglasses looked like a hipster celebrity trying to hide from the paparazzi, whereas Matt, whose white linen shirt matched the hat, looked like the dad you'd love to have a gentle flirt with at a school fundraiser.

But hats weren't the important thing right then. How had the afternoon gone?

'Who's this?' Alex waved at Arlo.

'This is my son, Arlo. He's one next weekend,' Lily said, greeting Alex with open arms.

'Matt said that you'd be here, so I thought I'd say a quick hello on the way home,' Alex explained. Was Alex *that* desperate for company in a new city? Or had Matt encouraged him to come along?

My spiralling thoughts were interrupted by a clinking sound. I looked down. The wedding band had fallen off my still slightly soapy hand and straight through a metal grate, into a drain.

Chapter 12

'Shit!'

A small pair of eyes lit up.

'Sorry, Evie.' I began to bend down but realised I couldn't with a baby strapped to me.

Everyone had stopped talking to look at me.

'The ring ... it just slipped off my finger and fell through the grate,' I explained. My heart began to race. Lily's custom rings were handmade. I couldn't just lose one, my one.

Both Matt and Alex wordlessly kneeled down on either side of the stormwater drain, peering into the darkness. My breathing became shallower.

'Maybe your mother is right. Maybe this wedding *is* cursed,' Dad said, with an amused chuckle.

'The symbolism isn't great,' Lily added wryly, though I could hear the catch in her voice as she realised one of her creations had been dropped into the ether.

'Google says that it's possible to get a ring out of a drain with a fishing rod and a big hook,' Matt read off his phone, pretending not to hear Dad and Lily. 'Do we know if Nick has a fishing rod?'

Despite the sick feeling in the pit of my stomach, a hollow laugh escaped me. Nick barely had time to see his kids and wife, let alone take up hobbies.

'I can make another ring. Leave it,' Lily said.

'Let's have a crack—'

'We'll get it—'

Matt and Alex spoke over each other.

My guilt transformed into panic.

Alice's face went red as she groaned. She then relaxed with a contented sigh.

'Okay. I've just got to change a nappy. No one do anything until I'm back,' I said, holding up my hands like the person in charge of stopping traffic near a construction site.

'What is happening, Alice?' I asked as I worked my way through most of a packet of wipes. She blew a raspberry by way of reply.

By the time I'd cleaned up my niece – which had necessitated an entire outfit change – and made it back outside, things had escalated.

Dad had evidently unearthed one of Nick's medical kits, and was tying knots in surgical thread. Alex was kneeling next to him on the gravel driveway, using pliers to shape wire into a large hook.

'Are you going to use a horizontal mattress stitch?' Alex asked Dad without looking up.

'Lock stitch,' Dad replied, not breaking focus either.

Matt was sitting on the doorstep next to Lily, a glass of red wine apiece. Arlo sat at their feet.

'What's going on?' I asked slowly.

'We're not entirely sure,' Lily said. 'John worked out that Alex is a doctor, and they haven't talked like real humans since. We think they're building their own fishing rod–style contraption out of medical supplies. It's like a deranged version of *Lego Masters*.'

My body stiffened. I'd barely been able to handle Matt and Alex spending an afternoon together. I could not cope with Dad and Alex acting like Chief Webber and Derek Shepherd.

'I knew Alex had studied medicine. But did you know he could do proper doctor stuff?' Lily asked.

'Yeah, I saw him in action. Once,' I replied.

I turned nervously to Matt, who had obviously been sidelined while I'd been gone. And knowing Dad, probably with zero tact.

'Matt … I'm sorry,' I said.

'It's okay,' he said, raising his glass. 'I'm also exercising my area of speciality.' Lily laughed at his self-deprecating tone but I couldn't force a smile.

After last night, I had never wanted to drink again. But a glass of wine, something to take the edge off this absurd situation of my own making, felt critical. Matt usually jumped at the chance to offer me a company wine, but he avoided my gaze. My stomach fizzed.

Evie appeared at the front door dressed in a miniature pair of scrubs, holding her toy doctor's kit.

'I want to play too!' she squealed. It was quite an astute observation – Alex and Dad did look like boys playing with toys. I felt a stab of guilt. Dad and Alex were just trying to help retrieve a valuable ring that I had lost.

'Do you want to watch some *Bluey*, Evie?' I asked. It didn't feel like Dad, in surgeon mode, had the bandwidth to supervise Evie. But, in what was an emerging theme, she ignored me.

'Don't touch anything sharp!' I said, and she gave me a look that felt far too withering for what a three-year-old should have been capable of.

'God, it's "Patient Presents" all over again,' Lily said, as she ran a bejewelled hand through Arlo's wispy hair.

'What's "Patient Presents"?' Matt asked, turning to Lily and topping up both of their glasses.

'You haven't told him about "Patient Presents"?' Lily glanced back at me, looking surprised.

'I feel like it's revelation central today,' Matt said. My heart sank. His tone was even. Lily wouldn't have noticed anything was off, but I knew he was upset.

'I remember the first time I went on a long car trip with the Evans family,' Lily said. 'We were all packed in together and John's voice boomed from the driver's seat: "Patient presents … with pain in their abdomen, a fever and low blood pressure." Then, I shit you not, the whole family each had a turn asking questions about this imaginary patient's symptoms. The winner was the person who guessed the correct diagnosis first. I suppose it made sense for a car full of doctors and aspiring doctors, but I felt very dumb that day. I guessed that everything was chicken pox, which was the only thing I'd heard of.'

Matt turned to me. 'You wanted to be a doctor?'

'For a while,' I admitted, with what I hoped was an air of nonchalance.

'That's a bit of an understatement. That was basically you for your whole childhood,' Lily said, pointing to Evie, who'd applied half a dozen Band-Aids to her legs and was now using her plastic stethoscope to listen to a giggling Arlo's tummy.

'Anyway,' Lily continued, 'while the rest of the world played "I Spy", this is what the Evans family did on road trips.' She laughed at the memory, and I forced a smile. I hadn't thought about 'Patient Presents' in forever.

'Our family just played *ABBA Gold* on repeat,' Matt said. 'Which probably explains why I love *Mamma Mia!* But also why no one trusts me with their heart.'

Lily snorted into her wine as I winced. I wanted to wrap my arms around Matt, but I knew that would make things worse.

I looked back at Dad and Alex, who were crouched over the drain and slowly pulling Frankenstein's fishing rod out of the grate.

'And … we've got it,' Dad said, in a steady, emotionless voice, as if he'd found a hole in an artery. On the end of the hook was a glinting, albeit slightly muddy, ring.

'Matt,' I said, but he either didn't hear me over Evie's excited shrieks or was ignoring me again.

Alex held my wedding ring to-be aloft like it was a Grand Final trophy.

'Thanks for saving the day guys!' Matt said to Dad and Alex, managing to sound grateful. 'Can I get either of you guys a celebratory nebbiolo? It's a really great one from a small winery the company just bought.'

'Am I still dreaming?' Stella appeared at the front door, rubbing her eyes.

'I really don't know,' I said, no longer feeling in control of the situation or my own mind.

Chapter 13

THEN

In the middle of the empty Exam Schools lobby, I held Alex for a few moments, then pulled away. I knew I needed to say, *Congratulations*, and then, *I should probably go.* He had just handed in his thesis, he probably wanted to sleep for a thousand years or celebrate with his college friends. And I was good at knowing when I'd had enough of a good thing: saying no to the drink that would tip me into being drunk, not watching one more episode so I'd get enough sleep, not ordering the side of chips that would make me feel too sluggish to study.

'Do you want to celebrate?' I blurted out instead. 'When else is every pub in Oxford open at eight in the morning. It's a sign! One glass of ... something?'

'Okay,' he said easily.

We walked from the Exam Schools to the King's Arms, then managed to snag a brown leather sofa almost hidden in a nook behind the main bar of the pub, which was in full party mode.

I fought my way through the very merry crowd and bought us drinks. I handed a pint of cider to Alex and raised my own.

'To Alex Lawson, PhD.' Our glasses clinked together.

'Almost,' he said. 'I have to pass my viva first.'

'Are you worried about that?' I asked.

'No,' he said, and we both laughed. I don't think I'd ever met someone so direct. It was refreshing. Sometimes it felt like my family only communicated in impenetrable riddles.

'What are you studying?' he asked.

'I'm doing a double degree in law and commerce.'

'I know absolutely nothing about either,' he said, and I smiled. I liked that he didn't have a shred of intellectual insecurity. 'Tell me something you've learned.'

I paused for a second as I ran through some options. I knew my degrees weren't the most exciting ones out there. But I wanted to rise to his challenge – to teach him something that would grab his mind.

I flicked through my mental Rolodex of options. Something from one of my economic classes, maybe the black swan theory. Or maybe one of the thought exercises from the philosophy course I'd taken over the last two terms – I'd love to hear Alex's thoughts on the veil of ignorance. Then it came to me.

'Okay, I'll tell you about my favourite case,' I said. 'It's one we studied in my contract law class.'

'I'm intrigued,' he said, looking as if I was about to impart a piece of scandalous gossip rather than a precedent relevant to contract formation.

'There's a case that went to the Australian High Court. It's about the legal principle of unconscionable conduct, but that's not the interesting bit.

'The case is about a man who was totally infatuated with this woman. He bought her heaps of presents, showered her with affection, and just generally lost his mind.

'Then, she told him that she was depressed, was going to be evicted from her house and would hurt herself if that happened. So the guy bought her a house.

'When his senses returned, he asked her to transfer the house into his name. She refused. It ended up going all the way to the High Court. And the court gave him back the house because they decided that she'd made him so emotional that he'd acted against his own interests.'

'So,' Alex said slowly, 'they basically made a law that means that if someone makes you emotionally dependent on them, and then uses that dependence to manipulate you into making decisions against your own interests – well, that's enough to invalidate a contract.'

'Exactly!' I got the sense that Alex would have been at the top of any class, across any faculty. Even by my fifth year most of my classmates couldn't summarise a case both as quickly and accurately. 'That's what the highest court in our country decided.'

'The law will undo the actions of someone who lets their heart overturn their head,' Alex said. I could practically see him turning this concept over in his mind, playing with its ramifications. 'What do you think?'

'In Contracts A it didn't matter what I thought. It's the law,' I said.

'But I'm not giving you a grade. What do *you* think?' he asked again.

I paused to weigh up my reply.

'I think the High Court made the wrong decision,' I said. 'Being carried away by emotions isn't a defence for making silly choices. If you can't control your heart, then that's on you.'

'Even if the other person behaves badly?' he asked.

'Even then,' I said. 'People are responsible for making their own sensible decisions. I don't think you get to blame someone else.'

I took a long sip of my drink. I waited for the expression on his face that would make it clear that I'd failed his test. Except his eyes sparkled and he held my gaze in silence as his mouth slowly pulled into a half-smile. My stomach did a small somersault.

'Can you tell me more about your research? Or do you never want to talk about it again?' I asked.

'I think it's the only thing I *can* talk about,' he said. 'I've lived and breathed it for the last few years.'

'So give me the idiot's guide,' I said.

'I don't think you need the idiot's version of anything,' he said. This time I felt my heart do a somersault.

'Okay, fine. But I only studied chemistry and biology until year eleven. So, you might need to go slow on the science side of things—'

Glass smashed a few tables over from ours, then there was a howl of pain. Alex froze.

'Can someone call nine-nine-nine? He's bleeding! Like a lot!' a plummy, but very worried, voice called. 'Is there, like … a doctor in here?' I could tell that she was slightly embarrassed to be using a line straight out of a medical drama, but on balance was too panicked to act cool.

There were a few glances across sticky pub tables. I could tell that a lot of people in the room were entitled to use the prefix 'doctor' but felt that a speciality in Victorian Gothic literature might not be needed.

I rifled through my bag for my phone before realising it

was in my pocket. By the time I stood up, Alex was out of our sofa and was kneeling next to the table at the epicentre of the drama.

'He's quite drunk.' The posh girl was wide-eyed as she explained. The whole room had fallen silent as we watched the drama unfold. 'And he accidentally dropped his glass. And I think one of the bits of glass bounced up and cut him.'

That was an understatement. Blood was pouring from her friend's long, thin arm that was poking out of a Jack Wills T-shirt. The arm's owner clearly had a pale complexion to begin with but right then looked ghostly.

Alex moved closer to him. 'Okay, mate. I know this is overwhelming, but I'm a doctor and I'm going to help you. The first thing I'm going to do is lift up your arm.' He spoke calmly but with total confidence. The girl looked visibly relieved that she was no longer in charge.

'Now I'm going to take my jumper and gently tie it around the cut,' Alex said. With the hand that wasn't holding the bleeding arm he pulled his university hoodie from around his waist and in one deft motion wrapped it around the bleeding forearm and then placed his hand around the material to hold it in place.

'Has someone called an ambulance?' Without turning around, he spoke to the crowd, which was still silently but avidly watching on.

'It's on its way,' one of the bartenders called out from the back of the room.

'Great,' Alex replied. 'Can you tell them that there's a deep cut to at least one artery, but it's been stemmed. Though it might have been a vessel and it's more than a couple of centimetres long, so it'll need stitches.'

He turned back to Jack Wills Guy. 'We're all under control. You and I are going to stay like this until the ambos arrive. The most important thing is that we keep this pressure on the wound and keep your arm elevated. Does that sound like a plan?'

The guy, now much less freaked out but still woozy, nodded.

The pub manager, with the authority of someone who regularly announced 'last orders', asked the gawking crowd to move into the main part of the pub. I hesitated for a moment, not wanting to linger but also not wanting to abandon Alex at his own celebration drink. I waited for a moment too long in case Alex looked up. But he didn't – he was totally focused on his patient.

'Who was *he*?' I heard a girl wearing a Teddy Hall scarf ask her friend as we all shuffled out.

I turned back and caught one last glimpse of him, and wondered the exact same thing.

Outside the pub, the dancers and musicians decked out in flowers and bells were gone and people who hadn't been up since dawn were bustling through the cobbled-stone square on foot and bikes, piles of books in their arms or satchels over their shoulders.

I slowly walked away from the picturesque pale pink building as an ambulance pulled up in front of the entrance. How many family events (and flights) had been derailed by someone in my family stepping in to take charge of a stranger's medical emergency. I half smiled. The morning had felt so uniquely English, but apparently the ability to lose yourself in a medical emergency was universal. I crossed Radcliffe Square alone, not knowing if I'd ever see Alex Lawson again.

Chapter 14

Two days later, I checked my pigeonhole in the porter's lodge. And there, among the usual flyers for student plays and club nights, was a thick creamy envelope with my name written on it. I ripped it open. It was an invitation to a dinner the next day to be hosted by the Shelley Society. And scrawled in black ballpoint ink at the bottom was a phone number and a note: *I have a lot of time on my hands now that I've submitted my thesis. I'm not very good at fun either – maybe we can learn together? Would this dinner make your list? If so, join me. Alex.*

I felt a flash of excitement, swiftly followed by a rush of panic. The dress code was black tie.

Given I lived in jeans and jumpers, I needed to enlist the urgent help of Lily. Oxford seemed to have two dress codes: scruffy casual or black tie, nothing in between. I owned a single black formal dress that had been a workhorse over the last two terms for college formal halls and events. But I didn't want to wear it to this dinner.

The next evening, I stared at myself in the mirror on the inside of Lily's wardrobe, which I'd raided. Did I look like someone else or like an enhanced version of me? I was wearing Lily's emerald-green dress, big gold earrings and sparkly deep-green eye shadow. Lily had used her hair straightener to create gentle waves in my hair. I looked like a grown-up woman.

'I can't believe you're going to a secret society event; I hadn't heard of it even after two years here,' Lily said. 'I'm so bloody jealous!'

It was a weird dynamic – Lily was normally the one invited to wild-sounding parties. She was the repository of anecdotes with a beginning, plot twist and end, and I was the audience. But tonight she was the godmother and I was Cinderella – out of my hoodie and into a gown.

Alex had been very blasé about the whole thing when I'd texted him to say I'd love to come: *Warning: It will be a bunch of undergrads pretending they're in* Brideshead Revisited.

Obviously this was not enough information, so Lily had done some digging. What she'd found out was that the Shelley Society was one of the college's oldest secret societies, one that had been around for hundreds of years, and the only one the college officially endorsed. It had its own set of silver. The members met twice a year for a feast in the dining room, which only the college's academics were normally allowed to use. The whole thing was totally archaic and intimidating.

Lily surveyed her handiwork (my face), added one more swipe of blush to each cheek and then poured us both a glass of our local shop's cheapest white wine.

As she studied my face again, I looked at hers. There was something off. Her energy wasn't at her usual full-beam. 'Are you okay?' I asked.

'We can talk about it tomorrow,' she said, looking away.

'We can talk about it now,' I said, putting my drink down. 'What's wrong?'

'I just rejected my place at law school,' she said. I stared at her for a moment. Lily had been at Oxford for the last two years as a Marshall scholar, doing a master's degree in art history. Then, she was meant to return home and go to law school.

'Right,' I said, trying to sound supportive yet neutral. 'Why?'

'Because I really don't want to be a lawyer,' Lily said. 'Or study law.'

'That's a good reason,' I said. 'So, you'll … get a job?'

Most of our friends from school had already started working in hard-won grad jobs or entry-level roles. We were already at the tail end of the gainfully employed. And in a few months, I'd be suiting up and joining everyone in the city back home.

'I've applied for another course,' she said, a hint of defiance in her voice. 'A jewellery design course at Melbourne Polytechnic. I want to have a crack at making art. You know … be in the arena and all of that.'

'Wow, amazing!' I said, trying to sound as enthusiastic as possible. I knew that I was the test balloon, that she was gauging my reaction before she told her family. Lily's parents had moved to Australia when she was a kid and devoted their entire lives to their daughters' educations. Law school represented the prize for all they'd sacrificed for their children – they'd be unequivocally devastated.

'Have you been thinking about this for a while?' I asked.

'Since high school,' she said, after a moment's pause. 'It's what I've always wanted to do.'

I blinked at her. I knew she lived for all things aesthetic: clothes, design, jewellery, makeup. But I'd thought art was an area of academic interest and the rest a form of self-expression.

'I just … What if I die and I never tried the thing I really wanted to do with my life,' she said. 'Do you remember in year eight when we did a unit on sculpture?'

I nodded, though it was a vague, distant memory. I'd made a vase so wonky that Mum hadn't even been able to pretend to use it.

'I designed a necklace. And I became obsessed. I learned to solder and use pliers to bend and twist the metal. I made and remade it so many times. I loved every minute of it.

'And then I stopped being able to make things because I had to sign up for smart-kid subjects: maths and languages and music. I knew that if I did commerce or science, or even undergrad law, I'd be totally miserable, so I fought to study art history. Mum and Dad hated what I'd chosen, but they got around it because I got a scholarship and I told them that it was more prestigious to do law as a grad degree anyway. I thought that studying art might be enough. But being creative adjacent … it doesn't scratch the itch. I want to do the thing. Make the thing.'

She took a long sip of her wine.

'There are so many kids here who come from generations of privilege. And their parents are encouraging them to follow their dreams – some of them are even funding it. And I just feel … I'm smarter than them. I might be more talented than them. I know I want it more than them.' She stopped to take a deep breath. I'd never seen her speak with such fire.

'And I get why my parents just want me to do something that's safe and stable and pays a truckload. That's what they never had. That's all they wanted for us. But I … There's something I really want to do with my life. And it's not drafting legal documents. Or making clever points in a courtroom. It's my life, right?'

'Yeah, of course it is,' I said, wrapping my arms around her. 'I'm proud of you, Lil.' It wasn't the choice I would have made for myself, but I supported her unequivocally. And I knew that even admitting how she felt, let alone doing anything about it, was mammoth. I squeezed her tightly. 'I'm sure your parents will get their heads around it.'

'Do you think?'

'Yeah, of course. It might be a journey, but they love you. And … you'll just have to marry someone with a fancy job instead.'

Lily laughed.

'Marry Nick! He's almost finished his training. Your parents would love a doctor in the family!'

She broke our eye contact for a moment then stepped back from me.

'Okay, this is probably not the right time, but you've given me such a ridiculously perfect segue, I have to tell you something. Promise you won't get upset.' She refilled our drinks right to the rims of the glasses.

'Not a fair precondition,' I said as my heart thumped. 'What is it?'

'Nick and Stella are dating,' she said. I could see her studying my face for a reaction.

'Like our Stella?'

'No, a random Stella you've never met,' she said, deadpan.

'Wow,' I said.

'They've been working in the same hospital. Nick recognised his little sister's friend, all grown up, and was smart enough to ask her out. It's been over six months. And I think it is pretty serious.' Lily pre-empted all my questions.

'Six months!' I said. 'They've kept it a secret for six months?'

I wanted to be happy for them, if they were happy. But I felt a familiar sensation of the rug of certainty being pulled out from under me, of being totally blindsided by unexpected family news. My brother and one of my best friends were together. And they'd kept it from me.

'Stella is really sorry about that. But she thought that if it went nowhere then it wasn't worth making things weird.'

I silently resolved to be nothing but excited and over-the-top supportive when I next Skyped with Stella. I wasn't sure how I felt about her dating my brother, but I loved both of them.

'Isn't he too old for her?' I asked. Nick was eight years older than me, than Stella.

'I think we're at the age when dating a thirty-two year old isn't a headline anymore,' Lily said. 'Dr McBrainy is around the same age, isn't he?'

Lily hadn't just done some digging on the Shelley Society. She'd also used her elite research skills to get the lowdown on Alex. He'd been doing his medical training when he won a Rhodes Scholarship to complete his PhD at Oxford. He was about to be double Dr Alex.

'Yeah … I guess,' I said, adding up the length of his degrees in my head. I hadn't thought about his age, or any age gap. It didn't feel important. I guessed it was the same for Stella – not that I could fully process it yet.

Lily leaned across the window seat at the edge of the room and peered out the window into the quad.

'He's here!' she said. 'Jesus, he's gorgeous. How did I miss him? Poor form from me.'

I giggled, bathing in her performative jealousy. I raced over to the window and kneeled next to Lily. God, he did look good in formalwear. Did men know how gorgeous they looked in a tux? Surely not or they'd wear them all day, every day. The suit didn't quite fit, his shirt was creased, and his bow tie was totally lopsided. But it didn't matter at all.

My jangling nerves, temporarily quelled by our conversation, kicked back in.

Chapter 15

'Matt, we have a million things to do today. We need to do the seating chart. We need to buy thank-you presents for our wedding party. We need to check all the honeymoon details. And next weekend we've got stuff on. And the one after, we've got our hen's and buck's.'

I looked up from our shared document (saved as 'Wedding McWedding'). 'But first of all, we need to work out what to do with these ...' I tried to keep a straight face as I held up one of the two hundred sculptural candles we'd ordered. We'd seen the idea on Pinterest – we would attach a tag with each person's name on it, and it would be a cute place card and a memento to take home. But when we'd opened the box earlier that week, we'd discovered they were less pastel pink and more flesh coloured than they'd appeared online. And the shape was slightly – well, very – phallic.

'I know we have to deal with the wedding favours that look like penises,' Matt said. 'But we also need a day off.'

I slowly shut my laptop. I owed Matt a day of doing whatever he wanted after the start of the weekend. He hadn't said anything when we'd got home from Stella and Nick's place the day before. But he'd been quieter than

112

usual. He'd gone to bed early. We hadn't watched a movie together.

''Course,' I said.

We went for lunch at our favourite spot on Lygon Street, mopping up enormous bowls of pasta with spongy white bread. After we'd braved the queue for Pidapipó ice creams, we decided to go for a walk, and without ever discussing exactly where we were going, we walked towards the Melbourne University campus.

The academic year hadn't yet begun so the campus was almost empty – a set without the players. Flyers, sticky-taped to noticeboards and bollards, all belonged to the year before. In a few weeks' time, everyone would return from pub jobs, internships, backpacking trips around Asia. But today it was ours.

'Can we have a look at Queen's?' I asked Matt. This was his alma mater but not mine. And while occasionally we walked around the university campus, he'd never taken me into the residential college where he'd lived for the first two years of his degree.

'Okay,' he said, and smiled. He led me across a quad framed with dripping pale purple wisteria. We walked past the student union, advertising protests and Bubble Tea, and down a narrow path until we reached Queen's College.

I stared up at the impressive sandstone facade. I'd never really noticed that it looked exactly like an Oxford college. It wasn't a coincidence – the oldest uni in the city, in what had once been a colonial outpost, had been modelled on Oxford.

'What were you like when you were here?' I asked as we walked through the entrance – a heavy wooden door under the stone tower.

He considered the question for a moment. 'I had a lot of fun, but I think I was … lost,' he said.

'In what way?'

'I didn't know what I wanted to study. Or what I wanted to do with my career,' he said. 'I felt like that for a long time … like I was floating through life. Like it was happening to me.'

'What changed?' I asked.

He stopped walking and took my hand. 'I met you,' he said, his eyes softening.

'What do you mean?' I asked, confused.

'You were the first person who thought I was someone … serious, or with any depth, I guess,' he said. He raced over the words 'serious' and 'depth', as though they were still descriptors he struggled to say out loud about himself.

He paused, as if he was deciding whether to keep speaking, how much he was willing to reveal.

I squeezed his hand, but didn't say anything.

'The wall behind the piano in my parents' living room – have you ever noticed it?' he asked then looked away from me.

'No,' I answered. Matt's family home looked like it belonged to one of Beatrix Potter's animals. And when we visited, we were mostly in Jane's cosy kitchen, being continually fed.

'There's a whole wall of Holly's and Ivy's certificates – every gymnastics and piano and horse-riding award, spanning their whole lives. Their degrees. Graduation photos,' he said. 'And that's great! I think it's important to celebrate the things. Except I've only got two frames on the wall, to their dozens. God, that sounds petty. But one is my degree, which is basically next to the piano stool, and the other is a photo that appeared in our council newspaper, and I'm a toddler in a clown outfit.'

He paused for a moment, still looking straight ahead. 'I mean, my parents named me Matt. Not even Matthew. What hope did I have? I'm a nickname of a person.'

His tone was still light but there was an edge of pain to his voice, as if it was almost killing him to even veer towards territory where he was critical of his family. I knew that this hurt was coming from someplace deep and raw.

How had I missed this? Of course this was his family's dynamic. His twin sisters were Matt's dad's doppelgangers – all sharp features, accounting degrees and not a hint of a sense of humour. (They never missed a mistake on a bill in a restaurant, but wouldn't recognise sarcasm if it hit them in their faces.) Whereas Matt, all softness (with the exception of his body) and charm, was their antithesis. I guess I'd just assumed that Matt knew that he'd won the genetic lottery. But my perspective was that of an outsider. I could see that from the inside, it had felt like he'd been sidelined his whole life.

He finally turned to look at me, his eyes wide and apologetic. I wrapped my arms around him, wishing I could absorb his pain. Our hug felt like home. Finally, we pulled away from each other, but I reached for his hands, not wanting any distance between us. This space felt important – a place to say the vulnerable things that we were afraid weren't likeable, safe in the knowledge that we'd love each other anyway.

'You are the best person I know. You're funny and you don't take yourself too seriously. But you're not a clown, Matt. Or a joke,' I said. 'And your sisters got themed names. So, I think that just might be a your-parent thing.'

'Thanks,' he said, his face relaxing, the golden specks in his eyes glinting again. 'Haven't we spoken about this before?'

'No,' I said, shaking my head.

Matt took a deep breath, gathering unspoken thoughts. 'I'd always felt like everything I'd got in life was because I was easy to have around, that I could get on with people. And I was just happy to go with the flow. I sort of stumbled into my major and then fell into my first job,' he said. 'Then, on one of our first dates, I mentioned that I thought I might like to do a more challenging job one day. And the next time we met up you brought along a list of jobs you thought I might enjoy – ones you'd come across on your cases. And another list of people I might want to have coffees with to find out more.'

'I think most people would have run screaming from the girl who turned up to a date with a career-focused list,' I said.

He smiled but not broadly enough to disguise that this conversation was simultaneously uncomfortable and cathartic for him.

'And of course I wanted to help,' I added. 'It was nothing. *You* were the one to follow through on everything.' Matt had done the real work of networking and hustling to get his current job, which he was brilliant at.

'It wasn't nothing. You inspired me to … take the steering wheel of my own life,' he said. 'It was the most romantic thing anyone had ever done for me.'

'I guess I'll return that red lingerie set,' I said in a teasing voice with what I hoped was a coy smile.

'Please never return that red lingerie set,' Matt said, with one of his deep laughs that made me melt.

'You know that if there's anything you want to do, I'll do everything I can to help you make it happen,' I said, wanting to make sure that he knew that I meant it.

'I know,' he said. 'I've always known that. And I'll always do the same. We're a team.'

I swallowed hard. 'I'm really sorry I didn't give you the heads-up about Alex that first time I ran into him,' I said. 'That was a bad judgement call. The promotion had just been put on the table and I think I … short-circuited or something.'

'You want it, right?' Matt asked.

'What do you mean?'

'Do you want to be a principal at Stern?'

'I mean, yeah. Of course.'

'Why?' He looked surprised that he'd asked this question.

'Umm … You know, I really like my job. It feels …' I searched for the right word.

'Safe?' he offered up in a neutral tone.

I nodded. 'That and … I just really love Excel.'

Matt laughed.

'And I do feel like I'm helping people,' I continued. 'With this case, when we get the technology into hospitals, it will save a lot of lives.'

Matt turned away for a moment then looked back at me. 'You didn't need to get my approval to work with Alex,' he said. 'I didn't need to meet him. Thanks for thinking of me. Of course you can work with whoever you want. Of course you can go after any job you want. Of course I trust you.'

We began to walk again, still holding hands, in no particular direction.

'Lily told me that the ring that went down the drain yesterday is called a trinity ring because the three pieces of metal represent the present and future and past combined,' I said. 'And I think that's perfect. Because the best part of my life is living in the moment with you. Not the big stuff but the random lunches and meandering walks and the conversations in bed when we're both too tired to be awake but we keep talking anyway. And I'm so excited for our future together. I know sometimes we'll want different things but because we believe the same things matter, we'll always work it out.'

I paused for a moment.

'But maybe the thing we haven't talked enough about is the past. Our family stuff. And our exes,' I said, after a few footsteps of easy silence.

'Okay, we're doing this,' he said.

'We're doing this.'

'For me, it's only one really serious one,' he said. 'Jess. We met here, actually.'

'So, she was your uni girlfriend?' I asked.

'Yeah. And then after that,' he said.

'How long were you together?' I asked.

'About six years,' he said. I took a short, sharp breath and felt a sting of jealousy at the idea of Matt being in a substantial relationship with someone else. Though I guess time wasn't always an indicator of depth. But still, six years wasn't nothing. I quickly did the maths – Matt would have been single for a few years before we met.

'What about you?' he asked.

'No one serious, really,' I said. 'I didn't date much in my twenties.'

Why? I waited for the inevitable question, but it didn't come.

'Why did you agree to go on a date with me?' he asked instead.

'I almost didn't,' I said. I'd never told him this. 'But then I changed my mind. I think I … I don't know … I think I instinctively knew you were a good guy or something,' I said.

Matt looked thoughtful as he led us down a long path through manicured lawns.

'Alex and I were together for less than two months. The word "boyfriend" or "relationship" hardly feels legitimate. Maybe "situationship" is better,' I said. 'He promised he wouldn't hurt me, and then he did. But we were kids – well, Alex was thirty – but I was pretty young. It was forever ago.' The words tumbled out.

'Short relationships can still be heartbreaking,' Matt said.

'Yeah, I guess. There was no clear beginning and no clear end. I guess … I don't thrive in the land of uncertainty. And because it was such a short amount of time, everything was heightened. I didn't know what was real or what was just a fantasy,' I said. I'd wanted to tell him about Alex, but now I'd started I couldn't seem to stop talking.

Luckily I was saved from myself by people streaming into the quad in cocktail dresses and dark suits. And at the back of the group were a bride and groom.

'Oh wow,' I said. I always loved stumbling across a wedding in the wild. Though this wasn't exactly a public garden – we'd sort of barged our way into this college, and it was clearly a private event. Though we were far enough away from the crowd that they wouldn't notice us.

As if we'd both had the same thought, we turned towards each other. Our lips met and I shivered in the best way – feeling ripples as his fingers ran down my neck and my back. His lips were soft, the kiss slow and gentle. There was no urgency. We had time – we had our whole lives to kiss each other. So, right then, we could kiss like we were students. I wound my arms around Matt and held him tightly.

The kiss stopped my mind from whirring. I stopped thinking about all the mistakes I'd made the day before. I stopped thinking about everything on our wedding to-do list. I stopped thinking about the email I needed to send to Miranda to tell her that I was more than happy to stay on the case. I tried to stop thinking about tomorrow, when I'd be at an offsite with Alex. And I especially stopped thinking about the night Alex and I had spent in a quadrangle almost identical to this one.

Chapter 16

It was not a normal Monday. To make sure that our project team and the client team would work effectively together, the powers that be (Miranda) had decided that we'd spend the first official day of the case at a team-building day. Personally, I thought that more progress would be made if we did less bonding and more work.

Apparently, money was no object, because the offsite was being held at Jackalope, an incredibly bougie hotel, an hour out of the city on the Mornington Peninsula.

We all caught a minibus from the office together because ... bonding. I practically hurled myself onto a seat next to a member of the client team to avoid Alex. He walked past, heading to the back of the bus, noise-cancelling headphones on. He predictably gave his backpack a seat so that he didn't have to share with anyone, and I could have sworn he was laughing at me.

I spent the next hour learning far more than I'd ever expected to about the various stages of med-tech approval, thanks to my new, very earnest colleague. But, in her defence, I had asked. The bus ride seemed to take forever, and I wondered if I could invent a crisis and spend the day working on my laptop in a quiet corner. But Miranda was there, wearing burnt orange and looking improbably rested after her camping trip, evidently ready for us to make a good impression.

The hotel was impressive. It was arguably more suited to an Instagram-friendly proposal than a corporate awayday, but I wasn't complaining. A cheery facilitator, Fiona, who had the upbeat energy of someone who regularly finished their workday at 5 pm, met us in a conference room.

We were directed towards tables that ominously contained nothing but butcher's paper and markers. I waited until Alex had picked his seat, again at the back, before I sat down at a table on the other side of the room.

'Now, for our first session, we're going to focus on working effectively with different personality types,' Fiona said.

I tried to look enthusiastic, but at that point in my life I'd had more personality tests than birthdays. When I'd received the link on Friday to complete 'a short questionnaire' I'd almost been tempted to go rogue and try to conjure up another personality type, just to keep things interesting. But in the end, I'd dutifully filled it out, answering questions to situations that I knew almost by heart.

I pretended to look interested when the facilitator's assistant placed my results in front of me. I knew what it would say: *INTJ*.

'Your concerted efforts to avoid me have been thwarted by Myers–Briggs.' I looked up and saw that Alex was sitting down next to me. While pretending to look fascinated by my results, I'd missed the group being shuffled around the room.

'They're sorting us based on our personality type animals,' he said. 'It's very Patronus coded.'

'Wow, that's a new spin on this exercise,' I replied, and he laughed.

'It's a bold move using something with such a tenuous scientific basis on a bunch of scientists,' Alex said.

'I wouldn't count on a mass revolt. People can't get enough of any activity where they get to talk about themselves. Trust me, I've sat through enough of these.'

I looked around the room. Sure enough, faces were bright and eyes gleamed as people earnestly considered whether they were indeed a 'dolphin' or a 'fox'.

'My respect for my colleagues has already significantly gone down,' he said. 'Was that the point of today?'

'Yeah, the stated aim is to foster judgement and leave doubting each other's abilities.'

He laughed.

'Surely there are other people in this group?' I asked.

'*I N*,' Alex read off the piece of paper in the middle of the table. 'Are we the in-crowd? I've always wanted to be at the cool table.' I knew with total certainty that this was something he'd never cared about. But I was glad we were talking about anything but the weekend. Or Oxford.

'It means we're introverts with intuition,' I said. 'Have you really never done one of these before?' I pointed at the booklet in front of him that would show his results.

'No. And I'm intuiting that this is the stuff that gives science a bad name,' he said.

'You enjoyed the neuroscience lectures we went to,' I said. We'd both been obsessed with a course we'd stumbled upon during 'Lecture Lottery' called 'Being Human and the Brain' and had become the professor's most enthusiastic unofficial students.

'I thought "Rule One" was no nostalgia,' he said.

Before I could reply, Fiona appeared behind us.

'Any more in this group?' I asked hopefully, ignoring him.

'Just you two!' she replied. 'Now you, Rebecca, are a wolf.'

'Ahh.' I did my best to sound interested.

'Why is Rebecca a wolf?' Alex asked.

Fiona nodded as she seriously considered the question, not noticing Alex pressing his lips together to suppress a laugh. 'Mm, great question,' she said.

I avoided Alex's eyes so I wouldn't giggle.

'This type of person is powerful and independent. They don't open up to everyone and are hard to read. Wolves are pack animals and are generally monogamous creatures, finding one mate to spend their lives with.'

'I can see how that's relevant information for this project,' Alex said.

Fiona missed the sarcastic edge to his voice.

'So true,' I said, ignoring him. 'And I've found my he-wolf. We're getting married in a few weeks.'

Fiona beamed. I'd known, with my wolflike instincts, that she was the type of woman who'd get around a wedding.

'Am I also a wolf?' Alex asked, the teasing edge to his voice replaced with what sounded like genuine interest.

'No, you're in Slytherin,' I said in a low voice, and was rewarded with a flash of mirth in Alex's eyes.

'You're an owl,' she said.

'Hoot, hoot,' he replied, then smiled.

I noticed Fiona run her hands through her heavily highlighted hair. His chiselled jawline hadn't been lost on her.

'You're wise, logical and analytical,' she said. 'You have a unique perspective and intense intellect.'

I groaned. His metaphorical feathers did not need any more stroking.

'Do I need a she-owl?' Alex asked.

Fiona practically swooned. 'A special type of owl,' she replied, her voice now an octave lower. She twirled a piece of her hair with a manicured finger. 'Your personality type needs a counterpart who can challenge their ideas. They want to spend their life striving for intellectual mastery. They hope that the person they love will not just share this vision but be their greatest supporter.'

Neither Alex nor I responded. I knew what he was thinking.

'So probably not a wolf then,' I said finally.

'Though they're both nocturnal,' Alex countered.

'Actually, that's a common misconception,' I said primly. 'What would an ENFJ be?' I knew that was Matt's personality type because he'd been subjected to almost as many of these tests as I had.

'A dog,' she replied.

'I can see that,' Alex said.

I glared at him.

'Because they care very much about other people's emotions, and always want to know how others are feeling,' Fiona went on.

'Mm. Caring, loving, spreading joy,' I said thoughtfully.

'A dog is the descendant of a wolf. The domesticated version. That's interesting,' Alex added.

Fiona looked at both of us, as if she knew that there was something slightly unusual happening in this exchange, but she couldn't quite put her finger on it. 'I might check in on the dolphin and monkey table,' she said finally, and moved towards a group of animated people, including Miranda and Lucas, enthusiastically talking over each other.

'What are you doing?' I hissed at Alex as soon as Fiona walked away. 'I thought we were going to be civil.'

'You're so angry,' he said softly, almost to himself.

'I'm not,' I began, but trailed off before I finished my thought.

If anyone had asked me a week ago what I felt about Alex Lawson I would have said, *Nothing at all.* At the very most I would have said I felt a smidge of resentment or a hint of disdain. I might have added that I never wanted to see him again. But that was natural – who wanted to reacquaint themselves with a person who screwed them over? This was something I never understood about movies that had payback as the goal – why risk a future on avenging a past?

But since I'd been around Alex, it had become clear that he did stir up certain emotions: irritation, frustration and, the tabooest of female emotions, anger.

'Yeah, okay, so maybe I am—'

I was interrupted by Fiona announcing the end of our

breakout time. It was time to come together and discuss what we'd learned.

I ignored Alex for the rest of the morning. Lunch, which was pretty much the point of the day and where the actual bonding would happen, was at Doot Doot Doot, the hotel's restaurant. It would be paid for by Miranda's corporate card. It didn't quite pass the logic sniff test to treat a company that was paying us enormous fees to lunch, but sometimes it seemed best not to question the inner workings of late-stage capitalism. A free multi-course lunch on a Monday was one of those sometimes.

The restaurant decor was part upmarket Australian winery, part Scandinavian ski chalet. Pieces of grey faux fur were casually draped across blond-wood furniture.

'They've skinned some wolves. Watch out!' Alex whispered in my ear, before he thankfully went to sit at the other end of the table, next to Miranda.

We'd been given a long table down the middle of the restaurant. I sat between the other consultants on our team, Lucas (personality type: ESFP / dolphin) and Adrian (personality type: ISTJ / cat). I was happy to have the chance, in an informal setting, to get to know them better before I ruined their lives by asking them to run models and fix up slides late into the night.

Our central table took up most of the dining room but there were still other people, mostly couples, dotted around. I felt guilty – I knew that a group like ours would suck up most of the oxygen in the room. We would drink expensive wine and order the most courses, and because we weren't paying the bill, we wouldn't treat it with the deference it deserved.

A waiter stood at the head of the table, cleared his throat and with a theatrical pause waited for us to give him our full attention.

'Today our chef has curated a special menu for you based on the concept of "Differences, working together".' Fiona beamed in a way that made it clear that this was her masterstroke. 'We've paired ingredients that at first glance might not seem like they would work together into a coherent whole.'

While I knew my face would read as enthusiastic I inwardly groaned and prepared my grumbling stomach for dishes like gorgonzola ice cream. My phone pinged.

Do you think there will be popping candy in anything?

He'd found me on the company Teams. There was no escaping him. I gave myself a silent pep talk. Boundaries and professionalism – they were the bywords of today, and the next few weeks. I could handle work–related emails but was chatting on Teams too intimate?

Almost certainly. I also think odds of edible flowers are incredibly high.

I stared at the message I'd typed out. My finger hovered over the screen. It would be unprofessional to ignore a message from a client. I pressed send.

I saw Alex check his phone and then smile.

Haha.

I exhaled. Then another messaged popped up.

I remember every part of that dinner.

So do I. I mentally composed a message I was absolutely not going to send then threw my phone into my bag under the table.

Chapter 17

THEN

'You came,' Alex said as soon as I reached him at the entrance to the quad. He tugged the hem of his tuxedo jacket as if he could stretch the fine wool into something less restrictive.

'Did you think I'd stand you up?' I asked. He shrugged as he smiled sheepishly. It was the first time I'd seen a chip in his patina of confidence.

'I wasn't sure if the Shelley Society was your idea of fun,' he said. There was colour in his cheeks as if he'd been exercising just before he'd pulled on his suit. It looked like he'd attempted to brush his hair: his normally tousled mane was smooth though still buoyant. And was it the early evening light, or did his hair look more golden?

'I didn't have you down as the kind of guy who was part of a secret society,' I replied.

'I'm not. It's all undergrads, but they have to invite one grad student to minimise the chance they end up in the *Daily Mail*,' he said.

'So, you're basically an overqualified babysitter?'

He laughed. I felt my spaghetti strap–covered shoulders relax slightly.

'Was that pub guy okay?' I asked.

129

'Totally fine. Just needed a few stitches,' he said. 'Sorry I didn't get to say goodbye.'

'It's okay. I know dealing with random medical incidents is part of the doctor thing.'

'I promise that tonight if someone starts to drown in their soup or lights their hair on fire with a candelabra, I'll ignore them.'

'Deal,' I said, biting my bottom lip to stop my smile.

'Should we go eat some free food?' he asked. He offered me the crook of his elbow, albeit in an exaggerated way, as if he understood that everything about tonight was inherently bizarre – the ancient buildings, the formalwear, the promise of an evening filled with archaic traditions. But at the same time, I was giddy. Maybe the English were onto something. Maybe they knew that if you conjured up a beautiful backdrop and put everyone in flattering costumes, the magic would come. I took his arm.

As if it wasn't enough that we were in a medieval dining room covered in an array of hallmarked silverware, the dinner had a theme. According to the embossed menu in front of me, every course would engage a different one of our senses.

Seated next to Alex, I could smell a hint of his lime shower gel and see the fire in his eyes as he quizzed the girl sitting next to him about her dissertation. I could hear his gravelly voice asking question after question. I could feel his pinkie finger occasionally brushing against mine. As the notion of taste made me blush, Alex turned to me.

'"Sight"?' Alex guessed. We'd each been delivered a salad that had been made to look like a garden – all flowers (edible, I guessed) and carefully selected pieces of micro-herbs. Dark oils were artfully dotted around the plate.

'"Smell",' I replied, checking the ornate menu. 'It features a lot of infused oils.'

'The primary sensation I'll be feeling tonight is hunger,' Alex whispered, and I laughed.

We whizzed through 'Smell' and 'Touch' (venison and popping candy wasn't necessarily a combination I'd be rushing to try again). Even though I was in a foreign environment, a place that couldn't have been more English and rarefied unless a member of the royal family had shown up, it felt familiar. This could have been one of the dinner parties or barbecues or birthday lunches that Mum would throw before she left.

I mean, obviously we didn't have silver candlesticks running down an antique table, and Mum didn't serve a themed degustation to guests in tuxedos. But the carefully prepared food, people laughing and talking over each other, time stopping in the best way – Mum had always been able to create a similar atmosphere.

I basked in the warm fuzzy feeling of being a part of something again. Maybe this was the point of all these societies at Oxford – to make you feel like you belonged to a thing bigger than yourself, far away from home. Or maybe I was overthinking it and it was just an excuse to drink lots and get dressed up.

'Should we make a plan to do something else on the "Salad Days List"?' I asked, emboldened by my perpetually refilled wineglass. 'I know you have a bit of a break before your viva.' The words spilled out on top of each other. I felt like I was back at high school asking if Alex could put me in his Myspace top eight.

'I did have another idea for the list,' he said with a broad smile.

'Will all your ideas require black tie?' I asked.

'I'd need tails for the Trinity Ball. Would that count?' I wasn't surprised that he could remember an item off a list he'd looked at for a few seconds days ago.

'I think that would work,' I said. I took a sip of the heavy red wine, which paired perfectly with the filet mignon ('Taste'). 'Do you have a ticket?' He shook his head.

'I can try to get you one if you want?' Every summer a bunch of colleges hosted balls but there was only one lavish, white-tie Commemoration Ball each year. This year my college was the host, and the sense of anticipation had already started to build.

'That would be great, thanks,' he said.

'So, we just have seven weeks to fill until then. What's your idea?' I asked.

'I'm warning you, it's geeky!'

'I'm obsessed already.'

'The name of my game is "Lecture Lottery",' he said. 'How it works is that we turn up to the Exam Schools at nine each morning and go to whatever lecture looks most interesting. It can be from any faculty, on any subject.'

I laughed giddily because I adored the idea so much. He wanted to spend his time with me in lecture halls, learning random things. That was *my* idea of fun.

We finally finished dessert: a hamburger made of a chocolate mousse patty and brioche bun ('Sight'). The silver jugs of coffee were passed around and the tapers had dwindled to stumps.

'I think I've fulfilled my babysitting duties. Do you want to get out of here?' Alex asked. The college staff were making a show of removing things from the table – eviction from the dining room was imminent, and a plan was emerging to kick on in the college bar.

'Yes, please,' I replied. I think we both knew that we weren't going to the bar with the others.

'We could have another drink?' he suggested, when we emerged from the Senior Common Room into the now-dark quad. 'The roof?'

'I'm not sure I'd trust myself on a roof right now,' I said, already slightly wobbly on firm ground. The wine had flowed all night and then there'd been port, which had been sticky and sweet and seemed to have just hit my bloodstream.

'Dancing in the Moonlight' wafted out of the cellar bar in the top right-hand corner of the quad. It should have been cringeworthy, especially because it was a full moon, but instead it just felt like someone had done a good job of scoring the evening.

'Dance?' he asked, offering me his hand.

I stared at him for a moment. I hadn't expected him to be the kind of guy who'd want to dance, ever. But I was quickly learning that patterns of how people behaved weren't helpful when it came to getting my head around Alex.

I took his hand, and he pulled me in against him. We swayed with each other to Toploader. For the first time I understood the point of dancing – it clicked why dancing had made all the difference for Anna and Vronsky, for Elizabeth and Darcy, in a way that I'd always thought was overwrought. For the first time, I understood why they'd begun to lose their heads.

He held the small of my back and I rested my hand on his shoulder. I wasn't particularly short, but against Alex's tall frame, I felt tiny.

We stayed like that until the song ended. Then I pulled away from him, feeling warm and slightly breathless. In the shadows of the quad at nighttime his pale blue eyes had darkened and looked more like sapphires. He leaned forwards and kissed me. As his soft lips met mine a part of me that I hadn't been sure existed roared into life. It was an overpowering force, like a tidal wave. My stomach clenched and my palms, wrapped around Alex's wool jacket, became clammy.

I took a step back, off balance in my heels.

'Thanks for tonight.' I crossed my arms tightly, even though I felt flushed.

I turned and walked down the path that bisected the quad. The college bells began to peal, because of course the clock had struck midnight. The stage had been set so perfectly I was tempted to do it justice and kick off one shoe.

Except, unlike Cinderella, I didn't want the fairy-tale ending. In fact, right then I wanted my perfect dress to magically transform into a tracksuit. If a fairy godmother appeared and asked me how she could magic up some help, I'd ask her if I could go back in time so that I hadn't agreed to have a drink in Lily's room when I'd got my grad job offer, then when she'd had to go to a lecture, climbed out of her window onto her college roof with a bottle of cava. Because then I wouldn't have met Alex Lawson, and he wouldn't have kissed me. And then I wouldn't be feeling the way I felt right now – totally terrified.

Chapter 18

The next morning, I woke up with a hangover. But it wasn't one that I knew could be fixed with a day of eating carbs and staring at the ceiling. I stayed in my bed for as long as I could, until the need for something fatty and fried became too urgent. I pulled on leggings – even jeans felt too restrictive. I didn't look at myself in the mirror but I knew what would be there – eye makeup collected under my eyes and a mat of formerly perfect waves.

I almost made it to the bottom of my staircase, but Alex was sitting on the final step.

'Are you the Sphinx I need to riddle my way past?' I tried for a light tone, but didn't pull it off.

'What happened last night?' he asked.

I wanted to give him an answer. I'd had the most magical night of my life. 'I don't know,' I said.

'There's something between us,' he said. 'I thought maybe, at the start, it was like … a meeting of minds. But it's more than that.'

He stopped but I didn't fill the silence. I didn't know what to say. Both my body and brain felt numb. The deluge of emotions I'd felt last night had faded to nothingness.

'I've always felt lonely with other people,' he said. 'Like I didn't understand them, and they didn't understand me.

But with you … I feel the opposite of lonely. You're smart but you wear it lightly, you're funny and gorgeous.'

He paused again as I turned my eyes to the dark stone walls, not knowing what to do with the compliment.

'Please look at me, Rebecca. Because I think you feel the same way about me,' he said. 'I mean, maybe not the gorgeous part …'

I exhaled the breath I'd held because I couldn't help but laugh. Alex was so beautiful that it wasn't even subjective – though I was willing to bet that the only time he ever looked in a mirror was when he was brushing his teeth. And even then, I was sure his mind would be a million miles away.

'I do,' I said, meeting his stare again. 'Including the gorgeous part.'

'I think you're scared,' he said with conviction – in a tone that I bet had impressed his med school interviewers and scholarship assessors.

'You're wrong. I'm not scared,' I said, then swallowed. 'I'm … bloody petrified.'

'Why?'

'Because of what we feel right now. This thing that feels … big and powerful,' I said.

He nodded.

'It hurts people,' I said, willing myself not to cry. 'I don't want to feel something so strongly that I can't … think clearly.'

'Your parents?' he asked after a moment.

'Yeah.' I sat down on a cold step above Alex. I cleared my throat.

'My mum left my dad for another man just before I started year twelve. She was my best friend – we were really close,' I said. 'And then she just blew up everything because she lost her mind and … fell in love.

'Not that any of that is the point. The point is that I felt like the most naive person in the world. I just … didn't see it coming at all. I knew that Mum got frustrated that Dad worked so hard and had to travel so much. But I thought she liked that it was just the two of us together. But, yeah, I was wrong.' I laughed bitterly, my feet resting on the edge of a stone step worn smooth with age.

'I asked Mum to stay. She'd always stayed home when I'd asked, whether I was sick or just overwhelmed. She would stay if I asked. Except she looked me straight in the eyes and told me that she couldn't. Mum was the constant in my life – the person I could absolutely rely on. And then she wasn't.'

I blinked my stinging eyes a few times and then ran my sleeve across my face when that didn't work.

'I know she loves me,' I said with an involuntary sniff. 'But it wasn't enough. The type of love she felt for *him* was bigger.'

'I can't imagine what it must have felt like for your mum to *choose* to leave,' he said. I felt a flood of relief. He didn't dismiss or minimise what I'd told him, or the pain I'd tried and failed to disguise. In fact, his tone bordered on condemnation. And I knew why. His mum had left too. But I knew that she would have done anything in the world to stay – to still be with her son.

I'd never spoken to anyone about this chapter in my family's history. Partly because it didn't feel dramatic enough to make a big song and dance over. I was the daughter of two doctors who'd lived pretty smooth lives.

So I'd had one little road bump to contend with when I was a teenager, one that happened to heaps of people. So what?

I never wanted anyone to see this dark and twisty part of my brain (or was it my heart?). I didn't want them to judge how I felt or encourage me to take a more generous position. Alex hadn't done that, he'd validated how I felt.

'What was it like when you lost your mum?' I asked.

A shadow crossed his face. He looked down and fiddled with a loose thread on his college tracksuit pants. Then he looked up, and his eyes, which looked almost inky blue in the darker light of the stairwell, met mine.

'I made Mum a promise before she died. She wasn't conscious or anything, but I told her that I'd fix the thing that broke her.

'I think that if I hadn't made that promise, a promise that felt bigger than the sadness, to focus on, I would have gone to a dark place. But there wasn't room for feelings when I had to top med school, then work a million hours as a registrar and get a scholarship to come here,' he said. 'I think having this thing to do for Mum sort of saved me. Who needs anti-depressants if you don't have time to think?'

I laughed even though it wasn't really a joke.

'I went down the medication route,' I admitted. 'I got anxious after Mum left. I'd always been a wound-up kid, but after she left, I started to have panic attacks. Not that I really knew what they were. Grandma Evelyn noticed, and a GP prescribed me Xanax for when things became too much.'

'Did it help?'

'Yeah, it did. But I was like a bingo card for side effects – I got nausea, fatigue, dizziness and blackouts. I took one of the pills the night of my year twelve formal, washed it down with a glass of champagne, and I don't have a single memory of the night. I'm in about a thousand of the photos that my classmates uploaded to Facebook. Lily and Stella said I acted totally normal the whole time, but I don't remember a thing.'

'That must have been really scary,' he said.

'It was the first time my parents had been in the same room since the split, so it's probably a good thing that I don't have any memories of the night,' I said lightly.

Alex didn't smile.

'I learned how to stay on top of the anxiety stuff without medication after that. I worked out that if I slept enough, ate well, stayed away from Mum, made lists ... I could manage it.'

There was silence between us, one that we both needed to metabolise the confessions we'd made, revealing the invisible cuts and bruises we were still nursing.

'You outsmarted your feelings,' he said.

'So did you,' I replied. 'Except when I'm with you, I feel a bit like I did back then. Like I'm not really in control of myself.'

I paused again to gather my thoughts, which had been careening around. But I knew that Alex understood everything I was saying.

'I grew up thinking that following your heart was the most important thing in the world. "Love your job and you'll never work a day in your life." "You only get one life." Dad used to say stuff like this all the time. He loves his work so much,' I said. 'But … I saw that love, love like Mum felt, and following your desire without thinking about anyone else, can hurt other people,' I said. 'I don't want to feel like she did. Ever.'

He turned his head away for a moment, his chin buried in his hand like *The Thinker* come to life. Then he looked back up the stairs at me.

'I think we're different from other people. So, let's promise that we'll do us differently,' he said. 'We won't lose our heads. We won't hurt each other.'

'We've only got this one summer term. After it ends, we're going to live on different sides of the world,' I said quickly.

'I know,' he said.

'How about we agree that we're just a … summer fling. No losing our heads. No hurting each other. Just … fun,' I said. I wanted to be with him. I wasn't sure I'd be able to stay away from him. But I couldn't just *be* with him. Not without a plan, not without some guarantees, some protection.

He smiled, lighting up his whole face. 'Okay,' he said.

I grinned back, then bounced my Lycra-encased bottom down one hard stair then another until I was next to him.

'No one gets hurts. I promise,' he said.

Our outfits were the opposite of glamorous, the dark stone staircase was the opposite of romantic. He leaned towards me and his lips met mine. I understood that energy followed the rules of physics. But right then, I didn't believe it because the release of whatever energy had built up between us over the last few days defied anything kinetic, nuclear or otherwise.

I moved into his lap, and my tongue moved into his mouth. I felt a silent groan vibrate from his soft lips. Something pulsed through me, the same thing I'd felt the night before – was that what proper, all-consuming desire felt like? I'd been certain feelings like it were a fiction, the stuff of books with swooning people on the cover and movies where lovers kissed in the rain at the end.

And, as I felt his arms wrap around me with far less hesitancy, I couldn't help but smile. From our first conversation our brains had fitted together. But now I knew that our bodies did too. And I fully intended to spend the summer making Alex's body my specialist subject.

Chapter 19

NOW

'Oh my god, look what's happening!' Lucas exclaimed as the second course of our awayday lunch was cleared away. His eyes were lit up, and he was holding his hands up to his face. I turned to follow his gaze across the restaurant.

At a corner table, a man wearing a blazer, almost shaking with nerves, had got down on one knee. A woman, dressed up as if it was a Saturday night, not a Monday afternoon, looked down at him. I guessed that she'd totally expected that this was going to happen today, but now that the moment she'd dreamed of had arrived, she was overwhelmed.

Lucas stood up and started filming them.

'Should we give them some privacy?' I asked.

'Trust me, a girl that wears heels that high for lunch has a strong social media game,' he whispered, and I smiled. I had no idea if Lucas knew anything about healthcare or pivot tables, but I knew that he would make me laugh if we were stuck together in the office at 2 am – and that wasn't nothing.

Our whole table looked on. The man finished his speech and then the woman began to furiously nod. He'd asked the question, and it was a yes. The room collectively exhaled, having absorbed the couple's nerves, and burst into applause. Even Miranda looked a bit dewy-eyed. I saw her whisper to our waiter and knew she'd be sending them a bottle of champagne. Glasses around our table were topped up too, and a lot of people who hadn't been drinking now said yes. The proposal had created a festive atmosphere around the room. I decided to join in.

I couldn't help but sneak a glance at Alex. I'd expected cynicism on his face, but he looked wistful, maybe even moved. Had he softened as he'd grown up? Or maybe he was in love with someone – I hadn't asked him if he was in a relationship. I'd assumed not, because he'd recently moved across the world, but of course he could have been in a long-distance relationship. I made a note to casually drop the question into our next conversation, in a not-weird way.

'Did your fiancé get down on one knee?' Lucas asked me, staring at my ring.

I laughed. 'No, he didn't,' I said.

'So how did it happen? Tell us the story!'

'We'd been dating for about a year. And one night we were at my place watching a movie together and at the end, as the credits rolled, Matt handed me a ring box and said, "Marry me?" And I said, "Yes." I opened up the box and inside was a piece of paper.'

'He proposed with a piece of paper?' Lucas asked. I couldn't help but giggle at his very underwhelmed face.

'Well … sort of,' I said.

People often asked Lily whether, in her professional opinion, it was better to buy the ring before or after someone proposed.

'Do you know how I know when a couple are going to make it?' she'd ask.

'By how expensive the ring is?' someone would joke, and she'd ignore them.

'How?' they'd ask.

'It's got nothing to do with how much a ring costs. It's not whether they've picked out something for a surprise proposal, or if they wait to pick it out together. No … I always know when a relationship is going to last when they want to make the choice that will make their partner the happiest.

'Some people want to buy the biggest ring they can afford to show off their success. Some want to buy the cheapest thing they can get away with because they think the whole thing is unfair. But the ones who are going to live happily ever after just want their partner to be happy. That's the beginning and the end of it.'

After Lily had shared her engagement ring theory, some people would be starry-eyed while others would be surreptitiously eyeing off their partner's hands, running their own motive through Lily's lens. When I'd opened the ring box Matt had given me, I'd wondered if he'd heard her speech. Because it was the perfect proposal. Inside the box was a piece of paper titled *Qualities Rebecca Wants in Her Engagement Ring* with a numbered list for me to fill out. Matt had given my list to Lily, and we'd bought a ring from her together.

'He knows I love lists, so he proposed with one,' I said. Lucas looked bemused, but Adrian, who I was beginning to suspect was a romantic, looked moved.

Had that only been nine months ago? I'd felt so sure about everything then. But that was before every decision we made about the wedding seemed to blow up in our faces. That was before the curse seemed to linger in the background of conversations.

As I inhaled a mouthful of lunch, I snuck a glance at Alex. He was engrossed in conversation with Miranda, whose face was animated. They'd both stuck to water so were probably in the middle of a razor-sharp deep dive into something off-the-charts complex. I'd forgotten what a good listener Alex was, that he was at his most handsome when he was really absorbed in trying to understand what someone was telling him.

I pulled my focus back to the couple drinking the champagne that had arrived at their table, cheeks flushed, totally in their own world. They were probably also talking about what their dream wedding would look like. I mourned the naive, hopeful version of myself that I'd been at the start of our engagement.

A few courses later, my suspicion that wildly different flavours didn't complement each other had been confirmed. But alcohol and a corporate AMEX *did* go together. The team had very much bonded at the hands of the bottles of local wine, which had been flowing since the proposal. Most people were flying. I feared for Fiona's afternoon session.

'Are you okay?' Adrian, who I guessed missed absolutely nothing, asked me. Had I got carried away and had a glass too many?

'You've gone a bit … blotchy,' he said carefully.

As I put my hands on my cheeks, I realised that I didn't feel very well. I felt hot, and my mouth was tingly. I looked down at my plate and realised what I'd done. While I'd been distracted, surreptitiously watching Miranda and Alex, I'd loaded my plate with food from the communal platter, ignoring the special one that had been put in front of me.

'Shit,' I said, my heart beginning to pound. 'I think I'm having an allergic reaction.'

Chapter 20

I pulled my handbag from under my seat and frantically rifled through it, looking for the EpiPen I always carried but had never had to use on myself. My fingers touched a lipstick, then a tampon before finally finding it. My mouth felt like it was on fire, and I was afraid that if it got much worse, I'd struggle to breathe properly.

Everyone sitting around me had gone still. I stared at the EpiPen. 'Sky high.' That meant the blue bit pointed upwards, I was pretty sure. Flashes of the training sessions I'd done a few times played through my head. But I'd only practised on a doll with a fake pen.

I steeled myself. I liked oxygen more than I feared jabbing myself.

'Now I'm going to need that,' a commanding voice spoke over my shoulder. Alex held his hand out for the EpiPen.

'No, I can do it,' I said. Well croaked, really.

'Rebecca, shut up, do what I tell you and answer these questions,' he said. 'Can you breathe?'

'Yes,' I wheezed. 'But it's ... tight.'

'Do you have an allergy?' he asked.

'Yes,' I said again. 'Capsicum.' Of course, as an adult I'd developed the least sexy allergy on the planet.

He pulled the cap off the EpiPen and slowly pulled up the fabric of my skirt, exposing my thigh. Then he pushed the orange part of the pen into my skin and held it there. I felt a little sting.

'It's okay. The adrenaline will kick in soon and you'll feel much better,' he said in a soft, almost-soothing voice.

A restaurant full of people were watching us, a darker second act after the proposal, but right then it felt like it was just the two of us, that everyone else had faded into the background of the moody restaurant.

'Could you please call an ambulance?' Alex turned to Lucas, who already had his phone out. I hoped he wasn't also taking a video of this. I really didn't need this to make the Christmas party blooper reel. 'Tell the operator that a woman, mid-thirties—'

'Early thirties,' I cut in. Alex ignored me.

'A woman in her mid-thirties has had an episode of anaphylaxis. She's been administered a point-three milligram dose of epinephrine. She's able to breathe.'

Lucas echoed Alex's words down the phone.

'They said they can send an ambulance, but if there are no critical respiratory issues it might be quicker to drive to the nearest emergency department, in Frankston,' Lucas relayed the information back to Alex.

'I'll drive her in one of the hotel cars,' Alex said.

'I'd like an ambulance, please,' I said. Lucas looked between us, not knowing who to take instructions from.

'I'll drive. Alex can stay in the back with Rebecca.' Miranda, standing behind me, settled the discussion.

Was this really happening? Was I about to be taken to hospital by my boss and my ex-boyfriend?

'I'll be fine.' I tried one more time.

'We'll need to complete an incident report,' Fiona piped up. 'I would have preferred someone with first-aid training administer the medical assistance. Colleagues aren't meant to medicate each other under our policy—'

'It's okay, I'm—'

'He's my ex-boyfriend,' I jumped in to finish his sentence. I felt a strong need, from my position of helplessness, to regain some sense of control over this situation. I didn't want Alex to be the one to reveal to my colleagues that we'd once dated.

'I was going to say a doctor,' Alex said, looking bemused.

A wave of humiliation shot through me, competing with the drug full of inhibitors that had apparently lowered my inhibitions. Of course he hadn't been about to drop our former relationship status into the conversation. And I'd just outed us. I knew that one of the symptoms of anaphylaxis was mental confusion, but I hadn't imagined it would manifest like that.

'So, Professor McDreamy is also Dr McDreamy. Plot twist. Why did she break up with the hot doctor?' Lucas speculated to Adrian, slightly too loudly.

'Her fiancé does sound really thoughtful,' Adrian replied earnestly. I decided that he wouldn't be doing any all-nighters on this project.

'Fine, let's go to the hospital,' I said, trying to drown out my direct reports speculating about my love life.

By the time we arrived at the hospital, all the adrenaline from the EpiPen had worn off and I felt awful.

'I really just want to go home,' I said to Alex, as soon as the room was free of nurses. Miranda, after making sure I was okay, had wandered off to take an urgent client call from one of her other projects.

'You can't,' Alex said. 'You might be okay now, but there's a risk you'll have another attack even without further exposure.'

'That hasn't happened before,' I said. Though I also knew that I'd never had such a violent reaction. I'd been warned that my allergy could become worse with each attack.

'You might need more drugs or oxygen. And they'll probably want to monitor you,' he said.

'Do you actually know what you're talking about?' I asked.

'Yes,' he said simply.

We were interrupted by a doctor, a distinguished looking man with an aura of extreme competence, replacing the harried doctor (he'd barely looked old enough to have finished med school) who'd examined me in the ED. As Alex predicted, the older doctor considered out loud whether I needed an IV drip or help breathing. In the end, he decided to see if my body would be okay on its own, but that I needed to be monitored.

'We're going to take excellent care of you, Ms Evans,' he said, in a practised reassuring voice.

'Can I monitor myself at home?' I asked. I hated hospitals. 'If I feel even a tiny bit strange, my house is only a ten-minute drive from an emergency department. And I have a stack of in-date EpiPens.'

'We recommend that anaphylaxis cases are monitored here,' the doctor replied, thick brows furrowing.

'I'm a doctor,' Alex said. 'I can monitor her.'

The doctor now assessed Alex for the first time, as if he was a ghost who'd taken on a body.

'Well, in that case ... I'd be comfortable with a discharge if you're under medical supervision,' he said.

A discussion must have taken place in the hallway, but in the end I was informed that Miranda would return (reluctantly, she insisted) to the offsite, and that she'd booked an Uber to drive Alex and me back to Melbourne.

By that point, I didn't care how I got there, or who I was with, I just wanted to get home. I must have slept the whole drive because the next thing I knew I was being shaken awake. As I slowly came to, I realised that it was Alex pulling on my arm and that we were outside my house.

The hideous afternoon all came flooding back as I wiped dribble off my chin. I still felt like I'd been run over by a truck, but I was much less wobbly now.

'You don't need to come in,' I said, as I unbuckled my seatbelt. I thanked the driver and opened my door.

'Of course I do,' Alex said. 'Can't break my Hippocratic Oath.'

'What if I pinkie promise not to die?' I asked.

He laughed, joining me on the kerb.

I wondered if a night in hospital might have been preferable to an afternoon with Alex in my house.

'Is Matt home?' Alex had reached the front door before me, holding my work bag and my now-dead phone, and was poised to ring the doorbell.

'He's in Sydney for work,' I said. I hadn't told Matt about my reaction yet. His company had a massive investor presentation the following day, which he'd been working towards for weeks. I didn't want to distract him.

I rifled through the front pocket of the bag Alex was holding until I found my keys, and let us into the house.

'Do you want a drink or something?' I asked as I led him down the hallway.

'I want you to get into bed,' he replied.

I could see him taking it all in. Just after Matt and I had got engaged, we'd moved in together, renting a single-fronted cottage in a row of identical houses, only differentiated by whether they had a modern addition stuck on the back. Ours didn't, but we hoped one day we might be able to buy one that did.

'Fine,' I said. 'But you're staying out here while I'm getting changed. Make yourself at home. Help yourself to anything.' Why was I speaking like a hotel concierge? Next I'd be offering him an early check-out.

I quickly took off my work outfit. As my skirt slipped off, I remembered Alex pulling it up, the silk lining moving up my thigh. Had he needed to do that? Of course he had, the training had made it clear that the EpiPen needed to go into the upper leg muscles. I was worse than Fiona, writing up a mental incident report. He hadn't been feeling me up; he'd been trying to save my life.

I considered getting into my pyjamas, but that felt too intimate even if I put on my fluffiest flannel ones. Instead,

I pulled on a pair of Matt's tracksuit bottoms and an old college hoodie.

I curled up on my side of the bed and closed my eyes, hopeful that when I woke up I'd discover that it had all been a bad dream. I heard footsteps coming into my bedroom.

'Oi!' I said. 'You can't come in here.'

'I have to come in here. My job is to make sure you're breathing.'

He plonked himself down on the armchair in the corner of the bedroom, which most days was piled high with clothes that weren't dirty enough to wash but not clean enough for the cupboard. Matt must have tidied as he'd packed.

'You're bad for my respiratory system. The last time I struggled to breathe was the night of the ball. The night you dumped me,' I said. Evidently the adrenaline was acting like a truth serum on me; first, I'd outed my relationship with Alex to my colleagues, and then I'd started oversharing every thought I had aloud.

He stared at me with an expression that was the closest his face could come to perplexed.

'It wasn't an allergic reaction, though,' I said. 'Well, maybe I had an allergic reaction to your behaviour. But medically speaking, I had a panic attack. It was the only time in my adult life I lost control of my anxiety.'

'The night of the ball?' he asked. He leaned forwards, and I could see his gaze drifting off, as if he was trying to piece something together.

'Anyway, all I want to do is go to sleep,' I replied, kicking myself for opening up a conversation I absolutely didn't want to be having. 'Please, let me just fall into unconscious oblivion.'

'What do you think happened that night, the night of the ball?' he asked slowly, as if he was toying with a new concept, a new rabbit hole to go down.

I closed my eyes. I didn't have enough energy to engage in one of our verbal sparring matches.

'Rebecca, I need to know why you're treating me like I'm the devil incarnate,' he said.

I felt my hackles rise and a flame of irritation build. He was the human equivalent of bellows, breathing oxygen into the embers of resentment from times past. 'You want to know why I'm mad at you?' I asked, clenching my hands into a ball to stop them trembling. 'I'm mad because when I was with you, I did the one thing I'd promised myself I'd never do. I made a ridiculous decision based entirely on emotion. And then you put yourself and *your* career first without a second thought. You announced you were going to America as if what had happened between us meant precisely nothing. And then I never saw you again. I'd only just pieced myself back together and then you cracked me apart again … you broke my heart.'

I watched his expression change from my horizontal position. He had the audacity to contort his face to look shocked. As if I'd put his perfectly imperfect nose out of joint.

'But … that's not what happened,' he said.

'No. That is what *happened*,' I said. My voice rose at the end of the sentence. But it was a statement, not a question.

There was a cough in our bedroom doorway. Alex and I turned to find Matt standing there, his eyes flitting between us.

Chapter 21

THEN

It was the seventh week of Trinity term, and I was sitting with Alex on a rooftop. We were swigging champagne – well, incredibly cheap, soapy-tasting cava – from a bottle as we watched the sun still blazing over the dreaming spires.

That morning, Alex had got the call, the one he'd been working towards for the last three years. He now had a post-doc all lined up. All the long hours in the lab, the endless papers read, the epic thesis written – they'd all paid off. I felt proud, but also devastated and forlorn. In a week's time, Alex was moving to London. I was moving home.

I turned to Alex to see if he looked satisfied, but his expression gave nothing away.

'Are you okay?' I asked.

'Yeah, of course,' he said, then attempted a smile.

'It's just you look so sad … and you're on a roof.'

His smile widened. 'I'm celebrating,' he said.

'Are you still flat about America?' I asked. He hadn't said anything when he'd been knocked back by Harvard, but I suspected the rejection had hurt more than he'd let on.

'I'm flat because … I don't want you to go,' he said. 'I love you.'

I stared at him. 'But … you said we were going to do it differently. We were going to be together for just the summer. We promised that it wouldn't get …' I flapped my hands around as if there was a universal hand signal for falling head over heels in love with someone.

I loved Alex. Of course I did. I'd loved him for weeks, practically since I'd met him. We'd spent nearly every minute of the summer together and it still hadn't felt like enough. We'd been to a million lectures on random subjects. We'd debated everything. We'd talked endlessly about his mum, the lack of a dad in his life and my family. We had a favourite table at a pub (the one in front of the Bob Hawke sign at the Turf Tavern). We'd spent countless afternoons lying in the sun reading. We'd spent even more time in both of our single beds. I knew every part of his brain and body – the way he methodically could work through any problem, the small burn from a campfire on his inner left wrist, the promise he'd made to his mum before she died, the rough of the golden stubble on his jaw.

But the agreement we'd made – that we wouldn't lose our heads – had felt like a protective case between my heart and reality. If we never acknowledged our feelings, then we'd be able to walk away from each other and resume our real lives unscathed.

I stood up.

'Stay,' he said, and reached towards me.

'I'm getting cold up here,' I said, rubbing my bare arms as if to prove my point.

'No, I don't mean up here. I mean stay in England. Move to London with me.'

*

The next day I sat with Lily on a punt. She wore a white shirt with a wilted red carnation in her lapel, a rumpled black skirt and her hair was covered in confetti. She'd just finished her final exam.

'It's the end of Oxford. The end of the road that's not going to be taken,' she said as she lay on her back, staring up at the bright blue sky. Neither of us really knew how to steer a punt, so we'd stopped trying.

'Your parents will get their heads around what you're doing. They'll just need time,' I said.

'They can't believe I'm turning down a stable career when it's almost impossible to even get a bar job at the moment,' she said.

'Recessions don't last forever,' I said, reaching for the confidence of someone who almost had an economics degree. But I knew what she meant – the bubble wrap of our student days was about to be ripped off, and we both knew that the world wasn't in great shape to be starting a career.

'I'm going to prove them wrong!' she said, somehow managing to look fierce while covered in confetti. 'I'm going to pull it off, Becs. I'm going to do what I love and I'm going to make it work.'

'Maybe avoid the being fuelled by a need for vindication?' I suggested. I went to take another sip of my Pimm's and realised that I'd already finished it.

'Alex asked me to stay,' I blurted out.

'Here?' Lily asked, confused.

'In London, to live with him while he's at UCL,' I said. 'America was always going to be impossible with visas. But

I can get a working one and stay here. He asked if I'd try to transfer my grad job.'

'Can you do that?'

'I don't know,' I said.

'Do you want to live in London?' she asked.

'I don't know,' I said. I barely knew the city. I didn't know anyone there.

'Can you leave him?'

I don't know. I didn't say this out loud, but it hung between us.

'It just feels nonsensical to be even thinking about changing everything in my life because ... I met a guy seven weeks ago.'

Lily nodded but I could tell she didn't agree with me, that she thought that the 180-degree pivots were the stuff that life was made of.

'What do you normally do when you need to make a decision?' Lily asked. It was rhetorical question – she'd known me long enough.

It took me three days before I worked up the courage to make an international call to the HR department of my soon-to-be employer and ask if there was any chance that they could transfer my grad position to their London office. I was so nervous that I'd written a script for my side of the conversation.

The response I got was professional but frosty. Underlying the conversation was the sentiment: *Don't you know what's happening in the world? Don't you know how lucky you are to be allowed onto our consulting rocket ship?*

I took the Oxford Tube bus to London alone. I'd visited the city a few times over the last year but through the lens of a tourist, not as a potential Londoner. The city was huge and bustling and ancient. Could I thrive here or would I be swallowed up and spat out?

I sat in a Caffè Nero and wrote a list of pros and cons.

Cons:
- *Expensive*
- *Takes ages to get anywhere*
- *Don't know anyone*
- *Bad coffee*

Pros:
- *Alex*

I stared at the piece of paper until my acidic long black got cold. For the first time in years, a list wasn't helping me.

In any event, it was a wasted trip. When I got back to my college room there was an email – the transfer wasn't possible. Neither was the deferment of my place. The tone was officious and the implication was clear, that I was replaceable and would be shooting myself in the foot if I gave up my golden ticket.

Well that was that. I'd tried and it wasn't possible. I told Alex that night as we lay in his bed.

We slipped into silence. I knew that we were both playing out all the possible moves. Except it was checkmate. A long-distance relationship between London and Melbourne for years would be impossible. Especially when I'd have next to no time off for holidays and Alex would barely earn enough to survive in London. In less than a week, we were going to say goodbye to each other.

I looked up and saw that there were tears falling down Alex's face and his chest was jerkily moving up and down. I felt a jolt of surprise. Once again, he'd done the thing I'd least expected from him. He was crying.

He swiped at his eyes, almost as if he was trying to push the tears back in. 'I'm sorry,' he said, his voice thick. 'God, I haven't cried since Mum ... I just ... I'm sorry.'

I wrapped myself around him. If I held him tightly enough, could I squeeze the sadness out of him? Out of me?

I was in my room staring at the popcorn ceiling when my computer began to ring. I checked my watch – somehow three hours had passed since I'd last noticed. I did a quick calculation – it was late evening in Australia, so it was probably Mum. I moved slowly to my computer, hoping it might ring out, then sped up as I read the caller's name on my screen. It was Nick.

My heart began to race as the video connected. Was something wrong? Had something happened to Dad or Mum?

His face flashed up and I could tell that it wasn't bad news. His normally serious face was grinning.

'Becs!'

'Hey,' I said. I realised how terrible I looked when I saw myself in my camera. Alex had gone to London for a night to meet his new team. I'd decided the night apart would be a practice run for when I left. Except it was a test I was epically failing. Instead of starting to pack up my room, I'd just lain on my bed, feeling miserable.

'I've got good news,' Nick said.

'What?' I asked, his excitement penetrating my gloom.

'I got into the training program!'

'Seriously? Congratulations!' I squealed. 'On your first try? That's insane!' Nick had just finished his general training and wanted to be a surgeon like Dad, except one specialising in obstetrics. But we both knew that the specialist colleges were tightly guarded and admitted very few new doctors into their hallowed, lucrative spaces — particularly on the first try.

'And I'm moving to Cairns for my first placement,' he said.

'Wow!' I absorbed the news. Nick had gone to med school in Sydney, so I'd been used to him being away, but the top point of the country was seriously away. And I couldn't really imagine him in a tropical shirt with a tan. Though that probably wasn't a likely scenario because he'd be working all hours.

'And Stella's moving with me,' he said. 'Because … we got married today!'

Stella's face burst onto the screen just in time for me to attempt to morph my face from dumbfounded to thrilled.

'Oh my god! You're married?' I said, as a finger with a gold band on it popped up next to Stella's face.

'We eloped. It was very last minute, very romantic,' Stella said.

'We're sorry you weren't there,' Nick said. 'It was just, if we were married, Stella would be able to transfer hospitals with me, and doing a ceremony with just the two of us was …'

'Less drama,' I finished. 'I get it.' I didn't blame them for sneaking off. The idea of Mum and Dad getting through a whole wedding day without emotional fireworks seemed improbable at worst and emotionally exhausting at best. But they'd got married – one of my best friends and my brother.

'Tell me everything! I want to hear all about the day,' I said. They turned to look at each other. I noticed that Nick was in a dark suit with a small rose in the lapel and Stella was in a chic cream cap-sleeved dress with the same type of rose tucked behind her ear. They looked giddy and madly in love. They were in technicolour, and I realised, as I caught my own reflection on the screen again, that I was sepia – mourning the end of something that hadn't even ended yet.

I'd been so sure that following your heart only led to implosions. But had I got it wrong? There was a reason Nick was going to be trusted with life and death situations – he was smart, disciplined, focused. And Stella lived deliberately too, just in a quieter way. They were both the opposite of thoughtless – but still, they'd jumped.

And Nick had also seen the foundations of our family crumble. But maybe he'd learned the smarter lesson: to still try, but do it better, love harder.

When Lily had first told me that Nick and Stella were together, I'd felt a familiar pang of bitterness – I felt like I'd been blindsided again. As I watched them both, luminous with happiness, I realised that I didn't feel bitter, I felt jealous.

'Jealousy is an important emotion if you use it the right way,' Grandma Evelyn used to say. 'It tells you what you really want, deep down.'

I wasn't jealous of their love but rather that they'd moved towards that love, that they'd let themselves be together and happy. I was afraid and miserable and bracing for a broken heart.

After I'd asked them every possible question about their wedding day and said congratulations over and over, I used the dregs of my almost empty savings account to send Nick and Stella an enormous bunch of flowers. I showered, got dressed, ate then sat on the roof outside Lily's bedroom until the sun set, much later than it had at the start of the term.

I tapped out a long phone number, listened to the melodic international dial tone and took a deep breath.

'I'm moving to London with you,' I said. Alex had returned from London late the following day and had come straight to my room.

'They let you transfer?' he asked. I shook my head and saw his eyes narrow with confusion.

'No, apparently they barely made any grad offers in London this year,' I said as steadily as I could. 'I gave it up.'

'You gave it up?' he repeated.

I nodded. 'I'm eligible for a two-year Youth Mobility Scheme visa that will let me work. I'll apply for jobs here,' I said, trying to sound confident. 'Until I get one, I can try to find something casual in a cafe or a bar. Maybe do some tutoring.'

'You've already quit?' he asked. For the first time since I'd met him, he was acting like his brain didn't work at supersonic speed.

'Yep, I called them last night. It's done,' I said. 'You're happy, right?'

'Yeah, of course,' he said. I couldn't read his face. 'You're not leaving me.' He wrapped his enormous arms around me.

'You know, the first time you saw me,' I said when we finally pulled apart, 'you thought I was going to leap.'

He nodded at the memory with a smile that lit up his aquamarine eyes.

'I did want to,' I said. 'I mean, not off a roof. But just … in life. To finally do something that I really wanted to, even if it didn't make any sense. I wrote a list of whether I should stay or go. And the only logical thing to do was go back home. Except … I'm going to try to live without lists for a while, I think.'

He stared at me for a moment. 'Rebecca …' His eyes darted away from me. It was the first time I'd seen him lost for words. 'Thank you,' he said finally.

I tried to shut down my whirring brain. Maybe he'd been less thrilled by my news than I'd expected because he was just as aware as I was of all the difficulty that came with this decision. Alex had access to sparse uni accommodation – would it still be romantic in the dead of winter? How would we go living together when we didn't have college cleaners, or dining halls that served us food? How would life look when it wasn't just one big expanse of time to fill, when both of us were busy working? But no, I was going to try to live without risk governing every move, without lists and rules. I was going to try to be happy. To just be.

'I'm not naive. I know we've been living in a bubble. But I want to try real,' I said. 'And anyway, we still have two more salad days here.'

Alex smiled again and I melted into his arms.

Chapter 22

NOW

Matt paused in the bedroom doorway. I could see us through his eyes – Alex leaning forwards, his eyes lit up, and me sitting up against the bedhead, cheeks flushed. Had he heard our conversation? We hadn't been talking quietly.

'Are you okay?' He rushed across the room and kneeled beside me, taking my hand, which still had the hospital wristband around it.

'I'm fine now,' I said in what I hoped was a reassuring voice. 'I had an allergic reaction. The EpiPen worked, and they didn't have to do anything else at the hospital. I feel normal now, just exhausted.'

He visibly exhaled.

'What are you doing home?' I realised as soon as I'd asked the question that it was the wrong thing to say in front of Alex, that somehow, I'd revealed too much. I immediately wanted to recall the question, like an email gone to the wrong address.

'Your dad called me,' he said. 'He's your emergency contact.'

I felt a pang from somewhere deep. If Dad had known I'd been unwell enough to end up in hospital, for my work to call him, why hadn't he come to check on me? I shook my head. He'd probably been in the operating theatre standing over a cracked chest. An allergic reaction was hardly more of a medical emergency than a heart attack – when he finished his list, he'd probably call me on his way home. Or maybe when my phone came back to life, there'd already be a stack of missed calls and worried messages from him.

'Thank you.' Matt, still holding my hand, turned to Alex. 'I spent the whole time on the plane just thinking what if you hadn't been there and the worst had happened ...' His voice caught as he trailed off.

Matt must have raced to the airport, bought a ticket for the first plane leaving Sydney, and been white-knuckled the whole flight home.

I felt another shock of energy burst through my body, as if someone had stabbed me again with an EpiPen – except this time, instead of adrenaline it was a shot of guilt. Matt looked like he'd spent the last few hours wracked with worry because I hadn't called him, because he'd probably received some unclear call from Dad.

Why hadn't I updated my emergency contact when Matt and I got serious? When we'd got engaged? When we'd moved in together? I mean, the obvious answer was that I'd been working at the same company forever – I had a corporate headshot from my fringe era (a truly unfortunate choice), and an emergency contact set when Dad was my go-to person. But still, I should have been more on top of this stuff.

'I stabbed her then jailbreaked her out of hospital. I don't know if that really warrants thanks,' Alex said lightly as he pulled himself out of the armchair. Matt laughed and I was grateful that Alex had broken through the thick tension in the room. 'I think that we're out of the danger zone. Now that Matt's here to keep an eye on you, I might head off.'

'Yeah, of course,' I said quickly. 'Sorry I derailed your day.'

Alex paused at our bedroom's entrance and smiled. 'It's not a day I'll forget in a hurry.'

Matt smiled back at him; it was the type of comment that was meant to sound offhand and placating. Except I knew what Alex was actually implying – there was a day, well, night, that I'd apparently forgotten.

'Do you need anything?' Matt had returned to the bedroom after showing Alex out.

I started to ask for a glass of water, but instead burst into tears. I saw Matt look at me for a moment, surprised. I wasn't a crier.

'I'm sorry,' I said, trying to get a hold of my body, which was betraying me again as he moved towards me. 'I'm such an idiot for eating the wrong food. I never do stuff like that. I'm being ridiculous, having an allergic reaction is hardly a big deal. But I just ... hate hospitals. And it was just so ... so ...'

'Hey, hey, Becs,' he said soothingly as he climbed into bed, 'mistakes happen. That's human. It must have been scary.' He held his arms around me.

My body heaved with each sob. He silently cocooned me until my breathing returned to normal – for the second time that day. I snuggled against the length of his body while he gently ran his hand in circles across my back, as if

I was Alice, needing help getting to sleep. For the first time since the attack, I felt like I could properly relax.

'You work better than an EpiPen,' I said, my face still buried in his shirt. Alex was all nightshade, triggering responses in my body that I didn't want.

'When I was in the hospital, I was really freaked out,' I said, almost in a whisper, as if I was making a confession to the rider on his embroidered horse. 'The only person I wanted there was you.'

The circles on my back stopped for a moment and then continued again in the same pattern.

'I'm sorry I didn't call,' I continued, this time pulling my head up from his chest. His bright, warm chestnut eyes met mine. There wasn't a hint of recrimination or even hurt, just concern on his face. 'I knew how important this trip was for you. I really didn't want to ruin it.'

'My job is a job. You're my life. Love is turning up,' he said, as though this was the most obvious truth ever spoken out loud. I swallowed – my dad hadn't shown up. Again.

My head fell back onto Matt's chest. I could feel his beating heart beneath his crisp, ironed shirt. My breathing fell into his rhythm with each reassuring thump.

'I *am* cursed,' I said. 'All these things keep happening. All our wedding chaos. I'm forced to work with Alex. I end up in hospital—'

'You had anaphylaxis when a doctor happened to be in the room,' he said. 'I think that makes you the opposite of cursed. It makes you lucky.'

'I don't think people talk enough about how optimism can be quite an annoying trait,' I said. His chest rose and fell faster as he laughed.

'Go to sleep, Becs,' he said. 'I'm here. Everything's okay.'

I promise to focus on making our future the best version it can be. The vow sprang into my head. I closed my eyes so I could remember it.

Matt was my future. The past could stay in its box. Alex could drop as many bombshells into conversations as he wanted, but that didn't mean he got to shatter my carefully built world. And so what if Alex had a different take on how we'd ended. It didn't matter. The headline was the same – we'd ended. That was the important part.

No, I *was* in control of my life. And it was time to focus on what mattered, who mattered. My world was in this bed.

'*Question two: Was it love or lust at first sight, or a slow burn?*' Matt looked up from the piece of paper he'd been reading from. It was Tuesday mid-morning, and we were both still in bed. Miranda had ordered me to stay offline and out of the office and Matt, despite my attempts to reassure him that I was fine, insisted on taking the day off too. I felt awful that he was missing his work trip, but the silver lining was that we had time to finish the world's longest questionnaire, which Belinda had insisted that we complete and drop back with the official paperwork.

'Did you mean what you told Belinda the other night?' I asked. 'Did you just know?'

'Yes. After I met you I just … never wanted to not be with you again,' he said simply. 'But it wasn't like that for you, was it?'

'No …' I said slowly.

Almost two years earlier, I'd decided to accept Matt's invitation to go on a first date. I'd said yes to the invitation in the moment – it would have felt rude not to – but planned on politely backing out of it like I normally did.

Around that time baby Evie was struggling to sleep. I watched helplessly as Stella seemed to fall apart in front of me. Nick, of course, was a bit more sleep deprived than he'd been before Evie had arrived. But otherwise, his life looked pretty much the same – he went to work, he travelled to medical conferences, he taught at his old uni.

The day after I met Matt in the cinema, I visited Stella and Evie at a sleep school. I sat on the edge of Stella's hospital bed, watching her cry with exhaustion and guilt – full-bodied, rib-aching sobs. Stella loved Nick wholeheartedly. I witnessed what love had done to her – it had torn her to pieces. It tore everyone to pieces.

Stella had fallen head over heels for Nick. Mum had lost her mind when she'd met Dad, and then again when she'd met Hamish. I'd had a crush on Alex and then been swept off my feet. I didn't want that kind of love. If you fell head over heels or were swept off your feet, you'd land on your face or arse. To lose your mind was the kind of diagnosis that landed you in a psych ward. The only things that were meant to be crushed were banged-up old cars and pineapple.

And I also knew that love could catch you by surprise – I'd been caught off-guard before. I wondered whether maybe the best way to inoculate yourself against the contagion of all-consuming love was to embrace a gentler type. To not fall head over high heels, but take dainty steps from like to love in sensible flats. To spend my life with someone like Matt, who I'd already sensed was thoughtful and helpful and hopeful – all the good 'ful's.

I could feel Matt looking at me intently. I felt a sting of animosity towards Belinda; she was a licensed celebrant not a psychologist – where did she get off asking these intimate questions?

'For me, it was a slow burn. But in a good way, like a perfect winter's log fire,' I said.

Matt's smile widened as I wrote *The best kind of slow burn* on the form.

I hadn't realised how emotionally frozen I'd been until we'd been together for a while, and I'd begun to thaw. Matt was all warm embers, fireguard in place.

Alex had been a bushfire. He'd swept in, during the peak of summer, an uncontrollable force, destroying everything in his wake. I'd been a gum tree set ablaze, that had exploded and then been left a charred stump. Even if that's not how he remembered it.

'Are you feeling well enough to go out for lunch?' Matt asked.

'Does that mean we have to get out of this bed?' I asked as I rolled across the wrinkled sheets into his arms.

'Tragically, it does.'

Chapter 23

'Now, you have to choose one final side dish.' Lucy, our perky wedding venue's event coordinator (whose job to date had mainly been communicating bad news) looked at us expectantly.

'Fries, please,' Matt and I replied without consultation or hesitation. We turned to each other and smiled. Matt had organised a last-minute food tasting (take two), knowing that nothing would be better for morale than ticking something off the wedding to-do list.

'Great, well that's your menu sorted again. And' – Lucy, whose aesthetic was generational wealth and whose energy was real estate agent on a Saturday in spring, flicked her glossy hair as she paused for effect – 'the amazing news is that the renovations are on track to be finished by your wedding date. And, even better, the builders said it should smell way less smoky after they've painted it!'

I felt Matt kick my foot under the table and tried not to laugh. We both found Lucy's ability to deliver any information as if it was the best news ever, even though almost every update had been dripping with disaster, hilarious. Matt had even started sending me text messages in the style of Lucy that made me cackle at work. (*The great news is that only one of our toilets is blocked!!!*)

'Amazing! And I'm sure all the flowers will help with that too!' Matt added, pathologically incapable of not being the most positive person in a room.

Lucy left us alone at the small table in the corner of the commercial kitchen to finish all the samples of desserts we'd been given.

'Maybe things have turned around. I think from now, everything will come up Matt and Rebecca,' I said. Matt smiled, and it went all the way to the crinkles in his eyes. I could tell that my renewed positivity meant everything to him. I felt Matt's leg brush up against mine under the table and I felt my stomach flip.

'There's a theory called emotional hedging,' I said. 'I think we should apply it to our wedding, so no matter what disaster strikes, it's all upside.'

'I'm intrigued,' Matt said. I reached across the white linen tablecloth and took his hand in mine.

'So how it works is … we brainstorm all the possible bad things that could happen at our wedding and come up with a correspondingly good thing. This means that even if everything goes wrong, we're still happy,' I explained. 'So, say … a dog breaks into the venue and eats all the fancy charcuterie and cheese on the grazing table, then—'

'That night we do it doggy-style,' Matt said, a twinkle in his eye.

I snorted with laughter. 'Exactly, you totally get how the theory works,' I said, when I could speak again. 'Okay … the wedding day temperature is forty-three degrees so …'

'We do it doggy-style,' Matt replied, deadpan. This time we both collapsed into giggles.

'I'm loving your thinking. But I think we might need some variety.'

It was a sunny afternoon but I felt much warmer than I had a few minutes earlier. Matt gently twisted my engagement ring around my finger and all I could think about were his hands everywhere else.

'I like variety,' Matt replied, his voice a bit slower and gravellier than it had been. 'The three-tiered cake falls off the stand and smashes onto the floor?'

'Chocolate body paint?' I suggested, raising what I hoped looked like a suggestive eyebrow.

The sparkle in Matt's eyes transformed into a glint. 'My suit pants split open?'

'That's got to be anal,' I replied instantly. We both burst out laughing again.

Why hadn't all the wedding planning been this much fun? Could it have been if I hadn't lived in my own head so much, if I hadn't allowed little things that had gone wrong to become outsized in my mind? If I'd done what Matt had suggested and laughed off the curse as a bad joke?

'God, I hope it all goes wrong,' Matt said.

'Me too.'

'Should we sneak in next door?' Matt suggested. We'd been told we couldn't look at the venue itself because it was still a building site. But I could hear Lucy filming a TikTok in her office and surely the builders had finished for the day.

'Definitely,' I replied. This game, well the sexy version Matt had turned it into, had made me feel alive and reckless.

Giddy, I crept behind Matt through the kitchen and into the courtyard where, in a few weeks' time, we'd become husband and wife. It was still very much a construction site – there were tools and dust everywhere. But as Lucy had so emphatically promised, it looked like the repairs were almost finished.

'Rehearsal?' Matt asked, already walking towards the spot we'd designated as the end of the aisle. I nodded and moved to the entrance of the courtyard.

What would happen in this spot, the question of which parent would walk me down the aisle, had already caused me a lot of angst. But it didn't matter. They weren't there right then. It was just us.

As I moved towards Matt, carefully stepping over a few stray wooden offcuts and then skirting a paint tin, I felt silly. But then we locked eyes and it all felt real, like we were actually about to get married. I couldn't see the paint-splattered ladders or drop cloths. All I could see was him – the most handsome groom in the world. And under his gaze, wearing my ancient black cotton dress, I was the most beautiful bride that had ever existed.

I reached the end of the aisle where Belinda would be waiting to officially marry us.

'This is the part when I'll tell you that I can't believe how lucky I am,' he whispered and kissed the side of my already flushed cheek. 'Or maybe that my wedding suit pants have split open.'

I laughed.

'Let's go home. It was a ridiculous idea to leave our bed,' I said in what I hoped was a sultry voice.

Soon we were back in our bedroom.

'Isn't it weird to think that not that long ago lots of couples had sex for the first time on their wedding night?' I asked, slowly undoing the buttons on Matt's pale blue shirt. 'Imagine if, right now, you were getting undressed, out of your wedding suit, and I didn't know anything about your body.

'I wouldn't know that you loved to be kissed here,' I said, then slowly kissed the soft spot of his neck, just under his jaw, inhaling his soft citrusy smell. I gently ran the tip of my finger over his now-bare nipple. Matt closed his eyes and groaned. I smiled. 'Or that you lose control when I touch you there.'

'Imagine if you stood in front of me in your wedding dress,' he said as he opened his eyes again. 'But I didn't know that you'd like me to pick you up and take you to the bed.'

He folded his strong arms around me. I pressed my hips into him and I heard him take a deep breath. As our bodies became entwined, my brain emptied of thoughts. I kissed his neck again and rode the high of his cologne or pheromones or whatever his embrace did to me. He carefully placed me down on the bedcovers and then lay next to me. My whole body tingled.

'And then I'd pull off my wedding dress,' I said. I half sat up and without breaking eye contact, pulled my summer dress over my head. 'And you'd see me in my underwear for the first time.'

Matt's eyes widened when he saw I was wearing my red lingerie set. I smiled, biting my bottom lip.

'But I wouldn't know that when you start to eat your lips like that, it means you think you can't wait another minute,' he said with a glint in his eye. 'And I wouldn't know that you'd enjoy it more if I teased you a bit longer.' He ran his hand up the side of my body, and curled his fingers into my hair. I whimpered.

'I want you,' I said. My body was screaming for Matt. I could hear impatience in my voice. He moved his head forwards and his mouth met mine. My lips parted and it felt like the world was just us, our almost-naked bodies pressed up against each other.

'Is this where you want me?' he asked as he pulled his head back then gently kissed my shoulder. I shook my head.

'What about this?' He moved down to the inside of my thighs.

'I want you,' I said again, my vocabulary reduced to three words.

'You're going to have to wait,' he said as he slowly pulled the pair of lacy underwear, down my legs. I let my knees drop to the bed in response.

Matt knew how to turn my impatience into giddiness, how to take control in a way that made my toes curl.

'I want you,' I said, a final time. And then I stopped talking.

'I think we were always good at this, even the first time,' I said once I could finally speak. I lay on Matt's chest, recovering and wondering why everyone didn't spend Tuesday in bed with their fiancé. Our various limbs were entangled, the linen bedding twisted. Belinda's questionnaire, half complete, was scattered around us.

'Movies and books make it seem like sexual tension is the hottest thing in the world. But I think when we became each other's person and there was no more tension … that's when the fireworks happened.'

'I agree. When we started sleeping together, it was great because it was exciting,' he said. 'But I think it's better now that we know we belong to each other.'

I rolled off Matt's chest onto a few crumpled pages.

'I'll return the forms to Belinda in the morning and we can drop the cake stand at your parents' house on the weekend,' I said as I smoothed out the pages. 'You've told your mum there won't be cake toppers, right?'

'All taken care of,' Matt said, still catching his breath.

'And maybe let's not mention the decapitated groom cake topper to my mum. She doesn't need another reason to invoke the—'

'Don't say it—'

'Curse.'

Chapter 24

THEN

I had agreed to meet Alex at the Commemoration Ball on our final night in Oxford. I must have walked through the front gates of Trinity College hundreds of times over the last year, but this was the first time that my stomach writhed with excitement and anticipation.

Lily and I arrived together, flashing our nylon wristbands at the girls in gowns manning the entrance. The courtyard was almost unrecognisable. Circus performers, decked out in silver costumes, roamed around on stilts, enormous lanterns with real flames were dotted around, a string quartet played as trays of champagne circulated.

I'd barely had time to absorb it all when I saw him. Everything else disappeared – there were no violins, no fire, no swishes of satin. Just him. How did an Australian guy, who barely wore shoes most days, look so perfect in a tailcoat?

He saw me and smiled. Lily squeezed my hand and then peeled off to find her college friends. I took one step towards him then stopped, my hands fluttering to my turquoise silk dress. I'd bought it during my trip to London – I normally wore dark colours and I shouldn't have been spending money, but for the first time in my life, I felt properly beautiful.

He grabbed my hand, like he'd done on the May Day morning, and silently led me through the crowd until we reached my staircase. I noticed that my nameplate had already been taken down – ready for someone else's name to be put up at the end of the summer.

'No one's allowed back up to their rooms until the ball's over,' I said slowly.

'No one's allowed on our college roof either,' he said with a teasing smile.

The climb to my room on the top floor took a long time. We kissed on the step where we'd made out weeks earlier. He tasted like champagne, and I was sure I would taste like juniper from the gin I'd had with Lily while we got ready.

Finally, he pulled away and stared at me with soft eyes.

I took his hand again and led him to my door. 'Before I met you, I lived in my head,' I said. 'You make me feel like I live in my body too. Discuss.'

'I think this is a subject for an equation rather than an essay,' Alex replied, his voice huskier than usual. 'Maybe we can work it out together?'

I wordlessly nodded.

'I think we start with subtraction,' he said, closing my door behind him.

'Subtraction sounds good,' I said, though any words could have been coming out of my mouth.

I turned around, facing away from him. He slowly unzipped the dress and let go. It fell to the floor. I wasn't wearing a bra and my underwear was skimpy and sheer. But I didn't feel self-conscious in the slightest. I turned back to face Alex and his eyes lit up.

The insides of my body felt like one of the electron diagrams you learned about at school – everything zipping around, bumping into each other.

Classical music wafted up through my open window, accompanied by a chorus of laughter and chatter. This night felt different from our other nights together. I felt out of time, like I didn't exist in the real world. It wasn't real life.

'Now you,' I said. He smiled, accepting the challenge. He wriggled out of his jacket, but then got stuck pulling off his white silk bow tie.

'I had you down as a clip-on man,' I said, laughing as the knot tightened as he tried to yank it off. 'Let me.' I slowly coaxed the silk knot apart, pulled it carefully from under his collar and handed it to him.

'What should I do with this?' he asked, holding the piece of fabric in his hands. I raised my hands up above my head and held my wrists together.

'Are you sure?' he asked.

I nodded. We'd never done anything like this. I'd never done anything like this. But I wanted to do everything, try everything, feel everything.

He carefully tied the material around my wrists, gently tightened the knot, and then, with much less care, pulled off all his clothes. He stood naked in front of me, and I felt woozy.

'Can I do more subtraction?' he asked.

'Quickly,' I said. He hooked his finger under the left side of my underwear.

'Are you sure you're ready?' he asked. I nodded, and gasped as he picked me up and carried me to my bed. I wondered whether it was possible to die from desire.

An hour later, arguably less polished but both glowing, we sat at the top of a Ferris wheel, overlooking the ball. It was as if the world had been created only for us in that moment, and I admired the view below, where everyone was young and glamorous, wearing dyed wool and silk. In the morning, the suits would be returned to the rental companies, the dresses consigned to the back of cupboards.

It was easy to forget that the next day we'd be kicked out of our borrowed rooms – that over the summer they'd be home to executives doing short courses at the business school, and, after the summer break, they'd belong to new students. All I had tomorrow was Alex.

'I got into Harvard,' he said, interrupting my thoughts.

'What?' I turned away from the panoramic view to face him.

'Harvard changed their mind about the post-doc place. They realised they shouldn't have turned me down,' he said.

I stared at him. There was a steeliness to his voice – it was the voice you used when you'd made up your mind about your life and now had to blow up someone else's. I recognised it; I'd heard it before.

'They were too late,' I said. I could hear a pleading tone in my voice, which I resented. His expression turned to wounded, as if he was hurt because the first thing I'd said wasn't 'congratulations'.

'I said yes.' The Ferris wheel skirted the ground and rose for another spin. If I jumped off, would I land on the ground safely?

'What do you mean? We're moving to London together. Tomorrow.'

'I reached out to Harvard a few days ago, asking them to reconsider their position. I only heard back from them last night,' he said. 'But I can't say no.'

'Of course you can. You say, "No." Like I said, "I will no longer be taking up my very prestigious grad job." You just say it.'

He didn't reply. It was the same silence that had hung between me and Mum when I'd asked her to stay. It was the silence in which everything changed.

A few seconds before, I'd thrown my head and body back against the seat like a child on a swing. Now, I felt totally trapped, in a slippery polyester-blend dress and sweaty palms.

'I gave up my job. You can go with your second choice of prestigious university,' I said.

'Your job and my work aren't the same thing,' he said. There was a hardness to his voice I'd never heard before. 'I'm trying to fulfil a promise I made to my mum. You ticked things off a list!'

I stared at him, trying to understand if he really believed what he was saying or was only trying to justify his own decision. But his face had become an expressionless mask – one without a hint of remorse or guilt.

'I'm saying this all wrong,' Alex said, shaking his head as if he'd gone off-script. As if it was the delivery of what he was saying, not the substance that was the problem. 'When you told me that you'd quit your job, I felt awful ...'

'Wait. You'd already asked Harvard for another chance when I told you I was moving here, and you didn't say anything?' He looked away from me for a moment and I knew the answer.

'So, you're not moving to London tomorrow?' I asked.

'No. I met the team there and everything was … all wrong for the project,' he said. 'I can't, Rebecca. I have to go.'

I stared at him for a moment to make sure he wasn't joking. Except his eyes had narrowed and his arms were now crossed.

The numbness I'd felt since he'd started talking wore off and a wave of anger crashed through me. This wasn't going to happen again. I wasn't a naive teenage girl anymore. I was not going to let the siren's call of other people's passions and the actions driven by other people's selfishness bulldoze my life.

The Ferris wheel stopped at ground level. Our safety bar was lifted, and I jumped out of the seat. I ran. I could hear Alex calling my name, but I didn't stop.

I pushed through the crowds until I made it to my room. I took in the rumpled bedsheets. Then I looked at my suitcase and bags sitting next to my wardrobe. Everything I owned in this country was in them. Tomorrow I was meant to be zipping them up and starting a grand adventure. I was meant to be moving to London with Alex tomorrow. Except he was moving to America. To Harvard.

We'd rented a cheap flat until we could get access to his uni accommodation at the end of summer. I couldn't afford to live there on my own, not without begging my parents for a loan, something I knew both of them (in a rare show of unity) would disapprove of. And I didn't want to be in London on my own. There was nothing waiting for me there.

I gasped for a breath, then another. Was I? Yes, I was. I hadn't had a panic attack for years, since I was seventeen, but I still recognised what was happening.

I ran to the bathroom and tried to take regular, deep breaths. My head was pounding now. I rifled through my washbag and pulled out an unopened packet of Xanax. I wasn't meant to mix them with alcohol, but how else was I meant to manage what was happening?

I popped the small white pill out of the blister pack, swallowed it and finished a glass of water. I breathed in, then out. I lay on my mussed-up bed until my breathing had almost returned to normal. I had no idea how much time had passed – a few minutes or an hour. I finally got up and I stared at my face in the mirror. The girl who had never felt more beautiful in her life was gone; looking back at me was a heartbroken ghost.

I knew that I should lie back down. But it wouldn't be long before Alex would bang on the door, looking for me. And he was absolutely the last person I wanted to see.

I made a plan. I'd go find Lily. But I just had to do one thing first.

I opened my laptop. My instinct was to make a Skype call, but I was in a ballgown and that would raise questions. Instead, I opened my emails.

Hi Dad. I know I told you that I was staying here, but I made a mistake. Could you please book me a flight home urgently? I'll pay you back as soon as I can. I'll call you tomorrow. Love, Rebecca.

I pressed send and shut the laptop lid.

Chapter 25

NOW

For the rest of the week, I kept my head down. Alex was in some of the bigger meetings I couldn't miss, but other than that, I managed to avoid any direct contact with him. If our team had a burning question, I sent Adrian or Lucas to talk to him, making a note to add 'provides growth opportunities' to my promotion application. If the team noticed that I was actively avoiding my ex-boyfriend, they were kind enough to only talk about me behind my back.

The work was absorbing. When we were under the pump, I was normally pretty good at working out the twenty per cent of information I needed to get across and tasks that needed to be prioritised that would make eighty per cent of the impact. But with this case, I found myself reading all the materials that Lucas, whose chronic online-ness extended to brilliant research skills, had pulled together. I found myself filling pages of my notebooks with reflections in my still-schoolgirlish handwriting.

The weekend arrived much more quickly than I'd thought was possible. And on Saturday morning, Matt and I turned up to Arlo's birthday party right on time, converging at the front door with Lily's little sister, Mia, and her parents.

Mia was a junior lawyer at an international firm, but this morning looked like death warmed up. She wore pyjamas she was clearly hoping to pass off as a linen set. But given that most of her eye makeup was aligned with her nose and her hair was exploding out of her scrunchie, she hadn't pulled it off.

A few shrieks from presumably overexcited babies and toddlers wafted down the hallway and through the flywire door.

Mia turned to me, her eyes wide. 'Are there going to be kids here?' she asked in a concerned whisper. I laughed then realised she was deadly serious.

'Well, we're at a kid's birthday party, so I'd say yes.'

'Like more or less than five?' she asked, again without irony.

'I think Lily invited her whole mothers' group, so ...'

The colour drained from Mia's already washed-out face. 'Okay ... I'm going to need to get a coffee before I can do ... this,' she announced as she waved her hands at the front door.

She almost jogged back down the pathway.

I turned to Lily's parents, waiting for them to admonish their daughter for bailing on her only nephew's first birthday party.

'She had a client event last night,' Lily's mum said proudly.

'A box at the tennis,' her dad added, his eyes soft as he watched the back of his youngest daughter disappear down the street.

'Wow,' Matt said politely.

I loved Mia but it was slightly bizarre to watch her ascent to unequivocal favourite child after she'd gone to law school and then nabbed a job at a big firm.

We were saved by Lily's appearance at the door, with the birthday boy in her arms.

'Happy birthday! Congratulations on surviving the year!' I squealed, knowing that a first birthday was as much a celebration for the parents for making it through a year of the lowest lows and highest highs.

In the kitchen, Lily pulled open the cake box we'd brought and her eyes widened. Matt and I snuck a glance at each other and smiled. I'd baked a two-tiered Funfetti cake and Matt had decorated it with fondant figurines inspired by the circus-themed mural that Lily had painted on Arlo's nursery wall in her final trimester.

'You guys. This is incredible,' she said, looking touched.

'Everything looks amazing!' I enthused. The living room was already beautiful, painted peach and totally covered with framed paintings that Lily had bought online, at small galleries and from artists she met through work. It had been festive to begin with, but she'd leaned into the colour of their house and gone for a retro party vibe – all primary-colour balloons, streamers festooned from brass light fittings and bowls of nostalgic party food. Then I noticed someone from the past, helping himself to a Cheezel – Alex.

'What's *he* doing here?' I hissed at Lily as soon as Matt went to deliver Aaron a beer.

'He reached out and asked if he could drop off a present for Arlo. So I invited him,' Lily replied. I retreated to the corner of the kitchen, out of earshot of the rest of the guests. Lily followed me.

'So, he heard you mention Arlo's birthday last weekend, guessed there'd be a party and basically angled for an invite,' I replied. 'Jesus. He's at work. He's in my bedroom. And now he's bloody here.'

'He was in your bedroom?' Lily asked, raising her eyebrow.

'Well in a medical capacity,' I said, my tone tinged with defensiveness. 'I had a capsicum-based incident and he was keeping an eye on me until Matt got home.'

'Be careful,' Lily said, putting her flute of champagne down, her expression serious.

'What do you mean?'

'It's normal to get cold feet before your wedding,' she said, choosing her words carefully.

'I haven't done anything!' I said, my voice an octave higher than normal.

'You tracked him down at Parkrun. You invited him to coffee. You had him in your bedroom. I mean, what does Matt think of all this?' Lily asked. I felt a rush of exasperation shoot through me. Lily was painting a picture of the kind of woman who couldn't be trusted – the kind who inappropriately slid into DMs or touched an arm for a moment too long.

'I did those things to try to create boundaries,' I protested. 'And he was in my bedroom because I didn't want to die before my wedding! Or like, ideally, at all.'

'Okay,' she said, and held up her hands. 'I'm just saying that my therapist told me that heaps of people actually end up getting back together with their school or uni boyfriends later in their life.'

'Really?'

'It's a total thing. Which I thought you might be interested to hear in the context of your curse and Alex and whatever.'

'Wait. Did you speak to your therapist about me?' I asked.

'I plead the Fifth!'

'Not a thing here,' I said. 'You really should have gone to law school.'

She gave me a withering look then sighed. 'I have a working theory that if there's anything unresolved in your life,' she said slowly, 'planning a wedding will expose it. That a wedding is the event equivalent of that dye that's injected into your veins so doctors can see if there are any blockages not visible to the naked eye ...'

'An angiogram?' I clarified.

'The medical term isn't important for my theorem. What I'm saying is that ... all your family in one room, a weird relationship with money, body anxiety – a wedding will shine a giant spotlight on whatever you've spent your life not facing up to.'

'So, Alex is my ... blockage?' I worked through Lily's theory out loud. Lily shrugged as she topped up both our drinks.

I was my father's daughter – I knew via osmosis that an angiogram was a diagnostic test that looked for weaknesses in the heart. Was Lily right? Was that what wedding planning was – something to stress test your heart, to ensure it was strong enough to endure, for better or for worse, life with another person?

'So, what's your hang-up about marriage?' I asked, keen to deflect the conversation away from myself.

'Maybe there's a reason Aaron will be my boyfriend forever,' Lily said with a cheeky laugh.

'I'm going to talk to Alex,' I said, feeling resolute. 'I'm going to find out exactly what he's doing here.'

'Okay,' she said. She looked down at the cake and then across the room to where Matt and Aaron were cheering on Arlo as he attempted a few tentative steps. 'Just be careful.'

'I'm always careful!' I protested.

'I know you are,' she said, with a bit too much pathos.

I crossed the room to the trestle table where Alex was still manning the Cheezels bowl.

'These are exactly as good as I remember them being, which is a rare thing,' he said.

'Some palates mature with age, some don't,' I said archly.

'I can't believe Lily is old enough to have a kid. That she's a parent,' Alex said, watching Arlo proudly shuffle behind the walker he'd just received from Lily's parents.

'That's a refreshing take,' I said.

'What do you mean?' He turned to face me.

'Well … I feel like people are more surprised that I'm a woman in my thirties without kids, or at least a baby belly.'

'Do you want kids?' Alex asked. He seemed surprised by the notion, as if one of the experiments he was conducting had just reacted in a way he hadn't predicted.

'Yes,' I said, as usual struggling to be anything but honest under his inquiring gaze. Matt and I hadn't worked out an exact timeline – neither of us wanted to upset the gods of fertility. But I'd upped my health insurance to include maternity. And when he'd got his job, Matt had been thrilled by their generous paternity-leave policy. 'Do you want kids?'

'No,' he said, without hesitation. 'Though I guess I've only thought about it in the realm of the hypothetical.'

I stared at him for a second. If 'What do you want to be when you grow up?' was the defining question of our twenties, this question and its variations – 'How many?' 'When?' – was the question of our thirties. I'd only known Alex for two months in my early twenties. Of course there were a million things I didn't, couldn't, know about him.

The twenty-page questionnaire that Belinda had inflicted upon us had many categories: 'Approaches to money', 'Resolving conflicts', 'Work–life balance', 'Your future family'. Could Alex and I have agreed on any of those sections?

'Is it a coincidence that we're working together?' I finally asked Alex the question I'd come over to discuss, the one I'd convinced myself was my mind spiralling.

My phone started vibrating before he could reply. I looked down at the screen in case it was Miranda. My eyebrows involuntarily shot up with surprise. It was Dad.

'Sorry, I have to take this,' I said quickly. The house was heaving with people, so I ducked into the small nook Lily used for work to hear him.

'Dad! Hi!' I said.

'Darling. I heard you had a bit of a rough week,' he said in his booming voice.

'Oh, yeah,' I said. 'Sorry they disturbed you at work. I hadn't updated my emergency contact.'

'I rang my colleagues at Frankston Hospital to make sure you were getting the royal treatment as soon as your boss called,' he said. I felt a sting of remorse. I'd been quick to judge Dad for not checking on me but he'd been one step ahead. No wonder my very junior doctor had been quickly replaced with someone who was in charge, who'd had the authority to let me go home.

'Thanks, Dad!' I felt my eyes well up again – was I becoming a crier? Dad *had* shown up for me.

'I've just pulled into the hospital car park so—' The call ended abruptly. My calls with Dad had been cut off mid-conversation for as long as I could remember. He would have reached his designated parking spot, deep in the bowels of the hospital car park with no reception.

I stood in the nook for a moment. Lily's office was peak Lily – an old-fashioned roller top school desk, which she'd painted emerald, showcased a hot-pink U-shaped resin vase, holding two dahlias. The desk had a stack of what looked like bills on it. The letter at the top of the pile had *Final Notice* printed on it in an aggressive red that matched neither the desk nor the vase.

Was everything okay? I took a step towards the pile then paused. Lately, I'd been rushing to the wrong conclusions. I had to stop. It was none of my business. If Lily had forgotten to pay a parking fine or whatever, it was none of my business. If Alex wanted to spend his Saturday afternoon at a kid's birthday party, well, that was lovely. If Dad wanted to work every weekend, wouldn't his patients feel cared for. I needed to stop imagining every worst-case scenario. Like Matt said, I wasn't cursed. I was lucky.

The party, because it was a party hosted by Lily Li, was a triumph. Even Mia, who'd returned after inhaling a handful of Paracetamol and a strong coffee, looked like she was enjoying herself despite the many babies in situ.

We all gathered around a table as Aaron lit the candles on the cake, which fitted Lily's party aesthetic perfectly. Matt kneeled in front of them taking photos. I scanned the room. Alex was at the back of the crowd, standing by himself.

I shot him a friendly smile – the same kind I'd give Mia or her parents. But he didn't see me. And then I noticed his expression. He was staring at Arlo, flanked by both his parents, with the saddest expression I'd ever seen. I'd seen glimmers of this look before, when all the bravado, all the self-assuredness, had melted away, exposing a man who looked so vulnerable, so sad.

His mouth moved along with the final line of the birthday song, but I could see that he wasn't really in the room. As Aaron leaned forwards to blow out the candles and Lily kissed Arlo on the cheek, her eyes bright and face burning with love for her son, I could almost see the pull in his heart.

Ever since he'd reappeared, I'd been so focused on Alex as a concept: the ex, the client, the harbinger of the curse. I'd forgotten that he was just a guy. One I'd once really cared about. One I knew was a bit broken.

As people shouted, 'Hip, hip, hooray,' and one of the grandparents made a brave attempt at 'For He's a Jolly Good Fellow' I found myself moving through the crowd, following him down the hallway. I caught up with him as he reached the front garden and as soon as he saw me his mask slipped back into place.

'Birthdays are hard.'

'Always,' he said. 'I avoid them.'

'What did your mum do for your birthdays?' I asked.

'She didn't have a lot of time. Or money,' he said, still looking a bit dazed. Then he smiled as he remembered.

'But on my birthday every year, she'd stick candles into a watermelon. It was normally school holidays, so we'd do it on the beach and then we'd swim and get an ice cream.'

I could almost see the warmth of those days wash over him as he let himself bask in the memories.

'That sounds like an amazing tradition,' I said softly.

'I mean, it probably started because the beach was free and she didn't have time to make a cake,' he said.

'Doesn't matter. She made magic,' I said.

'Yeah,' he said.

'Do you still do it?' I asked.

'What do you mean?'

'Your traditions.'

He broke eye contact. 'My new tradition is to pretend I don't have a birthday.'

'When is it?' I asked. If he and his mum had spent the day on a beach then surely it was coming up soon, before the summer ended. Once again, I was struck by the strangeness of what I didn't know – that we'd never known the information about each other you'd need to apply for a passport. We'd just known each other, in all the ways that didn't have boxes on a form.

'Last week,' he said. 'Last Saturday.' His expression was now defiant. I worked hard to keep my face neutral, from looking even slightly sympathetic.

It made sense. I'd never bought the idea that he was lonely and was desperately trying to make friends in Melbourne. Alex was a lone wolf (or owl); he'd always been happy in his own company, in his own thoughts. But on his birthday … I could see why he jumped at Matt's invitation.

'Though I mainly went to the tennis with Matt because I wanted to see who you were marrying. And I really did want to say hi to Lily after all these years,' he said, pre-empting my questions. 'But yeah, I guess I didn't really want to be alone too much on that particular day.'

I remembered that Alex was acerbic, insanely smart, focused and looked like Jamie Dornan (when he wasn't playing a sociopath). But I'd forgotten he was also human.

'Happy belated birthday,' I said. 'Wait here, okay? Don't move.'

I ducked to the kitchen and returned to the front garden a minute later holding a paper plate. Alex laughed. On the plate was a slice of watermelon with a half-melted candle in it.

'Did you steal that from a child?' Alex asked. The watermelon slice had a single bite taken out of it.

'It was abandoned. And possession is nine-tenths of the law,' I said.

'And you want people to believe you went to law school?' he replied.

'Be nice or I'm going to sing at you, and we both know I can't sing,' I said. 'Just pretend to blow out the candle and make a wish.'

He went to take a breath then let it out. He looked up from the watermelon slice.

'I don't know if I should make *this* wish,' he said, his aqua eyes almost boring into me.

'Then make another wish,' I said firmly.

'My wish is that I want to be with you,' he said. 'I tried to forget that I did. But it's still what I want.'

Chapter 26

'You've got to be kidding me,' I said.

I stared at him. He'd said it in a totally matter of fact way, as if he'd casually brought up work. Since Alex had arrived, I'd been berating myself for doubting his motives, for even thinking that he might be here for me. The prick of vindication transformed into something more potent.

'That's not true,' I said. 'You don't mess up the lives of people you want to be with!'

He blinked a few times, and I didn't wait for him to speak.

'Do you know how much you messed things up for me back then?' I asked. Anger, lying dormant somewhere deep for almost a decade, rose up like lava. 'After I quit my job, they gave away my spot, and there was a big black mark against my name. The job market was a mess back then. Australia had barely avoided the recession. I'd missed all the application deadlines and I couldn't get a grad job anywhere. Miranda, the partner who'd interviewed me, took pity and managed to get me an assistant role. I spent a year arranging meeting rooms and booking travel, watching the grads who should have been my peers begin their careers, while I had to prove myself.'

'Wait—'

'But actually, it wasn't about the job,' I said, everything unspoken bursting out of me. 'I mean it was, that wasn't great. But you were the only person in the world who knew what Mum leaving did to me. I told you that I didn't want to be with you, to fall in love with you, because I couldn't handle getting hurt. And you promised that we'd be different. You promised me that you wouldn't hurt me. And then you asked me to trust you, to rearrange my life for you. And I did – I jumped.

'Then you chose *your* research, *your* work, over me. I was the person who wasn't chosen. I was the person who wasn't enough. I was the person who was left. You broke me open. Again.'

I stopped talking to catch my breath, drained after resecting almost a decade's worth of metastasised hurt.

'I didn't leave you. You left me,' he said. 'But … I think we might remember the end of that night differently.' His husky voice had softened and the expression on his face was gentler than it had been over the last week. He looked more like the Oxford Alex I'd known.

My heart began to pound.

'What's the last conversation you remember from that night?' he asked.

'The Ferris wheel. You told me you weren't coming with me to London,' I said. I could hear the tinge of uncertainty that had crept into my voice. 'That was the last time we saw each other. Right?'

He shook his head. We both stood in silence facing each other for a moment.

'Do you think … I had another blackout that night?' I asked in a quiet voice.

'A lot more happened. After the Ferris wheel,' he said, his voice still gentle. The fire of my anger and his acerbic tone were gone. It was just the two of us trying to work something out together. On the same team again. 'So, if that's your final memory of us then, yeah, I think you probably did.'

I'd woken up the morning after the ball and known I'd lost time after I'd taken a pill on a stomach filled with the ball's free-flowing champagne and the gin I'd drunk with Lily. I'd felt so much shame – I thought I'd cured myself of panic attacks, that I no longer had to rely on pharmaceutical help to manage my emotions. But, even more, I hated the idea that I might have temporarily lost control of my mind. That was the kind of thing that happened in dark psychological thrillers with moody covers or as a plot twist in a silly soapy melodrama.

And honestly, it wasn't a night I'd wanted to dwell on. I'd had no interest in worrying about memories I didn't want to cling to, anyway. Who wanted to remember the pain of the night their boyfriend left them? I figured that if anything important had happened, that if I'd seen Alex again, surely it would have penetrated my consciousness. And so I'd let go of thinking about that hole in my memory.

'You told me once, just after we met, that it had happened before. And after what you said the other day, in your bedroom … I wondered,' he said. I wasn't surprised that he was able to recall a conversation from almost a decade earlier. 'I came today because I knew you'd be here. And I wanted to test my theory. I needed to know if everything I've thought about how we ended was wrong.'

How had we ended? What had Alex thought for all these years?

'Do you want to know what happened that night?' he asked as if he could read my mind, his voice low and calm.

'Yes.'

He took a slow, deep breath. 'I was waiting for you at the bottom of your staircase. You finally came down and we went for a long walk, away from the crowds …'

Alex trailed off and I could tell that he was wondering if he should go on, that his mind was doing a quick evaluation of both the cost and benefit of continuing this story.

'I want to know,' I said.

He nodded. 'I told you that I'd done some research and that it was pretty easy to get an American working visa if you were married to someone with a student visa. And that I loved you and knew that I wanted to be with you forever. And I thought you felt the same way about me.' He paused and looked away for a moment. 'So then I got down on one knee and said, "Rebecca, will you marry me?"'

I felt my jaw involuntarily drop and my eyes widen with shock. Was I having a hallucination?

'You got down on one knee and proposed. And I said yes?' I asked. His expression morphed as he registered the shock in my voice. He looked like I'd physically hurt him.

'You did.'

'God, Alex. I'm so sorry,' I said. 'I was acting totally normal?'

'Yeah,' he said with a shrug, though a slight edge had crept back into his voice. 'You were shocked when I proposed, but then you seemed excited. We both were. We celebrated with champagne and dancing. And then you were tired, so I walked you back to your room. I left you sleeping. I was too wired to rest and needed to pack, so I went back to my room. And then when I returned in the morning … you'd gone.' His voice cracked.

A memory of the day after the ball surfaced from the recesses of my mind. I hadn't noticed that I was wearing a ring until I was on the plane home. Had I clocked that it had been on my left ring finger? No, I couldn't have. I'd borrowed my jewellery for the ball from Lily's enormous collection – I'd probably assumed it was one of hers, which I hadn't had a chance to return before I'd left the country.

'Did you give me a ring that night?' I asked.

'Yes,' he said. 'It was a ring that had belonged to Mum. She never had an engagement ring, but she wore it a lot. It wasn't valuable it was just …'

He didn't finish the sentence. I could tell he didn't want to make me feel bad for losing something of his mum's that had sentimental value. I swallowed. So, he'd asked me to move to America with him and proposed with his beloved mum's ring. And my brain had done the mental equivalent of the circle of death, like when my work computer ran out of hard-drive space.

But what had he been thinking? We'd known each other for two months. I was twenty-four – who got married at twenty-four?

Except part of me knew exactly what his thought pattern would have been – we loved each other, so why wait? I knew that Alex was the kind of guy who'd love a few things in his life and devote himself single-mindedly to them. And if he wanted us to be together, and the US would have granted me working rights if we'd been married, this would have been a logical next step. If I was happy to move to London and look for work, why not do the same in Boston? I could imagine that he'd have thought that there'd be even more opportunities for me in the US than the UK, that I might be thrilled.

'If you thought we were engaged, that we were going to get married, that I was going to move with you' – I could hardly believe the words coming out of my mouth – 'why didn't you reach out to me?'

'I did try,' he said. 'But you'd left the country by the time I realised anything was wrong. And I'm guessing you either blocked my number or changed yours when you arrived in Australia.'

Dad, with typical efficiency, had booked me on one of the first flights out of Heathrow after he'd received my email. I'd only had time to throw on a tracksuit, return my room key and zip up my bags before I'd needed to catch the bus to the airport. When I'd left, there were still people in ballgowns and suits eating breakfast and taking survivors' photos.

'I only had your uni email address. I did sign up to Facebook and message you. But you rejected my request. And I was … heartbroken.' His voice cracked. 'I thought that we'd just had this magical night and were going to go on this adventure and spend the rest of our lives together. And the next minute I find out from your porter that you've left the college.'

'I thought you'd ghosted me,' he said. 'I … went to a dark place after you left.'

'I'm so sorry,' I said. 'What happened, what I'd *thought* happened … it reopened a wound that had never really healed.'

'I know,' he said, gently. 'I'm really sorry I made you feel like that.'

'I'm sorry I made you feel like that too,' I said.

A woman holding a baby Arlo's age walked past us, an apologetic look on her face, as if she instinctively knew that she was interrupting something charged. We waited for the front gate to click behind her in thick silence.

He moved towards me. I took a step back.

'When I saw you in that meeting room I wondered, just for a minute, if it wasn't a coincidence,' I said. 'But then I thought – stop being so self-involved. Of course he's not here because of you. It was one summer, a million years ago.' I stared at him, refusing to break eye contact, even though I desperately wanted to.

'I had a lot of offers for my work,' he said. 'And when I got one, a competitive one, from a company based in Melbourne … I thought it was a sign.'

Since when did Alex Lawson believe in signs? Maybe when I'd started to believe in curses.

'And is it a coincidence that I'm on this project?'

My heart sank as I read his face.

'They were always going to hire consultants,' he said. 'I made sure you were one of them.'

He took a deep breath and I held mine.

'I still love you,' he said. 'I've never stopped. I just made myself so busy, for so long, that I didn't have to think about it. But then I sold my company and finally, for the first time, had space in my life. And I realised that what I felt for you never went away. I've never met anyone else like you. It's always been you.'

'I'm getting married in a month,' I finally replied.

'I know. I mean I didn't know when I decided to move here. But I know now,' he said. 'And if you tell me to back off, I will. I'll try and stay out of your way at work. And leave you alone otherwise.'

I took another step back. I was now backed up against the red-brick wall next to the front door.

I'd spent nearly a decade thinking that he'd been selfish and heartless. A door in my heart had swung shut when Mum left, and Alex had managed to find the crack that was still ajar and open it again. But when we'd broken up so abruptly it had slammed back shut. After Alex had left, I'd vowed to be governed by reason, not passion. It had felt like a rock-solid foundation for life, but suddenly everything felt more like quicksand.

I looked down at my left hand, and the ring sitting on it. In a few weeks' time, the trinity ring would be sitting next to it. I looked up into Alex's eyes, that were almost the same colour as the sky on this perfect summer's day.

'Yes, please,' I said, my voice resolute. 'Please stay out of my way.'

'Okay,' he said. And without going back into the party or even looking at me again, he walked out the front gate and down the street.

I hid in Lily's bathroom and tried to pull myself together. When most people had left the party for nap times (the toddlers and Mia), I busied myself cleaning up the living room, stuffing shredded wrapping paper and abandoned paper plates that were smeared with icing into a bin bag.

Finally, I stretched my face into a smile and found Matt in the garden, helping Aaron assemble the cherry-red wooden bike we'd bought Arlo.

'I was looking for you,' he said, glancing up from the wheel he was screwing on.

'Sorry I was just … cleaning up some stuff,' I said.

'Is everything okay with Alex?' he asked, and I knew he'd noticed that both of us had left the party, that maybe he'd seen us talking at the front of the house.

'Yeah,' I said. 'I think the party just made him miss his mum. She died when he was pretty young. He was a bit rattled.' Matt's eyes softened with sympathy, and I felt a stab of guilt for not being totally forthcoming.

'My boss called. There's a bit going on. China's being China again,' Matt said. 'I'm going to have to go up to Sydney. I might have to be there a bit for the next few weeks. I know it isn't ideal timing with the wedding prep.'

'Yeah, okay. Sorry things are kicking off,' I said, trying to sound as supportive as I could. I desperately wanted to go home with Matt and never leave. I wanted to hear his deep, generous laugh as we joked about Mia's arrival at the party. And pair a burger from our favourite place with popcorn I microwaved and a pink cocktail he invented for movie night, then go to bed a bit too late together and curl up against each other. But we had the rest of our lives for that.

'I have to fly up this afternoon. They want to get on top of the messaging. I'll tell you all about it when I can,' he said.

'Of course,' I said, knowing that he would. 'You just focus on that. I've got the wedding under control here.'

After Matt left for the airport, I dropped off the cake stand to Jane. While Jane made us cups of tea (it was impossible to leave their house without accepting a hot drink), I snuck into the living room and stared at the wall behind the piano. If anything, Matt had underplayed the extent to which his older sisters were celebrated. It was a shrine to their achievements and Matt was a footnote. Except Matt was a headline of a person. I felt a rush of protectiveness for him. Did Jane understand the impact a lifetime of treating him like a Labrador puppy had had on him?

Then, even more galvanised, I bought matching satin pyjamas for Stella, Lily and me to wear while we got ready. And pulled together a wedding playlist for the DJ. And knocked out a running sheet for the day.

I wanted to fulfil my promise to Matt to keep the wedding ball rolling while he was flat out with his work emergency. And I also wanted to not think, at all. I'd asked Alex to back off. That was that. Now it was time to focus on what really mattered – our impending nuptials.

By Sunday, having blitzed through wedding errands, I decided to change my RSVP to a conference Miranda had invited me to. The firm was a sponsor and a few of our senior partners were presenting, so sitting in the front row of their sessions wouldn't hurt my promotion case.

I arrived at the grand hotel on the edge of the city in time for the women's networking breakfast event. I slipped on my lanyard and filled my plate with a miniature cinnamon swirl, a miniature yoghurt parfait and a miniature bacon and egg tart (the barometer of corporate luxury being how many petite food options were available).

Our firm's allocated table was filled with female partners and clients in a rainbow of summery business-casual dresses. The breakfast's keynote speaker was the founder of a hugely successful makeup brand. The number of women in the corporate world had reached an important tipping point, which meant that we no longer had to pretend to enjoy corporate golf days or boxes at sports matches. Instead we got to listen to successful women wearing Alemais entertain us with insightful and pithy stories.

'Rebecca!' Miranda's face lit up as she ushered me into the seat next to her. 'I'm on a panel today. What's your excuse?'

'I'm mainly here for the gift bag,' I said with a laugh. I rifled through the enormous tote sitting atop my place setting. 'And actually … it's a really good one.' I pulled out a lipstick, one in a wearable shade.

'Did you know I was almost this company's first employee?' Miranda said, tapping her index finger on her own tube of lipstick, still encased in its trademark lavender packaging.

'Really?' I turned to her. How did I not know this? Miranda and I spent so much time together, I thought we'd exhumed every possible topic.

'My dream was to be a formulator. You know I left Stern for a few years, right?'

I nodded. Though I'd never thought anything of it – lots of people left consulting for a chunk of time, normally because the company had picked up the cheque for them to attend a prestigious American business school.

'I went off to do a PhD – the focus of my research was formulating cosmetics. I became a certified expert on lipsticks. At the end of my doctorate, I got two job offers: one to come back to Stern, and one to join a small Melbourne-based beauty start-up.'

'And you turned down your dream job?' I asked, confused.

'I did. I thought about it for ages,' she said. 'But I realised that consulting had, before I'd even realised it, become a great career for me. That I'd fallen in love with this all-consuming job that used every part of my IQ and EQ.'

'Do you ever think about what might have happened if you'd picked the other job?'

'Yeah, sometimes. When a client is being demanding or a member of my team particularly hopeless, I wonder if maybe the world of eyeshadow and blush might have been more satisfying,' she said with a small laugh. 'But my working theory on careers is that there isn't a perfect one, that you should aim to find the one that fits best and then seek out whatever bits are missing from other parts of your life. I think the same theory applies to men, actually.'

She stopped to eat a bite-sized pain au chocolat.

'Consulting wasn't my first choice either,' I admitted. 'It was medicine.'

'What happened?' Miranda asked.

I paused, not entirely sure how to answer the question. The summer before my final year at school I'd had a plan – the med-school deadlines were highlighted in my diary, I was enrolled in advanced maths, chemistry and biology. Then, just before the year began, Mum and Dad split up. Every time I opened my UMAT practice exam books, I had what I'd soon learned were panic attacks.

My parents were so distracted that they didn't even notice that I'd switched all my subjects – exchanged the sciences for economics and business studies. Neither of them had come to the careers evening (theme: Live Your Dream), so they hadn't seen me when I'd trailed Lily – who was following her parents – to sweep up all the commerce and law school brochures. By the time Mum asked me when I had med-school interviews, it was too late. I'd expected a fight, but she surprised me by quietly accepting that I'd changed my mind.

'I'm from a family of doctors,' I finally replied. 'And I think I just saw how much medicine requires of you. It's not just a job, it's a vocation, a calling, a … life.'

The room's lights were dimmed and two women in chic maxi dresses clacked onto the stage. It was showtime.

An hour later, everyone in the room felt upbeat about their gender and was ready to conference.

'I have to do my plenary session soundcheck soon,' Miranda said. 'I was going to email you my notes on the ATG presentation, but I may as well give them to you now.'

Miranda had no boundaries between work and life. I had lost count of the number of calls I'd had with her while she'd been at her kids' swimming lessons. So, I knew she wouldn't think twice before digging into a case on a Sunday morning.

She reached into her emerald leather handbag and pulled out a copy of the printed slide deck I'd sent her on Friday afternoon. The ATG executive leadership team had a meeting in a week, and our recommendations were going to be front and centre. I quickly flicked through the pages, skimming her handwritten mark-up – most of her comments were easy changes or questions I could work through with Lucas and Adrian.

I flipped to the final slide – the one where we were going to tell the company's leaders what we thought they should do with Alex's work – and froze. The team had spent the last week working up options one to three. But in Miranda's scrawl, there was now a fourth option – one we hadn't discussed. And next to it was a heading: *Recommended Option*.

I looked up and saw that Miranda was watching me. 'I'm guessing your first question is why are we blowing up your ex-boyfriend's career?'

Chapter 27

'Was shelving Alex's work always going to be a possible recommendation?' I asked.

'Yes,' Miranda said, and I could tell from her expression that not only was this always a possibility, but a probability. That all the work we'd been doing was largely ornamental.

'Why would they buy his company then sideline that company's main asset?'

'You tell me what you think,' Miranda said, leaning back in her chair.

'Because ... enormous companies that make their profits from intellectual property buy companies that have developed new tech all the time. But sometimes, when it comes time to sell the product they've bought, they realise it won't make them as much money as they thought it would.'

Miranda nodded. I'd got an A+. Though for once I'd rather have got it all wrong.

'This doesn't happen often. But it does happen,' she said.

'So why did they spend a fortune on Stern if they suspected they might not take the tech to market anyway?'

Miranda sighed then leaned forwards. 'I think they realised that the tech wasn't going to be the golden goose they'd hoped for soon after the deal was done. And, as you know, executives love to be able to point the finger at us, rather than admit that they're responsible for a bad decision. I think that's why they brought us in. Is this going to be a problem for you?'

I sighed, every part of me from my shoulders to my stomach feeling knotted. Instead of Alex's tool being used in hospitals all around the world to diagnose people at risk of heart disease, it would exist only in the loss column of a company's financial report and as a patent no one else could use.

'I didn't know he'd asked that I be staffed on this project until yesterday,' I said, not directly answering her question. 'Did you know?'

I could see her running a risk/reward analysis of all her possible replies.

'That the request came from him? At the start – no. But yes, I was aware that the company had asked for you to be part of this project.'

'Did you wonder why?'

She laughed drily. 'I assumed one of the executives had gone to uni with your dad or something. We get strange staffing requests all the time, and that's normally why.

'Look, I probably should have questioned it at the time, but I wanted to work with you. Then when I found out that there was a history between you and Alex Lawson, I did a bit of digging and discovered he'd made the request to staff you. I'm sorry I didn't give you the full picture. I had to put the client first, and ATG is a very exciting client for us. All of us.'

I nodded. 'Client first' was one of our company values. Miranda was just living by them.

'What happens to Alex if they decide to bury his research?' I asked then winced – I'd bit the inside of my cheek.

'Hanging on to Alex is part of their strategy. In many ways his mind was one of the most valuable parts of his company. They don't want him to go to a competitor and build something similar.'

But he trusted ATG with his work. It's not just a product, it's his promise to his dead mother, I wanted to protest. Instead, I nodded.

'I know I don't need to tell you this,' Miranda said, which meant she absolutely thought she needed to tell me this, 'but it's crucial that Alex doesn't get wind of what's happening. He's almost at the end of his six-month lock-up period, but there's a secondary retention bucket built into his agreement, which would tie him to the company for two more years. ATG are very keen that he takes up this option. They want his brain working for them.'

Alex had mentioned this the first time we'd spoken – that if things went well in the first few months, then ATG were going to fund more research. Except he'd assumed he'd be building on his work that was being sold to hospitals to help sick people whose illnesses might be missed. But if they took our recommendation, Alex would be unknowingly signing up for another two years stuck at the company that had killed off his life's mission, working on whatever was their priority.

'Wouldn't they be encouraging him to sign another contract under false pretences?' I asked.

Miranda laughed. 'Trust me, your Alex is as sharp as a knife. He would have known that this was a possible outcome, and if he didn't work it out himself, his lawyers would have explained it to him.'

I paused, gathering my thoughts.

'Look, nothing is set in stone. In my experience you can never second-guess what a bunch of executives will do,' Miranda said with a reassuring smile.

'Okay,' I said, feeling a small wave of relief. I'd learned in this job that nothing was over until it was over.

'There's something else I want to talk about. I didn't plan to ambush you on the weekend. But, now we're both here, it's probably a good thing that you'll have more time to reflect,' Miranda said. I braced, sensing this wasn't good news either.

'Sure,' I said, trying to sound as upbeat as possible. Like I wasn't completely rattled from the conversation so far.

'I've had preliminary conversations with some of the key partners about your promotion case,' Miranda said.

'Thank you,' I said.

'They're concerned that you're not aligned with a sector or practice group,' she said.

'But that's always been my value add. That you can staff me wherever. That I'm a jack of all trades,' I said quickly. The words rolled off my tongue because I'd been told them so many times.

'That's true,' Miranda said. 'At the more junior levels that's been incredibly valuable. But now you're on the cusp of a leadership role. You'll be managing teams. You'll be the go-to person for the client. You need to be an expert; you need to be a thought leader in a field.'

I stared at her for a few moments blinking, before I pulled myself together.

'Okay. Got it,' I said. 'I mean I've got a lot of experience in industrials—'

'You can't just throw a dart at a sector,' Miranda said with a laugh. 'Whatever area you pick, you'll have to be committed to it for the next few years as you build your partnership case. And then when you're a managing partner you'll be living and breathing the world of whatever you decide. Let me tell you from lived experience, you'll need to love your area or it will be almost impossible to stay in the race.'

I gulped. 'Have I left it too late?' I asked.

'No,' Miranda said. 'But the firm, well, the corporate services world, is moving towards a model of expertise. People don't want to pay what we charge for generalists anymore. They want people on the team who know their industry inside and out.'

'I get it,' I said. I'd been hoping that I could be the exception – the human skeleton key they kept around for when they ran out of people who had let themselves care about something.

'Let's have another conversation when we're both in the office,' she said with a smile that was so empathetic it made me want to scream. 'And have a think about the healthcare sector. You've been a natural on the ATG case.'

'Oh no, I don't—'

'Becs,' she said. 'Just think about it. At the risk of sounding unprofessional, I really care about you. You're like a daughter to me. Except one that does everything I say. And I don't want you to make any rash decisions that you'll have to live with, without really thinking them through. Now, I have to go wow a bunch of fellow nerds with my speech.'

I watched Miranda and her billowing lime-green dress disappear out of the hotel's ballroom. Then on autopilot I walked to my first session of the day.

I pulled my conference emblazoned notepad and pen out of my gift bag. *To Do*, I wrote a heading at the top of the first page. What was I meant to write next? *Pick sector to fall head over heels in love with for rest of professional career. Decide whether to tell Alex that his dreams could be shattered.*

I made it through the first five minutes of the session before I realised that I wasn't going to be able to concentrate, so I snuck out. Had I ever left a lecture or a work event early? Probably not.

Without really thinking about where I was going, I walked to the river and collapsed onto its grassy banks. It was a crisp sunny morning that would turn into a steaming, languid afternoon. I called Lily.

'Do you have a minute to talk?' I asked.

'Not really,' she replied. 'But given that tone of voice, absolutely.'

'You know the night Alex told me he wasn't moving to London with me?' I started.

'Of course,' she said. 'Whenever I had bad breakups, I'd console myself with the image of you being dumped on a Ferris wheel in a ballgown. Sorry.'

'That was false consolation. Because it didn't happen like that,' I said. 'I had a panic attack that night. I took a pill after drinking gin and champagne. I had another blackout.'

'Wow,' Lily said.

'There's more wow. A way bigger wow,' I said. 'The part of the night I don't remember is … when Alex asked me to marry him.'

'Holy shit!' Lily almost yelled down the phone.

'I mean, it was so I could get a visa and go to Harvard with him,' I added quickly.

'And you don't remember this? Like, any of it?' Lily asked.

'No, nothing,' I said. There was a pause down the line as Lily processed this version of events.

'If I hadn't seen you in a blackout before, I wouldn't believe this,' Lily finally said.

'He told me he loved me and still wants to be with me,' I said. 'At Arlo's party.'

'I was totally right about why he was here!' Lily said. 'God, there's so much to unpack here. But before we get into excavating your temporary amnesia about a core-memory situation, I just want it noted that I can still throw parties with drama. Who says that motherhood changes you?'

'I told him to back off,' I added, before Lily could ask. 'He's going to stay out of my way at work. Except …'

I paused. Except I held the power to potentially upend his professional life. I needed to tell Lily this to give her the full picture, to ask for her advice. But I couldn't. This was confidential information. I wasn't allowed to tell her. Or Alex.

'… nothing,' I finished. I had to work out what to do next on my own.

After I ended the call with Lily, I stayed sitting on the banks of the Yarra. The brown river gently flowed a few metres from my feet. Could you stand in the same river twice? I'd written an essay on this question for a philosophy subject at Oxford. What precocious conclusion had I reached?

'To tell Alex.' I plucked a yellow petal off an almost-naked dandelion I'd pulled out of the grass. Grandma Evelyn had taught me this game when I was a kid, mainly in the context of trying to work out whether the widowers in her bridge club were madly in love with her.

If I told him what our advice for ATG was going to be, he'd be able to reject the option to keep working for them. He could take his enormous brain and everything he'd learned to another company. He wouldn't lose two years of time being paid a bloated salary to do work he didn't care about. This would be a lot of people's dream, but I knew it would be Alex's nightmare.

And I didn't want to hurt him again. I knew how he must have felt after I'd left — heartbroken, bereft, unsure how life was meant to work anymore.

I didn't want to make a decision. I understood that even the smallest, most random choices had the potential to change the trajectory of a life.

What if I'd done something different during the Trinity term?

What if I hadn't run away from the Ferris wheel, had let Alex continue to explain his thinking to me? What if I hadn't had anxiety medication with me at Oxford? What if I hadn't asked Dad to book me a flight home?

What would, what could, our story have been?

Would we have got married that summer in Oxford, in one of the college chapels or the town hall? I bet we would have decided to elope, so we didn't have to confront the absence of Alex's family and the complexity of mine. Then, would we have applied for visas and moved to the US?

Would I have even found a job? Would I have become a consultant? Would I have celebrated all the days he made a breakthrough? Would I have picked him up on the days when it seemed like his research would never work out. Would we have made all the ordinary days count? Would our conversations have stayed in the realm of ideas or would they have descended into the banalities of running out of milk and having to change the sheets occasionally?

If I'd followed Alex, I wouldn't have been asleep in the cinema that day. I wouldn't have been gently woken up and asked to dinner. I wouldn't have said yes.

If I'd married Alex, I wouldn't have met Matt.

I felt my throat tighten and my heart clench, as if it had missed a beat. I took a deep breath then pulled the final petal off the flower. 'To not tell Alex.' The flower had spoken.

I told myself that firstly, if anyone found out that I'd leaked confidential information, I'd lose my job. And secondly, Alex had made the decision to sell his company to a giant conglomerate whose only real obligation was to its profit-hungry shareholders. Surely, as Miranda said, he'd been advised that this exact scenario was one of the possibilities. And finally, when the executive team met next week, they might totally ignore our recommendation. In fact, saying anything to Alex about it might aggravate the situation.

I stood up and brushed down my navy linen dress. Doing nothing was the right thing to do.

'I was sad that we had to cancel our dinner this week,' Jane said, stretching in a floral tracksuit. We'd had to postpone while Matt had been stuck in Sydney.

I really wished I was wearing something other than a rainbow, eighties-style aerobics one-piece a size too small for me when talking to my future mother-in-law, who thought that mixing navy and black in an outfit was risqué. I pulled at the fabric as if I might be able to stretch it out into leggings, or at least properly cover my bum.

Outfit aside, so far Lily and Stella had organised a really fun hen's party. It had begun with a relaxed lunch in the private room of a pub. Mum had sat with Jane and the twins, Holly and Ivy, and whenever I snuck a glance at them, they seemed to be having a good time.

After the lunch finished, I'd been sent to get changed into the multicoloured leotard that cut off circulation to most of my limbs. Then we'd all been shepherded to a nearby park where a bunch of bubbles were inflated, waiting for us to begin playing bubble soccer.

'I know, we were sad to miss dinner too. Matt's been dealing with a lot at work,' I said.

'Oh, there's a big wine emergency, is there?' she asked with a wry laugh.

Yes. A shortage of affordable savvy b! The Boomers will start picketing soon. I knew that's the self-deprecating answer Matt would give.

'Actually, it is,' I said. 'China's put another trade embargo on Australian wine. Matt's helping to prepare the disclosures and public response. It's a pretty big deal.' I might have slightly invented the details, but I was pretty sure that was the gist of what was happening. Matt had been so busy that we'd barely had time to talk all week. His best man had picked him up from the airport the night before to drive him to his buck's weekend, at a house they'd rented on the coast. I knew he'd be exhausted after a huge week, but if anyone could rally, it was him.

Jane's smile flickered. There had been a bit more edge to my voice than I'd intended. We were saved by the bell, or in this case, a whistle.

The twins were stretching out each other's hamstrings, looking like they were warming up for the Olympics. I scanned the edge of the oval until I found Mum. She wasn't in gym gear – I don't think she'd ever owned a pair of sneakers. I guessed she planned to watch us.

I was the first one bundled into an inflatable soccer ball and soon we were all oscillating between hysterically laughing – giddy from cocktails – bumping into each other and panting wildly from the exertion.

I'd never been big on organised sports. But the idea of being encased in what was effectively a giant piece of bubble wrap and blowing off some steam was exactly what I needed. It was nice to live in the moment, to not think, to focus only on staying upright and trying to get a ball into a goal.

This was the point of weddings and all the events around them. To doggedly revel in all the good things in life – the people who loved you and had been there for you, too much food and too many cocktails, to wear outfits you never normally did. To stop the merry-go-round of daily niggling worries and decisions and irritations, and celebrate your people.

Holly, who even through the plastic casing I could see had the focus of a Matilda, kicked the ball to me. There was no one between me and the goal so I clumsily dribbled it and with a dramatic kick it went straight into the net. I hooted with joy.

My celebratory cheer reverberated around the reinforced plastic. I turned around to find Stella and Lily so they could see how much I was enjoying myself. Except everyone was huddled together in the middle of the pitch. My stomach fell.

I wriggled out of the straps around my shoulders and pulled the ball over my head then jogged over to the group.

'Is everything okay?' I panted. Stella, who'd kicked into nurse mode, was kneeling on the ground next to someone who was groaning with pain.

'It's your mum,' she said without turning around. 'She needs some help.'

Chapter 28

'They need to do some scans to see if anything's broken,' Dad said. 'I'll make a few calls – get you bumped up to the top of the queue in the morning.'

'Thanks so much, John. I really appreciate it,' Mum said sincerely. How strong were the drugs she'd been given? Dad smiled at her.

I'd messaged Dad on the way to the ED and he'd been waiting for us when we arrived. And apparently triage didn't apply if you were related to a senior doctor because we'd been taken straight to a private room and Mum had been stuffed with painkillers. Though there had still been hours of waiting – even Dad couldn't magic up a queue jump for an X-ray on a Saturday afternoon. An emergency doctor, after conferring with Dad, had declared that Mum was going to have to be admitted and stay overnight.

I'd internally groaned. Obviously I wanted Mum to have the best care. But I'd successfully managed to avoid hospitals for over a decade and now, for the second time in as many weeks, I was stuck in a place I really didn't want to be.

'Is she going to be okay?' I asked Dad when it was finally just the three of us.

'Things fracture, they break. We fix them,' he replied without looking away from Mum.

'Great,' I said, biting my bottom lip. Before I knew what was happening, Dad had wrapped one of his big hands around mine and Mum had reached up and grabbed my other one from her bed. I froze.

'I'll make sure she gets the best care—'

'Of course I'll be fine—'

They both tried to reassure me at the same time.

'Thanks, Dad,' I said. I coughed to clear my throat then pulled my hands free of their respective clasps.

'I'm just going to check on those scans,' Dad said, which left Mum and me alone together for the first time that day.

The industrial-strength painkillers she'd been given had evidently kicked in because she no longer looked grey with pain, just tired. Now that I knew she was comfortable, I felt concern for her transform into something else.

'What were you doing in that stupid ball?' I asked, my voice almost a whisper. 'You were wearing heels!'

'It was a low wedge,' Mum said dismissively. 'It was your special day – I wanted to join in. I didn't want to stay on the sidelines.'

'Well, if you wanted to participate, you should have been prepared. Like Jane was. Like everyone else was. You don't just get to decide halfway through to sub in and mess up everyone else's fun. God, Mum – you just do exactly what you want. You never think about who might get hurt,' I said, unable to stop now I'd started. 'But people do get hurt! You got hurt. And you made *my* day about *you*!'

'I make everything about me?' Mum said, matching my tone. 'Stones in glass houses. You got drunk at my birthday dinner. And now I'm in a hospital bed and you've picked a fight. And I don't make everything about me. In fact, Hamish and I didn't even have a proper wedding, a real celebration, so we wouldn't upset anyone.'

'Well, maybe you should call Hamish. How would he feel about the fact you're batting your eyelashes at your ex-husband while he's on the other side of the world visiting his daughter?'

'Is that really an accusation you want to make?' Mum asked sharply.

We stared at each other, both of our mouths open in disbelief that the other had stooped so low. It was like I was a sixteen-year-old again and Mum and I were having one of our shouting matches. We'd go head-to-head over something stupid, like a curfew. Then we'd apologise to each other and be hysterically laughing minutes later.

But we never fought like this anymore. After she left, we'd barely spoken for a year. She lived with Hamish, and I lived with Dad. Then we'd slowly drifted back into each other's orbits and rebuilt a relationship. But it was a very different dynamic from what we'd had – we held each other at a civil distance, where emotions always stayed in a calibrated range.

'Mum, are you okay?' Nick appeared at the door, breathless. He was in scrubs, the lanyard from his hospital still around his neck, his auburn hair mussed in a way that made me suspect it had been recently under a scrub cap. His work clothes suited him – I couldn't imagine him in a suit or high-vis. Even though it looked like he'd raced here and was worried about Mum, he emanated a practised aura of calm and competence.

'I just had a fall,' Mum said in her most reassuring voice.

'I thought you were meant to be at Matt's buck's?' I asked.

'Yeah, I was really hoping to get down there but—'

'You had to work,' I finished his sentence before he could.

'Becs, I don't decide when a patient goes into labour,' Nick said in the tone he'd once used to explain to me why, because he was so much older, he got the front seat, the better bedroom, control of the remote. 'I can stay with Mum. You go back to your party. Stella's put so much work into it. It's not fair to her if you—'

'That's what's not fair to Stella?' I felt something that had been stretched too tightly inside me snap as frustration ratcheted up to anger. It felt like my eyebrows were almost at my hairline. He was really telling me off for leaving Stella in the lurch. Was he blind to the fact that the struggle of trying to care for both a newborn and preschooler single-handedly had left her an exhausted wreck? Did he not understand how unfair it was that he gave all his time and energy to his work and almost nothing to his wife and family? Were the Hippocratic Oath and hypocrisy a package deal?

'Becs …' Nick began to speak but a nurse appeared at the door. I could see her take the room's temperature.

'I'll come back in five to take your blood pressure,' she said to Mum after a moment, then quickly left. I was glad she wasn't taking my blood pressure, which I knew would be through the roof. I turned back to Nick.

'Let me translate this into the language the Evans family understands. Patient presents—'

'Becs …' Nick tried again, with a weary sigh, but I was on a roll.

'Patient presents as a mother of two with head and muscle aches. Difficulty concentrating. Extreme fatigue. Dehydration. Anxiety. Overwhelm.'

'Take a deep breath. I can see *you're* overwhelmed right now,' Nick said in an irritatingly calm voice, ignoring everything I'd said. He spoke as if I was one of his patients — except instead of birthing a baby, it was a bouncing bundle of histrionics.

'The answer is maternal exhaustion. Or for those of us without medical training ... leaving my friend, your wife, to sink,' I said.

I turned to face Mum, who looked bemused (or possibly high from her pain meds). 'I leave you in capable hands.'

I stalked out of the room with as much dignity as was possible while wearing a leotard.

By the time I'd walked through kilometres of hallway to reach the hospital's main lobby, I'd calmed down. My finger hovered over Matt's name on my phone's screen. I didn't want to interrupt his night of fun, just because mine had been cut short. But he'd also told me that he was the person I was meant to call when things fell apart.

He picked up after a few short rings.

'Do you want me to come home?' he asked once I'd filled him in on the slightly dramatic end to the party. 'I could see if an Uber could drive me back?'

'No, no, I'm fine. I mean ... I'm acting kind of like an emotionally incontinent person. But hearing your voice is helping,' I said. His offer to be by my side if I needed him was like a windbreaker, protecting me from the squall of familial drama. 'Anyway, I just wanted to check in. Let you know that I'm in the hospital,' I said.

There was a pause.

'Okay. I'll keep my phone with me. Can you message me updates?' he asked. I could imagine his eyes crinkling with concern, that he'd be running a worried hand through his silky hair.

'Yeah, of course,' I said. I heard some cheers in the background – Matt's night was clearly heading towards a crescendo.

'You go,' I said. 'Have fun!'

'Give my love to Helena,' he said. 'And sorry about your hen's.'

'I feel bad for Lily and Stella, they put so much work into today,' I said. Nick's comment about Stella might have been hypocritical, but it still stung.

'Aaron just showed me a photo of the two of them at the hotel with a tray of food in the king bed you were all meant to end up in. They're having a great night,' he said.

'That's good,' I said, relieved. Stella and Lily both had grandparents helping them with their kids this weekend, and I was glad that the hen's day had, at the very least, been a chance for them to have a break from the churn of their lives. 'Now go – enjoy your night!'

I ended the call then checked the time – it was almost nine. If I hustled to the hotel, they'd rally. But it was also past both of their usual bedtimes and they more than deserved a night of uninterrupted sleep.

I decided I'd say goodnight to Dad then go home.

I wandered the hospital corridors towards his office, muscle memory taking over.

I hadn't been there since I was a kid. I used to love it when Dad brought me to work with him. The magic of the doctors and nurses helping to heal every person who walked through the hospital's doors – with stitches, medicine and plaster – had seemed more potent than the stuff in the Harry Potter books I'd abandon on Dad's office couch so I could sneak through all the wards. The maladies solved with X-rays and MRIs seemed far more interesting than any of the mysteries I watched with Grandma Evelyn.

When I was little, I felt like all you could want from life was at hospitals. They were a complete world – birth, death, drama, food. I could understand when I was there why some doctors barely left, why Dad barely left.

The door to Dad's office was ajar and the light was on, but he wasn't there. I stepped inside. Very little had changed since I'd last been there. Behind his desk was a series of medical textbooks, and on the wall an array of framed degrees hung, his name inked in twirly lettering. Every other space was filled with thank-you presents from people grateful that he'd helped their brothers, sisters, dads and mums. I wondered, in some parallel world, if Dad had seen Alex's mum before it was too late, what Alex would have sent? And what Alex would have got back, how his life might have unfurled.

On one corner of Dad's desk were two framed photos. These had changed – when I was young, it had just been a single group shot of Mum, Nick and me. Now Mum was gone, and Nick and I each had our own frame.

Nick's photo was his graduation portrait. Mine was one of me at Oxford, grinning in front of the Radcliffe Camera. Alex had been standing near me, but he was out of the shot. There we were – Dad's two overachieving kids. Did he look at these on a busy day and silently congratulate himself for doing such a good job?

Before I could stop myself, I picked up my frame and threw it at the wall. It landed with a crack and then fell to the carpeted floor with a dull thud. I stared at it, shocked at myself. Had I developed an overnight anger-management problem? What had happened to my usually overflowing cup of impulse-control?

'Is everything all right?' An Irish nurse, who though young had already mastered the art of authoritative brisk movements, burst into the room. Her face darkened when she realised that it wasn't Dad throwing things around, but rather a woman dressed like an eighties aerobics instructor. 'You can't be in here.'

She had the expression of someone about to call a Code Black, the code for a safety risk. Was it normal that I'd known all the code colours, almost as early as I'd known the colours themselves?

'I'm John's daughter,' I said quickly. 'He knows I'm here ... My mum got admitted tonight and I'm a bit upset.' She gave me a half-smile but I knew she wasn't empathetic – I'd distracted her, no doubt, from an understaffed night shift.

'I can't leave you here on your own,' she said.

'I'm leaving now,' I said. I picked up the frame from the floor. There was a crack down the middle of the glass. I carefully placed it back where I'd found it on the desk.

I didn't sleep at all that night. After hours of tossing and turning and then a few more trying to dissociate on many social media apps, I drove to the market and chose two thank-you bouquets: a riot of colour for Lily and an enormous bunch of peonies for Stella. And then at the last minute I added a bunch of tulips for Mum. I dropped Stella's bunch on her doorstep – her mum's car was still in the driveway and I didn't want to interrupt their family time. Then I crossed the city to Lily's store. Since having Arlo, she worked on Sundays.

Lily Li Jewellery in Brunswick was like Aladdin's cave. It wasn't totally surprising that it was empty – it was only just after 10 am, which north of the river on a Sunday was the equivalent of dawn.

'Lil?' I called. I heard a sniff and decided to go through to the back, hoping I wasn't about to terrify one of her casual staff. Maybe she and Stella had decided to have a lazy morning in the hotel room.

Then I spotted her. She tried to plaster on a smile when she saw me in the doorway, but it was too late and too obvious that she'd been in the middle of a proper cry.

'Are you okay?' I asked.

'Yeah,' she said. 'I mean … not really.'

'What's going on?' I asked. Was Arlo okay? Was something going on with Aaron?

'I'm so embarrassed,' she said, flopping down onto the stool next to her workbench.

'About what?' I asked gently.

233

'The business is … not doing well,' she said, dropping her head into her hands. 'Actually … it needs to be taken off life support.'

'God. Okay,' I said. 'I'm sorry.'

She slowly lifted her head, vertebra by vertebra. 'Before Arlo, I was able to give it my everything. But now it's impossible to be totally on top of it. And no one is spending money on stuff they want but don't need at the moment. Small businesses are shutting all over the city. It's all just, I don't know. I think we're done.'

'You're going to shut Lily Li?' I asked, trying to keep my voice as neutral as possible. But I was shocked – this business felt like it was part of her. It had originally been a market stall, and then when her designs had blown up on social media, she'd opened the store. The brand had instantly taken on cult status and developed a following among the coolest people in the city. She'd bootstrapped the whole business into the success it was. Or had been.

'I need to get a job,' she said in a small voice. 'Our rent's gone up. Our basic bills just keep getting bigger. And the little bit of maternity leave I took ate into our savings. We want to start saving for a house, though that feels like a pipe dream at this point. Aaron can't work any harder – he's already onsite all day and then doing handyman stuff after work and on weekends. And I want Arlo to have a sibling.'

'I can—'

'Don't offer me a loan,' she said quickly.

'It wouldn't have to be a big deal,' I said. I'd been saving for a deposit too – Lily could borrow whatever she needed.

'It would only be a Band-Aid anyway,' Lily said. 'There's no point keeping someone alive if they won't make it.'

'What kind of job do you want?' I asked.

She laughed, a resigned one. 'I don't know. Something entry level,' she said. 'I'm not really qualified to do anything.'

'That's not true! You have a master's degree. You've run your own amazing business. You're one of the smartest, most talented people I know,' I said. I reached out and held her hand.

'Could you get a job as a jewellery designer for someone else?' I asked.

'People kill for those jobs,' she said, and sighed. 'And I need a part-time job or the childcare gets too expensive. I'll need something with proper benefits – nothing vaguely creative has those. Maybe I'll go to law school, Mia might hire me to be her paralegal.'

I didn't reply, fighting my instinct to try to solve the problem, to try to think through the issue. Maybe what Lily needed was someone to listen, a shoulder to cry on.

'I used to judge you,' she said, smiling as she rubbed at her nose with a tissue. 'I thought the way you insisted on enrolling in a degree and getting a job you didn't care about was so unbelievably stupid. Like you were willing the world to make you miserable.'

I looked at her. Is that what she thought? Is that what I'd done?

'But now, I think you're a genius,' she said. 'I followed my dream and it's all crumbling around me. I can't give my son the things I want to, or even show him that it pays off to go after the thing you love. And it hurts … it hurts so much.'

She held both her fists against her chest, almost bent over as if she was recovering from a physical blow to her stomach.

'I should have listened to my parents. They wanted me to go to grad school so I could always fall back on a steady job. But I was so stubborn, I thought there was no way I'd want a mortgage or the white picket fence or private health insurance or a car that's not falling apart. But now I do. I actually *really* want those things. But you, you've always been a realist. You've always listened to your head. And look at you – you're killing it at work, you're marrying the nicest guy in the world, you don't have to worry every time you tap your credit card.'

I opened my mouth, about to tell her all the many ways that I'd failed. But then I closed it. This wasn't about me.

'God, how's Helena? Sorry, I've been talking about myself when she's in hospital.'

'I'm so glad we talked. And I want to keep talking, okay? Whenever you need to,' I said. Lily reaffixed her smile as she wiped her eyes with the back of her ring-covered hand.

'Dad messaged this morning to say that the X-ray showed that it's a pretty bad fracture. Mum's seeing the foot doctor today, so they'll be able to tell us if she needs surgery. I'm going to see her now,' I said. I paused for a moment, wondering whether to tell her about the fight I'd had with Mum. And Nick. Or that I'd acted like a brat in Dad's office.

'I'm sorry yesterday got cut short. I did have an amazing time,' I said instead. My phone lit up. I smiled, expecting it to be Matt telling me all about his night and checking in on me and Mum. Except it was Belinda.

'Sorry, I just have to take this …'

I stepped out into the shop, which was still empty.

'Hi Belinda,' I said, in the brightest voice I could muster. Though I could feel my heart beginning to pump faster. To date, unexpected phone calls from wedding vendors hadn't yielded great news.

'Rebecca, I don't know how to tell you this,' she said. 'But you can't get married on your wedding day.'

Chapter 29

'There was a problem with your paperwork,' Belinda said as I concentrated on breathing. 'I got a voicemail from the Registry on Friday, but my cat hasn't been well, so I only just listened to it.'

'What was the problem?' I asked, in my steady dealing-with-a-disaster-at-work voice.

'The intended marriage notice wasn't properly completed,' she said. 'Normally, I check everything. But you dropped it off just before the deadline and I was in such a rush and you two seemed so … reliable. I didn't check it.'

'What was the issue?' I asked. I'd had a bad feeling about Belinda from the minute we'd met – what kind of person used a wine bar for their office?

There was a short pause.

'You forgot to sign the form,' she said. I stared at the acid-green wall in front of me for a moment, not knowing what to say. I'd stuffed up the form. I never messed up forms. I always read paperwork from start to finish, and then again just to make sure I didn't miss anything. I was diligent, vigilant even, about things like that.

My brain whirred back to the day I'd been dealing with the forms. It had been the day after I'd had anaphylaxis. The day after Alex had been in my bedroom. The day Matt

238

and I had spent the afternoon in bed. I'd been distracted that day in a way I normally wasn't. I hadn't been totally myself.

My stomach fell. It was my fault. This time I couldn't blame the curse. This was on me.

'Can we still get married?' I asked and braced myself for the response.

'Maybe,' Belinda replied, which didn't fill me with confidence.

'How can I fix it?' I asked.

'You can apply for an exemption to shorten the notice period,' she said. 'I'll provide you with a letter to say I'm willing to marry you on your original date.'

'Thank you,' I said automatically. 'Can I do it without Matt finding out?' I asked, before I could think of a better way to phrase the question.

'No, he needs to sign the application,' she said sharply. 'And legalities aside, I don't think the foundation for marriage is a lie.'

'Yeah, of course,' I said, chastened. 'I'll fill in one of those forms and lodge it tomorrow.'

'Okay,' she said. 'It should take a few days before it's approved or rejected. Please let me know as soon as you're informed of the outcome, so we can look at my availability for other possible dates.'

Other possible dates. These words hung in the air after the phone call ended. Our wedding was in less than three weeks' time. Invitations had been sent out (twice), dietaries gathered, flowers had been ordered, outfits paid for, a honeymoon booked. But apparently none of it would be happening.

I felt sick. I knew that there were options. We could go ahead with our wedding party and get legally married later. Matt would be devastated – I knew that this moment, when we bound ourselves in front of all the people who loved us, was the bit that mattered, the part that meant everything to him.

God, how was I going to tell him that I'd stuffed up like this?

Matt called me as I was grating parmesan.

I'd decided to break the bad news and then apologise profusely as soon as Matt arrived home. I had a plan: I was going to cook (pesto pasta counted as cooking) and make a bright pink mocktail and a bucket of buttery popcorn. Then, I'd mention that there was a teeny palaver with the legal part of the wedding, but that I was totally across it and he just needed to sign a form. And then we'd watch a movie and cuddle up together.

I quickly pressed the green button on my screen, eager to know how far away he was, and how long I had until it was time to break the news of our latest wedding road bump.

'Sorry. The traffic's been insane. And I stayed with the guys to pack up the house,' he said. I smiled despite my pounding heart. Of course Matt had helped clean up after his own buck's night.

'Oh, no worries, fine, no rush. Though, I thought I'd cook dinner, so how far away are you? Just so it's not cold because there's nothing worse than—'

'Becs,' he said. 'Is everything okay?'

I took a deep breath, fighting the strong urge to continue to filibuster. 'Well … um, there's been a bit of a wedding hiccup,' I said. 'But I'll fill you in when you get home.'

'What's wrong?' he asked, and I could hear an undertone of concern enter his voice.

'Am I on speaker?' I asked, knowing that one of Matt's friends was giving him a lift home.

'No.'

I took a deep breath, willing my years of mindfulness training to kick in. 'So, I stuffed up the wedding form, the one we need to get legally married,' I confessed into my handset far too quickly, my words running into each other. I'd wanted to achieve a tone that made it clear that while I was aware of the seriousness of my mistake, I absolutely had everything under control. Instead, I knew I sounded both guilty and manic.

'Okay,' he said slowly. 'What happened?'

I swallowed hard. 'I didn't sign it. I just … missed it,' I said. 'There's a way to fix it. We need to go through an exemption process. It might … it probably will … be okay.' I tried to sound as upbeat as I could, but I knew it wasn't the most convincing performance. I imagined him in the passenger seat of one of his groomsmen's cars, absorbing the news.

'I'm really, really sorry,' I added.

'It was a mistake. They happen,' Matt said quickly. 'We've fixed everything else. We'll fix this.'

'Yeah, exactly,' I said, and exhaled. It was the same thing he'd said when we'd found out there was a nationwide shortage of roses and then when our videographer cancelled on us because she'd gone viral on TikTok and was throwing herself into full-time content creation. 'I've prepared the form. It just needs your signature when you get home.'

Matt didn't reply.

'Hello. Are you still there?'

There was no reply. He was probably on a highway with patchy reception. Had we been cut off?

'Hello! Matt?' I tried one more time.

'Yeah, I'm here. Sorry. That's what I was calling about,' Matt said. 'I just checked my email, and I have a meeting first thing in Sydney tomorrow. I think I'll need to be there for a few days. I'll have to get the last flight out tonight to make it in time. So, I'll need to ask the guys to drop me straight to the airport – I won't have time to come home.'

All I wanted was to fall into Matt's arms, to inhale all the good summery things he'd smell of after a day of cricket and swimming at the beach – sun, salty air, sunscreen, fresh grass. Except right then I wasn't in a position to get upset or be anything but supportive – I'd just thrown a grenade at our wedding plans.

'Yeah, okay,' I said. 'I hope you can get some rest on the flight. I'll email you the form to sign?'

'Great,' he said. 'I better go.'

'Love you,' I said, but the call had already ended.

'The CEO decided to accept our recommendation,' Miranda said. It was Monday morning, the ATG executive team had just met, and Miranda had pulled me into her office straight after the meeting.

So ATG had decided to shelve Alex's work. His tool would never be used in hospitals and clinics. Patients, with hidden but diagnosable heart conditions, would be left untreated.

'The good news is that Alex Lawson is going to be offered an extremely generous salary to stay on at ATG for the next few years.'

'I assume they're not planning to tell him about their plans for his work before he signs his new contract?' I asked, trying to keep my voice level and neutral.

'There's no legal requirement for them to disclose commercially sensitive information during contract negotiations,' Miranda said, a slight edge to her voice. 'And there's excellent news,' she barrelled on, before I could make a rebuttal. 'ATG were so impressed with our frank advice that they've given us a new, much more substantial case. They want us to do a review of all the companies they're considering buying in the context of their overall strategy.'

I tried to look thrilled. And normally I would have been. To gain an interesting piece of work from an enormous client was a win. I felt numb.

'I want to keep the same team on this new project. Are you going to be able to lead this new case?' Miranda asked me with a meaningful stare. I picked up the subtext: was I able to do my all for this company given my relationship with Alex and the outcome of our advice?

Could I? My job checklist had been the true north on my career compass, for almost a decade now:

1. *Work with smart people on interesting problems.*
2. *Earn enough money to eat, etc.*
3. *Help people.*

To date, I'd felt confident that all my criteria remained checked. Of course I helped people. Some of my colleagues even described our job as being like doctors for businesses. People gave us their problems and I worked with a team to solve them. I'd done a pro bono secondment at an organisation that ran the biggest food bank in the country. I did charity fun runs every year in a T-shirt emblazoned with the Stern & Co logo.

But while I knew that I'd helped ATG to make a decision to move their company forwards, right then I was struggling to *feel* that. Right then, I just felt like I was working for a company that was about to throw away groundbreaking research that could actually help people. That could have saved Alex's mum.

I checked my phone in my lap. There were no new messages. I felt a pang of worry in the pit of my stomach. Matt hadn't called that morning and he hadn't messaged me the night before either. He usually did when he travelled, even if it was just to say he'd landed and got to the hotel safely, good night and that he loved me.

I looked up from my screen. 'Of course, I can lead the team,' I replied, meeting Miranda's stare head on.

Alex had made decisions about the trajectory of his own life and career. It hadn't been my decision to sell his work to a giant biotech company. He could have retained control of his research. He'd been so blinded by his vision for the work he cared so passionately about that he'd made risky decisions. And in doing so he'd blown up everything he'd spent his adult life working towards.

Unlike Alex, I knew how to look at something dispassionately. I knew how to overrule feelings with thoughts. I knew how to see the wood, and not just the trees.

ATG's positive impact on the world was monumental – their technology had saved thousands of lives, millions maybe. ATG knew what they wanted the future of their company to look like. They had to make tough decisions sometimes.

'Okay. Are you happy to tell the team that it's pens down on the current project, and that we'll be regrouping for the new case next week?' Miranda asked.

'Leave it with me,' I said in what I hoped was my capable leader voice. 'And I thought about our conversation the other day. After giving it a lot of thought, I've decided that I'm keen to join the banking practice.'

Miranda gave me an approving nod. 'Talk me through your decision-making process,' she said with an encouraging smile.

'I like the industry – the regulatory side means it's always changing.'

'Good start,' she said.

'There's room in the partnership – particularly for a female partner.'

She nodded again, evidently agreeing.

'And all the banks' head offices are based in major cities on the east coast. If Matt needs to move for work, I can make that happen. And if I have kids in the next few years, I don't particularly want to be flying to the Pilbara every month.'

Miranda smiled as I finished running through my list. 'Well reasoned. No notes,' she said.

I sat at my desk triple-checking that I'd filled out the notice shortening application form correctly. I'd planned to scan and email it to Matt that morning so it could be lodged as soon as possible. But as I carefully checked the instructions (because there was no way I was going to miss any details again), I sighed. The form needed a wet ink signature because apparently the registry operated as if technology hadn't progressed beyond quill and ink.

I came up with a new plan. One of the best perks of consulting was that when work slowed down, or when there was a pause between cases, there really wasn't anything to do. We called it being 'on the beach', and during this time you were pretty much allowed to do whatever you wanted. (Lucas had left the office for a Japanese-spa afternoon, dragging Adrian along with him, about two minutes after I'd told them the news.) It didn't really make up for the long nights or working on weekends, but it was something.

I searched for flight options. I knew that flying to Sydney to have a form signed was excessive. But I also knew that Matt was a guy who appreciated a gesture. And we'd both been so busy I'd barely seen him over the last few weeks. I missed him so much it was beginning to feel like an ache.

Two hours later, I was on a plane headed north. All I had with me were the clothes I'd worn to work and my laptop bag. It all felt a bit wild. Except, for the first time in weeks, I felt that I could see things clearly. I knew what was important. I knew what I wanted.

Normally I worked on flights. Some of my best thinking had been done at cruising altitudes. But today there was no urgent work that needed to be done. I opened my laptop and created a new document: *Rebecca's Wedding Vows*.

The writer's block was gone. All the thinking I'd done, half snippets of vows that had come to me in emotionally charged moments over the last few weeks, coalesced. The words poured out almost faster than I could type. When the announcement came that we were preparing for landing, I looked up from my screen, dazed and surprised. I'd been in such a state of flow that I hadn't noticed the entire flight had passed by.

They were finished. I could now tick 'Write vows!!!' off the checklist. Why had it taken so long?

For the first time since we'd got engaged, I could *see* the wedding. I could see myself in the dress that was finally the right size and ready for me to pick up, facing Matt looking gorgeous in his tailored deep-navy dinner jacket. Everyone we loved would be there as our witnesses: school friends, uni crew, work colleagues and extended family. I could feel the moment when we'd look into each other's eyes and forget that anyone was watching us. I could hear the song we'd picked to walk back down the aisle ('It Had To Be You'), I could smell the pale apricot rose petals being thrown at us. I could even see the phallic-shaped candles on each plate, which we'd decided would be a fun icebreaker.

I quickly scanned the page before we were asked to stow our laptops and tray tables away. I stopped and read the final line again – *Matt, I'm all in. I promise to love you forever* – and grinned.

I arrived at Matt's Sydney office just before five. I debated whether I should surprise him or not – I didn't want to make him feel like he needed to finish up his day early. But at the same time, I knew he'd like the romance of it all. I decided I'd go say hi and then assure him that I was happy to wait at his hotel until he was ready.

I stood in the lobby and called him, but he didn't pick up. I tried his work mobile.

'Matt's phone, Jen speaking.' Matt's second in charge, whom I'd met at the company's (surprisingly fun) Christmas party, answered his phone.

'Oh hi, it's Rebecca.'

'Hey! Matt's calls have been diverted to me,' she explained.

'Is he still in meetings?' I asked.

'Oh, um no ...' She sounded a bit uncomfortable. Did she think it was unprofessional to disclose her boss's movements? Even to his fiancée? 'Matt diverted his calls to me because ... he's on leave.'

Chapter 30

'Leave,' I repeated. 'Sick leave?' Was Matt under the weather? Was he still feeling dusty from the weekend and had decided to have a doona day? Is that why he hadn't replied to my messages?

'Umm ... a day in lieu, I think,' she said. 'We've all been working such long hours, so we got given some extra leave to make up for it. Matt emailed the team last night to let us know that he was taking a few days to get on top of wedding stuff. Oh shit ... maybe that was a surprise, and I've ruined it!'

'Don't worry, Jen, I'm a good actress,' I said with a forced laugh. 'I'd better go. I just had a break between meetings and wanted to say hi to Matt.'

I made it out of the lobby before I began to breathe heavily. I stood on Castlereagh Street in the shadow of skyscrapers, hoping that no one I knew would spot me. Where should I go next? I'd planned to go to Matt's hotel room and wait for him to finish his workday.

Our Sydney office was just around the corner. I knew that I could go there, find a spare office and regroup. No one would question why I was in Sydney – our staff were always popping up in random offices with wheelie bags.

No, I didn't need to regroup. I just needed to know where Matt was. I needed to know that he was okay. What was he doing here? Or was he in Sydney at all? Had that been a lie too?

Matt. Are you okay? I just turned up at your office. In Sydney. But you're on leave, doing wedding stuff? Where are you?

I didn't really think about what I was writing, I just tapped furiously and pressed send. My phone lit up almost straightaway. It was him.

'Matt, what's going on?' I asked before he'd even had a chance to say hello.

'Are you really in Sydney?' he asked. Did he sound a bit nervous? Or guilty? Or just himself?

'Yes, on the street outside your office,' I said. 'Are you up here?'

'I am. In Sydney. Not in the office,' he said. 'Can we meet?'

'Yes! Of course we can meet. That's why I'm here – to see you,' I said.

'I'll meet you on the Woolloomooloo Wharf in twenty minutes,' he said.

'Okay,' I said. 'But Matt—'

'Let's speak in person,' he said, and ended the call.

I walked the familiar route to the wharf, the place where Matt and I often had dinner when we were both in Sydney for work, knowing that it would help to clear my head. By the time I arrived, exactly twenty minutes later, I felt calmer. There were lots of reasons why Matt might not have been in the office. Maybe he'd arrived in Sydney for the meeting, realised he was exhausted after a huge weekend and decided to take a day. Or maybe he was working on a secret squirrel project that his colleagues weren't meant to know about. Or maybe he had been doing surprise wedding preparations.

By the time I arrived and saw Matt, waiting for me at a restaurant where he'd already nabbed a table, I was convinced that I had overreacted and there was almost certainly a logical explanation.

Matt stood up when he saw me, and before he said anything my heart sank. Matt never looked worried – he existed on the emotional spectrum between joy and contentment. It took a lot to ruffle him, and right then he looked flustered.

'Hi Becs,' he said, but he didn't lean forwards to kiss me, on the lips or at least on the cheek, like he normally would have. He sank down into his seat and took a sip from one of the glasses of wine that he'd already ordered for us.

I took the seat opposite him and stared at him expectantly with the same feeling of anticipatory dread I got before performance reviews, where I needed to brace myself in case I received bad news.

'I didn't have a meeting in Sydney. I've taken a few days of leave and I'm staying with one of my old uni mates who lives up here,' he said, his face as serious as I'd ever seen it.

'Why?'

'I thought it might be a good idea to give you some space,' he said.

'Space?'

'To work out whatever you need to work out,' he said. 'With Alex.'

'There's nothing to work out with Alex,' I said quickly.

He raised an eyebrow. 'I saw you guys talking at Arlo's party. And when he was looking after you at our place. There's *something* between you two,' he said.

'We had some stuff to talk about, sure,' I admitted. 'But I've done nothing behind your back. Yes, I should have told you about him the day he turned up at work instead of ambushing you at breakfast the next day. But I've already apologised for that. We talked that through.'

There was a pause as Matt stared intently at his drink. 'You're right, it's not about Alex,' Matt said. He finally looked up at me. 'I think he's just another thing that you've been using to keep distance between us.'

I stared at him.

'I wasn't giving you space. I think *I* needed some space to think,' Matt admitted. 'I never understood why you were so obsessed with the curse. I didn't get it. You're so rational, and this fixation was so *irrational*. But on the way back from my buck's, when you told me that you'd made a mistake on our wedding form ... well, I did just enough psychology at uni to wonder if maybe sometimes a mistake isn't a mistake. That it's a manifestation of what we unconsciously, secretly want.'

I felt like I was on one of those theme-park rides where the bottom fell out from under your feet. Except my solid ground was Matt. Or it had been. My cream silk shirt began to cling to me as I broke into a nervous sweat.

'And the one question,' Matt continued, 'I'd kept pushing down for the last few months finally came to the surface and just kept circling around my mind: Does she believe in the curse because she doesn't want to marry me?'

He reached for the stem of his glass with a slightly shaky hand but didn't take a sip.

'I'd been flying to Sydney for work so much that I think I convinced myself that going to the airport and buying a plane ticket wasn't really a big deal. I knew that if I went to stay with my parents or one of my sisters, I'd have to tell them what was going on. And I knew that if it was easy to come home and be with you, then I would. And I wouldn't be able to think clearly. I'd just keep organising our wedding, stay busy checking everything off our list. But I did need some time to think.'

I stared at him in shock. Matt had fled to another state. Because he'd needed space. From me. Because, deep down, he didn't think I wanted to marry him.

As I took a sip of my own wine, I felt that door deep inside me, wide open for the first time in decades as I'd poured my soul into my vows, slam shut. I'd thought that Matt was the one person who would never, ever blindside me. I'd been wrong. I couldn't taste the chablis, which was almost certainly excellent.

'The curse is broken.' I could see his face fall when he realised that I hadn't protested, that I hadn't screamed, *Yes, of course I want to marry you, Matt!*

'What?' he finally asked, looking confused.

'It turns out that Alex proposed to me on our last night together in Oxford,' I said quickly. 'I didn't remember it because I'd taken a Xanax after drinking, and I lost a few hours.'

'You got engaged. But you were so high on prescription drugs you don't remember it. Actually, that's a good thing because you broke your family's curse, which you don't believe in except you really, totally do.' Matt neatly summarised exactly what I'd said with a dangerously steady voice.

I nodded. I could tell that he was annoyed, that by mentioning the curse I'd flung petrol onto the flames of his doubt.

'But that's not good news, Becs. If we follow the logic of the curse, I'm the second fiancé, so we'll make it down the aisle. But we'll be the ones in a terrible marriage. I'll be your alcoholic, emotionally repressed grandpa. Or your workaholic, self-centred dad.'

I felt every muscle in my body stiffen.

'I think we're getting distracted here,' I said. 'You lied to me. You ran away to another city instead of talking to me about our relationship. I had to chase you across the country to try to fix a mistake.' I pulled the form, a bit crumpled after a day of travel, out of my bag. I pushed it across the table towards him. Matt's face fell.

'Yeah, I'm sorry, that was really shit of me,' he said. 'Sometimes I'm not … very good at facing up to things. My instinct is just to smooth things over. I thought if I gave us some space then, I don't know … everything would be okay.'

Matt hated conflict. He would always give someone the benefit of the doubt, to decide that something wasn't worth kicking up a fuss about, to try to see the bigger picture. I knew that tendency made him so excellent at his job – he instinctively knew how to forge a path through tricky situations. It was one of the qualities I admired in him.

He picked up the piece of paper sitting in front of him. To an outsider, it might have looked as though he was reading it carefully. But I knew him well enough to see that his mind was elsewhere, that he couldn't even see the words on the page in front of him.

'Can I have a think about this?' he asked. I felt my stomach churn. Matt looked surprised by his own words.

Not again. Not you, Matt. Please don't leave me. Everyone always leaves.

A wave of nausea rolled through me. I felt like someone had turned off the light switch in my brain, as if everything was darkness. I bit my lip and didn't reply. Because I knew that whatever I said would be a version of *please stay* – in this case *please marry me*. And I couldn't, not again.

'Why don't we have breakfast together tomorrow morning?' he suggested. There was no invitation to stay with him. I didn't even know the friend he was staying with.

I wanted to say no, to tell him that I had to get home. But I recognised the expression on Matt's face, I'd seen it once before when he'd talked about his childhood, about a lifetime of being overlooked. I felt something in me soften slightly.

'Okay,' I managed to get out.

'How's your mum?' Matt asked.

'She's having surgery on her ankle tomorrow, but she'll be able to go home the next day,' I said. 'She's been at Dad's hospital.'

'That must have been weird for you,' he said.

'Yeah,' I said. I knew that he was trying to comfort me. The fact that he knew how this situation would affect me felt like salt in the wound rather than a balm.

'I'll see you tomorrow,' I said, standing up and turning away from him quickly before he could see the tears welling up in my eyes.

I didn't sleep that night. Everything about the hotel room — the adjustable temperature, the high thread count sheets, the soft lighting — felt hostile. I'd been single for years before I met Matt, but I'd never felt lonely. But for the first time since I'd been a visiting student I felt consumed by homesickness. Except the one person who felt like home, the person I loved most in the world, had blindsided me.

I'd had a twilight sedation, once, and this felt similar. The conversation with Matt had been the prick of the injection going into my arm, the burst of ice-cold liquid in my veins. And then came nothingness. That's how I felt — as though nothing could touch me, as if every sensation in my body had gone into shutdown mode.

He offered to meet me in the hotel's cafe for breakfast. We were both early.

'I can't do it,' he said, before he'd even said hello.

'You can't sign the form?' I asked. I knew what he meant, I just didn't want to.

'I can't get married,' he said.

'But our wedding's in less than three weeks.' I could hear the numbness that had enveloped me since the day before in my voice.

'Forget the wedding. The wedding is just … a day. We need to think about the rest of our lives,' he said.

A waitress came over to our table.

'Can I get you guys anything? A coffee to start?' she asked with a professionalism that was no doubt drilled into all the hotel chain's staff.

'That would be great,' Matt replied. 'An oat piccolo for me, and a long black?'

I nodded.

'Thanks so much.'

Even in the middle of the tersest, most emotionally fraught conversation we'd ever had, he was able to be polite and warm and friendly to a stranger. I wracked my brain – I realised I'd never seen him be rude to anyone.

As soon as the waitress left our table Matt turned back to me.

'Becs, I love you with every part of me. I think you are smart and funny and beautiful. I love the way that you treat every single task in your life as if you're painting the Sistine Chapel. I love that you only have a few friends but would die for them. I love that you only wear navy or black or beige but in private everything is bright pink or red or turquoise.

'When you agreed to go on a date with me, I thought I was the luckiest guy alive. When you said yes to my proposal I was the happiest man in the world …'

He trailed off, clearly considering his next words. He took a small sip of his water as if he was about to swallow a pill. My mouth was also dry but I knew if I reached for my glass I'd smash it by mistake or miss my mouth and spill water all over myself.

'I've always felt that you were holding back, but I ignored it. I think I wanted to believe that it was just how you are.' He paused. 'But then I saw you talking to Alex last weekend, and I knew that I'd been kidding myself. I could see that you'd never let yourself be in love with me the way you were with him.'

Matt spoke with a strangled voice and his expression was so stony that his dimple had disappeared.

'Matt—' *Please stay. Please marry me.*

'I've spent my whole life being second best,' he said. 'But I can't be second best in my marriage.'

'Please—'

'The other day,' he said, 'at my old college, when we were talking about your career, you admitted that you wanted to stay in your job because it made you feel safe. And I think that's how you feel about me … like I'm the safe option. But I can't be the guy you settled for, I deserve more than that. And so even though I'm breaking my own heart by saying this … I want to marry you, but I've made up my mind and I just can't.'

I stared at him. He loved me. He was leaving.

'I'm sorry I lied to you. I'm sorry I ran away. That was really shitty, childish behaviour from me. You deserved better than that,' he said.

'I'm flying home today,' he added. As the enormity of what had just happened hit, I stared at Matt in shock. In a relationship, on the cusp of your wedding, it was 'up or out'. You didn't decide that you weren't getting married so would just stay boyfriend and girlfriend for a bit longer and see what happened. We were breaking up. And we lived together. We rented a house together. We owned mutual things: a toaster, a TV, a bed that cost the same as a master's degree.

'I can stay at Mum's, I think,' I said quickly. 'She's going to need help for a few weeks anyway and Hamish is still visiting his daughter.'

'I can move out. Move home,' he said. Would Jane be devastated or thrilled? I wondered. Possibly a bit of both.

She'd be devastated on his behalf but thrilled to have her beloved son back under her roof.

'Can we … not tell anyone for a few days?' I asked.

'Some people are travelling for the wedding. We need to give them the heads-up,' Matt said. As always, it was other people that were at the forefront of his decision-making.

'A day or two won't make a difference,' I said. 'I just … I need a bit of time to process everything.'

'Yeah, of course,' he said.

I stood up and pushed back my chair. The coffees hadn't arrived yet, but I needed to leave.

'Stay, Becs,' he said, reaching for my hand. 'We should talk.'

'I just … have to go,' I managed to blurt out.

Chapter 31

I didn't cry in the lift, or in the hotel room, or on the plane. I held it together until I reached Mum's hospital room.

She was awake and looked like herself again — colour back in her face, eyesore of a dressing gown on and a full face of makeup, including lipstick, firmly in place. Of course she'd felt the need to look glam for surgery.

'Oh, darling,' she said, as I sat on the seat next to her bed and burst into tears. If Mum had accused me of pulling focus on the day she was due to have surgery, it would have been a fair accusation. Instead she offered me a tissue from the box by her bed.

'Can I stay at your place and look after you?' I asked between sobs.

'Of course you can, darling. I'll tell Hamish not to cut his trip short,' she said in an even voice. Neither of us mentioned that I'd never stayed at her and Hamish's house. When I'd moved out, Dad had sold our family home, and his spare room was an office. I didn't want to be an imposition on my friends, and most of them had more kids than bedrooms. I had nowhere else to go.

'Now, I've heard rumours of a French bakery across the street. And I'd love to have something that doesn't taste like institution waiting for me when I come to.'

I'd expected another sleepless night in Mum's guest room, but I passed out almost as soon as my head hit the pillow. As the initial shock of Matt cancelling the wedding wore off, the feelings flooded in. In fact, all I did for the next two days was sleep and cry. I picked up Mum when she was discharged, got her comfortable and brought her meals and pills. Then I collapsed back into the spare bed with a box of tissues. I made Mum simple food – soups and sandwiches – but I had no appetite. I'd never understood it when people said they couldn't get out of bed, but now I did.

Mum had fractured her ankle and been discharged from the hospital with a pain management plan and a rehabilitation team. But no professional had given me advice on how to manage the all-consuming body aches, or the moments when I'd wake up in the night feeling like I couldn't breathe or when I missed Matt in every part of my body. No physio was booking an appointment to rehabilitate my broken brain, and life, and heart.

I made languid attempts to make myself feel better. I tried drinking – but wine reminded me of Matt. I tried to distract myself on my phone but found myself scrolling through his social media and photos on my camera roll. I blasted podcasts to drown out my thoughts, but he'd recommended most of my favourite ones.

Occasionally I checked my messages but no one needed me. Matt hadn't reached out. Nothing was on fire at work. I felt like a ghost, like I couldn't feel anything real, like I wasn't part of the world.

On the third night I awoke with a start. I checked my phone – it was 3 am. I rolled over and closed my eyes, willing my body to take me back into the blissful state of nothingness I'd been in temporarily. But my brain had kicked into full gear; I knew there would be no more sleep for me.

I opened my laptop. As I was already awake, I thought I might as well be productive. Maybe doing would numb feeling. I opened a new document titled: *Cancel the Wedding.*

1. *Tell family.*
2. *Tell friends.*
3. *Email all guests.*
4. *Cancel venue and catering.*
5. *Sell dress.*
6. *Cancel hair and makeup.*
7. *Cancel photographer.*
8. *Cancel Belinda.*

I looked at the list once I'd finished drafting it and mentally allocated roles. I didn't really want to do any of it, though I knew I'd put my hand up for half. That's how our breakup would go. We'd both zealously try to do the right thing – split the tasks, split the bills. It would all be excruciatingly amicable.

I clicked on the 'Share document' button. I typed in Matt's email address and stared at it for a few seconds. Then I hit delete. Maybe in the morning, the real morning, I'd feel stronger. Or maybe the day after.

I stared down at the diamond perched upon my left hand. I felt a wave of despair break through the nothingness.

I yanked it off. There was a slight indent above my knuckle and my finger looked naked. Even my hand missed being engaged.

I knew the right thing to do was give it back to Matt. But I also knew he wouldn't take it. In which case, what was I meant to do? Sell it? No, I couldn't do that. This piece of metal and colourless stone meant too much to me.

Then I had a thought. I rolled out of bed and opened the spare wardrobe. When Dad had sold our house, I'd left a few boxes of stuff at Mum's place.

I slid a bunch of clothes in dry cleaner's plastic wrapping down the railing and there they were – Mum hadn't moved them. I pulled out the box at the top of the stack. It was full of old school stuff. The first layer was my diaries, then a smattering of school reports. Under these were a stack of UMAT practice test books. I don't think I'd cracked the spine of any of them. But I'd kept them. Had I felt bad about how much they'd cost? Had I thought I could pass them on to someone who needed them?

I stuffed everything back into the box and opened the next one. This one was from uni, though I hadn't kept very much, considering it had been a six-year chunk of my life. Most of the box was filled with stuff from Oxford. From my final term at Oxford.

I picked up the menu from the Shelley Society dinner, then the fabric wristband from the Trinity College ball, then a photo of a tree at dawn. I'd been heartbroken when I'd packed this stuff away. Part of me had wanted to burn it. But I think I'd also needed proof, tangible proof, that it had happened.

I sighed as I pulled the final notebook, the one with the 'Salad Days List' in it, out of the box. And then I spotted it. There it was, glinting, loose in the corner of the box, half tucked under the taped-down flap.

I picked it up. It was a delicate silver band with a tear-shaped turquoise in the centre. As Alex had said, I could tell it wasn't expensive. But I must have instinctively known when I was packing up this box that it wasn't junky costume jewellery that had been bought at Claire's or Primark. Had I tried to give it back to Lily? Had she said it wasn't hers and then I stuffed it into this box with the rest of the Oxford mementos? Or had some part of me known that it meant a lot to someone? I truly didn't remember.

I slipped the ring onto my bare finger. It had only been there for a few hours. Hours that had been lost to the ether. How could this ring have any meaning? Why did we let these inanimate pieces of metal and stone take on so much emotional significance?

This ring didn't mean anything to me. But I knew it meant a lot to Alex.

I pulled out my phone.

Do you have time to meet up today? I asked. Then I realised it was only 5 am – an antisocial time to message someone.

Yes. What time? He wrote back instantly. So, he still didn't sleep.

I stared at my phone.

Lunchtime? Let's meet somewhere near the office.

In the end we met up at a cafe between our houses. He was wearing shorts, a T-shirt and Birkenstocks – I guessed he'd been working from home. I hadn't seen him since Arlo's party. His summer tan had deepened since then. How had that only been two weeks ago?

'I know we were going to steer clear of each other,' I said. 'But I wanted to return your mum's ring. I found it with some stuff I'd kept from Oxford. Sorry I had it for so long.'

I carefully placed it on the table. He paused for a moment then picked it up. The ring looked even more dainty in his large hands.

'So, you really did propose that night?' I asked.

'Yeah,' he said, 'I did.'

'I always wondered who did that. People who met someone and just … whipped out a ring,' I said.

'Well, now you know,' he said with a shrug.

'I always thought that it was so …'

'Romantic?' he offered.

'Silly,' I said. He laughed.

'I'm really sorry I hurt you that night. You took a leap of faith, you opened yourself up and asked me to live life with you, and I left. I know, after what happened with your mum, how losing someone you loved with no warning would have been horrible. So, I'm sorry,' I said.

He looked down at the ring and then finally met my eyes. 'Thank you,' he said.

'Did someone give that ring to your mum?' I asked.

'I don't know,' he said. 'I don't even know if she ever loved anyone. Or if anyone ever loved her …'

'I know she had a great love,' I said.

He looked up at me blankly.

'*You*. I never met her. But I just know, because I know you – that you were the great love of her life.'

'Yeah. She loved me with … everything,' he said, slowly nodding. 'But I still wish I knew the story of this ring. Did she wear it because she just liked it? Or because it meant something? I wished that I'd asked her so many questions about her life. There's so much we never got to talk about. I was a teenager when she died. I didn't know what questions I'd need to ask back then. And then, I ran out of time.'

He paused for a moment and I could tell that he was collecting his thoughts. 'I gave you a bum steer that summer,' he said finally.

'What do you mean?' I asked.

'You were hurt. You were grieving that your family had fallen apart. I wonder if part of our gravitational pull towards each other was that we could both sense that we were processing a whole lot of buried pain and confusion,' he said. 'You were still angry at your mum. And I encouraged that, I think, because I was still mad at my mum for leaving too. And maybe it was easier for us to be angry and hurt together, or something. But our situations were, and are, different. She loves you and you still have her. You can still ask her all the things, you know?'

I nodded. But did I agree? The anger and hurt that we'd shared that summer had been so comforting. That he had changed his mind, had softened, had processed some of the pain he'd felt, somehow felt like far more of a revelation than what had happened the night of the ball.

'I'm glad I got to see you again,' he said.

'Me too,' I said, then felt a stab of guilt, because I hadn't told Matt that I was here with Alex. Matt was no longer my fiancé, I reminded myself. Here I was, alone again.

'I also wanted to tell you that I think you're really good at your job,' he said. 'It almost kills me to say this. And I mean it in the least patronising way possible. But I've been seriously impressed.'

I looked at him, searching for an edge of judgement in his voice. But for the first time ever when talking about the job I'd chosen, there was none.

'So, you don't think I wasted my brain, time, energy and life?' I asked.

'Not if you don't,' he said with a wry smile. I felt another stab of guilt. Because I was good at my job, I couldn't tell him that his job was about to become a nightmare.

'Matt and I aren't getting married,' I said. I felt an enormous frog in my throat as I said it out loud for the first time. 'We broke up a few days ago.'

'I'm sorry,' he said.

'Are you?' I replied, then laughed – a slightly more bitter one than I'd intended.

'Of course I am,' he said. The lines around his eyes crinkled in concern. 'Are you okay?'

'Not really,' I said. 'I'm … a mess. This is the first time I've got out of bed or dressed since it happened.'

'What happened?' he asked. 'You don't have to tell me, obviously. Only if it's helpful.'

'He said that he didn't think that I was all in. He said he deserved more than that,' I said.

Alex stared at me for a second and I could see his brain rolling through all the permutations of the things he could say.

'I meant what I said the other day. I've never stopped loving you, Rebecca. I want to be with you. I knew from the minute I met you that you were my person. I stayed away for a long time because I was hurt by how we ended. Except deep down I must have known that I didn't have the full picture.'

He moved into the seat next to me and stared at me with his piercing blue eyes.

I turned away from him. I couldn't have this conversation. How could I let him comfort me, open up to me, when I was basically betraying him? I felt a sudden, desperate urge to tell him what was going to happen to his work.

'I have to go,' I said. I couldn't do it. I'd just lost Matt. I couldn't lose work too. My job was an ark in this emotional storm raging around me. It was the one place where things made sense in a life without Matt. I felt my stomach churning.

'I just ... everything's been changing really fast,' I finally said. 'I'm a mess right now. I only came here today to return your mum's ring.'

'I've waited for nine years,' he said, his eyes twinkling but his deep, husky voice serious. 'You've just called off a wedding. I know you've got a lot to work through. But when you've had a chance to process your breakup you should think about giving us another chance. I can wait for as long as you need.'

I took a small sip of my sparkling water.

'So, are you free tomorrow?' he added, and in spite of myself, I smiled.

Chapter 32

I messaged Stella as soon as I reached my car: *Any chance you're in the market for a chat?*

I was feeling fragile, and I knew that she'd be gentle.

That would be lovely! Thank you! Visiting hours start soon.

Stella was at sleep school again. I'd totally forgotten that she was booked in after the hen's weekend, that her mum had stayed on to look after Evie.

I ducked into a cake shop en route and bought a box filled with slices and tarts — she was a patient at a private maternity hospital for people with expensive insurance, but there were still limits on edible hospital food.

'Becs!'

I was on the ramp leading up to the hospital when I heard my name. I turned around. It was Nick, walking towards the entrance, a few steps behind me.

'Hey,' I said then I felt a ripple of unease as I remembered the last time I'd seen Nick. 'What are you doing here?'

'I'm guessing the same thing you are,' he said, looking slightly amused.

'You didn't have time to visit when Evie was here,' I said.

'Yeah,' he said, taking my snark on the chin with an expression that looked very similar to remorse. I realised that he wasn't wearing scrubs or his hospital lanyard. 'But then my little sister said some things that hit a nerve.'

'If it's any consolation, I basically yelled at everyone that night,' I said, and couldn't help but grin, disarmed by Nick's candour.

'Do you have time for a coffee?' Nick asked.

'Aren't you going to see Stella?' I replied.

'She's used to me letting her down,' he said wryly as he shrugged his broad shoulders.

'Okay,' I said. We walked through the mostly residential streets until we found a small strip of shops and an open cafe. I let Nick buy my drink the way he'd always bought me little treats when we were growing up.

'You were right,' Nick said, as soon as we sat down at a table. 'I thought I was doing a good enough job. I was topping up Stella's super while she wasn't working. I dropped Evie off at kinder sometimes. I added items to the online shopping cart. And I thought that everything was okay. Stella's so stoic. And Mum helps her out so much …' He paused, fiddling with a sugar sachet.

'And I told myself that I didn't have a choice. Medical training is brutal. Obstetrics jobs aren't flexible. That I had to get lots of rest because what I do is a matter of life and death. But after Saturday night, and your unfiltered feedback imparted by way of a nostalgically nerdy family game …'

Despite the seriousness of this conversation, I giggled and Nick snorted. For a second, we could have been kids again – me a precocious eight-year-old, Nick a gangly, studious teenager.

'Well, I've done some thinking, some soul searching, this week,' he continued when we'd stopped cackling into our drinks. 'And all of that is true. But the thing is, the biggest role model I've had is Dad. And you know what he was like: "Love what you do—"'

'"And you'll never work a day in your life,"' I recited, finishing Dad's oft-recited catchphrase.

We both laughed again.

'Except, I think he uses love as a Trojan horse for selfishness. I think Dad is an excellent doctor but also a very self-absorbed man. And I don't want to have a life like his. I don't want to miss my kids' childhoods. I don't want my wife to resent me. To leave me.'

'So, what are you going to do?' I asked. All the judgement, intentional or unintentional, was gone from my voice.

'This is actually what I was coming to tell Stella,' he said. 'But I don't think she'll mind if I tell you.'

He took a deep breath.

'Today I got a new job as part of an obstetrics group,' he said.

'Congratulations!' I said. 'But what's that?'

Nick laughed. 'It basically means that I'll be one of five obstetricians who look after a big group of private patients. So, we all meet every woman during the course of her pregnancy and then whoever is on shift delivers the baby. Which means no overtime, no being called into the hospital during the night or on weekends, no more crazy hours. I'll work the occasional weekend and night shift, but otherwise I'll be home a lot more. I can do pick-ups and drop-offs and birthday parties and swimming lessons and date nights.'

'Wow,' I said. 'And what does this mean for your career?'

'I don't know. It'll probably slow things down. And it'll be less money,' he said. 'But maybe I'll be less exhausted. And Stella will be less exhausted. And I'll have time with the kids. And I think that when I'm not running on empty, I'll be able to be a better doctor.'

He looked completely daunted, but I could also see a glimmer of hope in his eyes.

'I'm sure you'll be an incredible doctor,' I said. 'And husband. And dad.'

'How did you escape the family curse of becoming Dr Evans?' Nick asked. I suppressed a laugh at hearing him invoke the C word. But maybe this was *his* family curse. Maybe 'curse' was just a synonym for 'baggage from your childhood you have to undo'.

'I wanted to study medicine so much. I think I would have loved it,' I said slowly. 'And that's why I didn't let myself do it. I didn't want to care about something, to love my job, as much as I knew I would. It felt too dangerous.'

'Yeah, I think Mum felt like that about losing her career,' Nick said. 'I don't think she ever really got over it, wanting something so much and not getting it.'

'What do you mean?' I asked, confused.

'You haven't talked to Mum about her career?' Nick looked equally perplexed.

'No. What happened?' I asked. I knew everything I needed to know about Mum's career, didn't I? She was a GP. She worked at a women's clinic where she helped women whose lives were being held hostage by their bodies. Her patients adored her. She ran her clinics around her life – catching up with friends, looking after Evie and Alice, travelling with Hamish.

'Mum was the superstar. She was brilliant while Dad was … fine.'

I stared at him. This was not the narrative I'd grown up with.

'Her dream was to be a heart surgeon,' Nick went on. 'She got accepted into cardio training way before Dad did. And the colleges rarely let in women back then.'

'But she didn't—'

'She got pregnant with me. She had to give up her place. They didn't hold spots for something as banal as pregnancy. Dad got to live out her dream.'

Mum had retrained as a GP when I was a toddler. I'd thought that it was admirable that she got to do it all. I hadn't considered that it had been a compromise.

'I didn't know that,' I said, as I scanned my memories for any hint of a conversation with Mum about this. But there was nothing. And we'd spent my whole childhood talking.

'I better go see Stell, tell her the good news,' Nick said, draining his coffee. 'Do you want to come?'

'I think she'd prefer to see you than hear my problems,' I said.

'Your problems?' Nick studied my face, his expression all brotherly concern.

'Another time,' I said, forcing a smile and handing him the box of pastries. It didn't feel like the moment to tell him that my wedding was off, and that my ex wanted to get back together, and to ask him to workshop the path forwards with me. He'd had enough life-changing decisions of his own to grapple with this week.

'Okay. But … let's do this more.'

'Yeah, that would be good,' I said as he wrapped his arms around me.

'And do one thing for me,' he said, as he let me go. 'Go talk to Mum.'

I picked up Mum's prescription refill on the way home from the sleep school.

As I made us both dinner, the revelations from the unexpected conversations I'd had that day kept reverberating around my head.

'Thanks so much, darling,' she said, when I left a bowl of soup and her pills on her bedside table. 'I know you've got a lot on at the moment with work and the wedding, so this means a lot.'

In her old, faded (albeit still fairly outrageous) flannel pyjamas, and her red hair pulled back in a bun and no makeup on her pale face, she looked uncharacteristically vulnerable. She looked like the version of the mum only I ever got to see when we lived together – the mum I'd crawl into bed with during the middle of the night, the mum who woke me up for school every morning, the mum who would make pancakes on weekends when we had nowhere to rush to. The one who'd always been there.

I knew that it was now or never. I climbed onto the other side of her bed and lay down next to her.

'What happened with you and Dad?' I asked. Even though I was looking straight ahead I could see her turn to me. Then she moved her head into the same position mine was in, both of us staring at the ceiling.

'What do you think happened, darling?' she asked in a soft voice.

'That you fell in love with another man and then left,' I said.

'That did happen,' she agreed.

'But I think that maybe it was more complicated than that?'

'Mm.' She made a neutral noise.

'Was I one of those "let's have a kid to try to save the marriage" babies?'

Mum sighed. 'No. You were so wanted,' she said softly. 'You were the baby we were going to do differently. Your dad had barely been around when Nick was little. But I just thought … that's what happens. None of my friends really expected much help from their husbands. And there wasn't room in a family for two surgeons. Not with kids.'

She paused for a moment, slowly twirling one of the rings that wasn't on her ring finger.

'I had thought about leaving. Things got pretty bad between us. And I finally told your dad how miserable I'd been, how alone and resentful I'd felt. And that if something didn't change, I was scared that all the simmering anger would metastasise. And for a while, things got better. He pulled back at work for a bit, travelled less. And we decided to have another baby. We were so excited. We spent the whole pregnancy talking about how this time it was going to be different. Your dad was going to drop his caseload, and I was going to have another go at getting into speciality training. We were going to do a better job of sharing looking after you, and go on family holidays and—'

'I don't remember Dad ever being home,' I said.

'I still don't think he's ever changed a nappy. And he didn't change at all. So, for a while I got angrier. And then I just couldn't handle all the feelings anymore. I emotionally checked out of our marriage,' Mum said in a flat voice. 'But the story had a happy ending – because you became my life. And the life that the two of us had together was magic.'

Even though I wasn't looking at her face I could tell that we were both smiling as we remembered.

'I didn't expect to fall in love with another man. I didn't even know that I ever wanted to again,' Mum said. 'As you were reaching the final years of school, I realised that you were almost grown up. Well, it hit me that you'd be leaving soon, and that you couldn't be my whole world anymore. That you were going to have your own life.

'Hamish and I had known each other for a while. I think we sensed a loneliness in each other and eventually we became friends. I didn't mean for it to become anything more, not until you were older at least. But then it did.

'I wasn't going to leave your dad or make any changes to our life until you'd finished high school. But one day your dad found messages and then it all came out, and our marriage ended.'

I continued to stare straight up at the ceiling as I processed her version of the story.

'Do you believe in the curse?' I asked after a pause. I was sure she knew what I was really asking. Did she take responsibility for the decisions she'd made, the actions she'd taken?

'I know Mum did,' she said slowly. I was relieved that she hadn't belittled the question or made a joke. 'Her relationship with my dad was so dysfunctional that I think that it helped her to believe that she wasn't wholly responsible for a marriage that had made her so miserable and that would have been so difficult to leave.'

She sighed and gently shook her head.

'But no, I don't,' she said. 'Mum and her sister lost the men they were going to marry in a war. My cousin got engaged because she thought she was pregnant and then when she wasn't she moved on.

'And I think I ended my engagement because … I thought that love was meant to be this dazzling, all-consuming force. And I felt that when I met your dad. I suppose I believed that it wasn't right to be with someone when I was able to feel the way I did about him.'

'You really loved Dad?' I asked, though I already knew what her answer would be from the warmth in her voice as she remembered.

'So much,' Mum said, and I could tell that for a moment she'd drifted off into memories of heady days. 'Except what I didn't understand then was that all the qualities that I found so intoxicating when I fell in love with him – ambition, drive, focus – would be the ones that made our marriage toxic in the end.'

'I'm angry at Dad,' I said. I pursed my lips together as if I might still be able to catch those words and shove them back in. But it was too late, they were out there now. I'd known it for a long time but had been too afraid to admit it. Matt had called him self-centred, and Nick had called him self-absorbed – it had felt like somehow this had been enough of a green light to feel what I'd tried not to feel, at least openly.

'I know,' Mum said.

'Matt says that love is showing up. And Dad didn't show up for us,' I said. 'But then … you didn't show up for me either. Why didn't you stay when I asked you to stay?' I felt like every piece of oxygen in my lungs had been expelled with that question, the one that had haunted me for so long.

'At the time, I convinced myself that I was doing what was best for you.' Mum began to answer my question straightaway in whole sentences, as if she'd had the answer ready, had spent a long time thinking about it. 'I knew that if I insisted that we stay in our house your dad would force it to be sold. If he couldn't have it, he wouldn't let me have it either. And it was your final year of school, and I knew how hard you needed to study and focus to get into med, and I wanted you to have as much stability and support as possible.'

'But it wasn't the house that was home, Mum. It was *you*,' I said.

'I know,' Mum said, and I could see she was trying desperately not to cry. 'You were my home too. And I'm so sorry I hurt you.'

For so many years I'd believed that Mum hadn't cared, that she'd fallen madly in love and been reckless and done whatever she wanted, not worrying about who got caught in the crossfire or if my life imploded as a result. But she had cared. She'd made a mistake, but from a place of confusion and concern and hurt. And love. And I now knew that it was possible to make a mistake, or lots of mistakes, which hurt the person you loved the most. Even if that's the very last thing you wanted to do.

I opened my mouth to say something but instead a howl came out.

Mum held me until the tears stopped flowing. I had no idea how long I'd cried for – it could have been minutes or hours.

When my breathing finally returned to normal, I cleared my throat. 'I think my engagement ended because … I fell slowly and deeply and madly in love with the one man I wasn't supposed to … my fiancé,' I said, almost in a whisper.

'Oh, darling,' Mum said in a soft voice. She began to stroke my hair, just like she used to do when I was a girl.

'I thought Matt was the safe guy. I thought there would be limits on how much I could love him. But the more I got to know him, the more our lives intertwined, the more I just … kept falling deeper and deeper in love with him,' I said. 'It snuck up on me. And then I loved him so much that I couldn't imagine life without him. And that terrified me. I was so scared of how much I loved him that I began to pull back. I don't think I really knew I was doing it.'

I sniffled then sighed.

'He called off the wedding because he thinks I don't love him enough. But the truth is, I was trying to hide the fact, maybe from him, I think mainly from myself, that I loved him too much.'

I bit my lip to stop myself crying again. Mum didn't jump in to fill the silence.

'Why did you bring up the curse after I got engaged to Matt?' I asked. I knew my thoughts were careering in a way that wasn't close to linear. But I needed to keep asking all the questions.

'I only mentioned it a few times as a joke. To try to cheer you up when there were hiccups during the wedding planning,' Mum said. 'You have many strengths, but a relaxed approach to event planning isn't one of them.'

Even though my body was emotionally short-circuiting, I laughed. And then Mum did too. And soon we were both hysterical. We both tried to speak but we couldn't get anything out between guffaws. I hadn't laughed this hard since … well, I couldn't remember. I'd probably last laughed like this with Matt. He was always able to make me laugh, belly laugh, even when I was at my most wound-up.

'You're right, Becs. You weren't imagining it, I probably did start to bring up the curse over the last few weeks,' Mum said when we'd both caught our breath. 'You kept mentioning it whenever we talked about wedding plans. And I started to wonder if everything was okay with you and Matt. So maybe I used it as a way to see if you wanted to talk about whatever you were feeling. I wanted you to know that if you changed your mind about him or about the wedding then it wouldn't be a big deal. That plenty of women in your family hadn't made it down the aisle either, me included.'

She sighed and then reached for my hand, the one with no ring on it anymore, and pulled it to her chest.

'I should have just asked you straight out if you were okay, if everything was okay,' she said.

I finally looked up at her through my puffy eyes.

'Oh god, Mum, you're in pain,' I said. I sprang out of bed, grabbed the packet of painkillers and her glass of water. 'You need to take this.'

'I'm okay,' she said, but I knew she wasn't.

'I love you, Mum,' I said, and pushed a tablet into her hand. I looked down at the packet of Endone in my hand. If I took one, would I stop feeling all the feelings that were swooshing around me? In spite of myself, I smiled. No, not feeling hadn't worked out that well for me.

I put the packet back on the bedside table. Life wasn't so bad that I had to steal my mum's prescription meds. And anyway – it was time for me to feel some things.

Chapter 33

I fell asleep next to Mum and woke up later than I normally did. When I finally came to and checked the time on my phone, I realised that if I didn't hurry, I was going to be late to meet Alex.

We'd planned to meet at Parkrun. I think partly because something in the daylight and so wholesome felt like neutral ground. But also, Alex's life was one of routine, even in the midst of an emotional maelstrom.

We both ran around the lake, Alex at the front and me in the middle of the pack, then walked in companionable silence to the market. As we ordered coffees at Padre, I wondered how it was possible for so much to change over so few weeks. Again. We carried our long blacks to our table and sat down.

'It's a no, isn't it?' he asked.

'Yes.' I paused for a moment and took a sip of my coffee, even though it was still scalding. 'I'm sorry for making things weird yesterday, for giving you the impression that there was hope for us. But I was doing the thing that I do when I get scared – I run towards the person who won't hurt me.'

'Ouch,' he said, with a smile that didn't meet his eyes.

'I'm sorry,' I said again.

'I'm sorry too,' he said. 'That I came here and messed everything up for you.'

'Have you signed your new job contract?' I asked.

'No, but I'm going to,' he said. 'But don't worry, they have labs all over the world – I'll leave Melbourne.'

'ATG aren't going to commercialise your work, they're going to mothball it,' I said.

'Shit,' he said. His face morphed from sadness to despondency. That I wasn't in love with him had bruised him. This news had broken his heart. 'I knew that was a possibility, but I thought—'

'That if you had a consultant on the inside to advocate for your work, you'd reduce the risk of that outcome?'

'That's not the reason I asked for you to work on this project,' he said. Then he looked up and his bright eyes met mine. 'It wasn't the *only* reason.'

I smiled. Because, in a way, it was reassuring to know that Alex hadn't only come back into my life because he'd been harbouring a flame for me all these years. Maybe that was the story he'd told himself. But on some level, he'd sought me out because I was someone who could help further his agenda. Alex had grown up and changed. But some things hadn't – his work still came first.

'I've only known about ATG's plans since Monday. Because they knew we had history, I was kept out of the loop before then,' I said, with a shrug. 'I should have told you earlier this week.'

Alex took a sip of his steaming coffee as he processed what I'd told him. I knew that part of him would enjoy the feeling of his tongue burning, to validate the emotional pain he was working through.

'You know that now you've told me what they're going to do, I won't sign my contract. I'll go to one of their competitors and I won't rest until I create something brilliant,' he said. His tone was flat and his eyes were aflame. What he was saying wasn't hyperbole. With his brain and work ethic, fuelled by a need to exact revenge, I had no doubt that he could do exactly that. 'And they're smart enough to know that the information that changed my mind came from you. You'll be fired.'

'I know,' I said. 'I'm not going to ask you to protect my career. But I am going to ask you to think about yours.'

His eyes narrowed.

'Your whole life's work has been in your mum's memory,' I explained. 'But … from what I know about her, from what you've told me, she would have only wanted you to have a happy, fulfilling life. I don't think she would have wanted every part of you to be a shrine to her tragic death.'

Alex's jaw tightened, and the knuckles of his hands became white as he clenched them tightly around his mug.

'I think purpose can be incredible,' I continued. 'But only when it enhances your life, not when it cannibalises all the other good things in it too.'

I'd never seen him lose his temper before, but for a moment I wondered if he was going to leap up from his chair and storm off. Then he crumpled. For a moment I caught a glimpse of the lost, lonely, grieving boy he'd been. The one who was still inside him. I reached across the table and took one of his hands and held it in mine.

'I think one of the reasons you enjoyed our summer together is that we spent so much of our time in lectures, learning things. During "Lecture Lottery", you came alive.

I remember watching you talking with undergrads about what they'd been studying and you were always so genuinely fascinated by those conversations. And they blossomed under your attention. Over the last few weeks, I've seen how brilliant you are at speaking and teaching – in a world where no one has an attention span, you can hold a room.

'I think if you spend your life enjoying your work and passing on everything you've learned, because of what happened to your mum … well, I think that would be an incredible legacy.'

I paused for a moment, letting him process what I was saying.

'My instinct is still to go with the devote-every-fibre-of-my-being-to-revenge option,' he said.

'You do you. And don't worry about me,' I said, taking my hands back.

'Don't worry, I won't,' he said. And although he'd grinned as he'd spoken, at the end of the day he'd always do what he needed to do.

Alex had given me a ring because he'd wanted me to move to the place he wanted to be for his work. He loved me, but the ring represented *his* dreams for *his* life. He hadn't passed Lily's engagement ring test.

After we'd finished our coffees, as I walked out of the darkness of the covered market and into the sun, I knew that I'd never see Alex Lawson again.

I spent the rest of the weekend letting my family and friends know that the wedding was off, trying and failing to hold back tears. Then on Monday I went to work. Not my work – our team was still on the beach – I went to Lily's work.

'Now, I'm here today to be *your* consultant.'

'You don't look so well,' she said, looking concerned. 'And I can't afford you.'

'Firstly, I know,' I said. I knew my skin looked blotchy and my eyes were raw and red. I hadn't been able to muster the energy to wash, let alone blow-dry my hair, so it was a knotted tangle of greasy curls, and not the fashionable kind. 'Apparently, this is what you look like when you're heartbroken.'

'Yeah, sometimes,' Lily looked at me, her eyes dull. She'd still managed to dress in one of her outfits: a linen waistcoat and cargo pants with totally hideous oversized runners. But I could tell that today it was a uniform rather than a form of her creative expression.

'And secondly, I basically owe you this to thank you for the work you did on our wedding rings.'

'Which you won't be using and that you paid for,' she said.

'You didn't charge us enough,' I said. 'Pricing is one of the things I'm going to be focusing on today.'

'Is there a world where I get to say no?' she asked weakly.

'No.'

'Fine. Though it's too late, anyway,' she said.

'Lil, I think that there are only a few people in the world who feel like they can't *not* do something. That there's this one thing that makes them feel truly alive.'

She stared at me for a moment then slowly nodded.

'Yeah, I love it,' she said. 'But sometimes, like right now,

I just really wish I didn't. I wish I wanted to have a good-enough job and then like ... play pickleball on the weekend.'

'I understand that there are practical realities. You have a kid, you and Aaron have to pay for childcare and all of Arlo's ... nappies and mush.'

'He doesn't eat mush anymore,' Lily said, smiling for the first time.

'Not really my point,' I said, smiling back. 'I'm not minimising rental payments, emergency savings, electricity bills and dentist trips. I get that you have to do what you have to do for your family. But I'm really good at thinking through problems. And before you totally give up on the thing that makes you spark, and that I suspect makes you a better partner and mum ... let's go through all the numbers? Just in case.'

'Okay,' she said, and I felt the energy in the room shift.

We spent the whole day, when there weren't customers in the store, going through years of paperwork. I searched through endless drawers of questionable filing to find the relevant numbers that I needed to plug into my Excel spreadsheet. I wished, as I tried to remember the models that had come as naturally to me as breathing in my first few years as a consultant, that I had Lucas there to do the heavy lifting.

By the end of the day, I'd pulled together a good snapshot of Lily's business. Lily had been quiet all day. I knew how vulnerable she would be feeling – I was doing the business equivalent of rifling in her lingerie drawer. I also had the experience to know how to make her feel okay about it.

Lily closed the store at 5 pm. Without asking, she poured us both a glass of wine.

'So …?'

'Obviously, I need to spend more time looking over everything – but I think you might have options.'

'Really?' she asked. I could hear a trace of hope infiltrate her voice.

'Yeah. So, let's start with the bad news: you're right that the shop has to go. The rent has gone up, staffing costs have gone up. The numbers don't work for being a bricks-and-mortar business.'

I saw her swallow, but she didn't let her face betray any emotion. 'Okay,' she said.

'But most of your revenue doesn't come through the store. You sell quite a bit online,' I said.

'Yeah, I guess,' Lily said slowly.

'And your highest margins are on your cheaper products and also your custom designs,' I said.

'With the less-expensive stuff, I do the design then get them manufactured. And people don't mind paying a premium for their engagement rings or birthstone rings or whatever.'

'Exactly. If you were fully online and focused on high-volume less-expensive products and then used your studio at home for meeting clients and making bespoke pieces – I think it could still be a really viable business,' I said.

I turned my laptop around and showed her the projected revenue range I'd modelled. 'Obviously, these numbers aren't a promise. Just my best guesstimate,' I said. 'Whatever you do next is totally up to you. And Aaron. But this is just … more information to help you make the decision for how you want to live your life.'

'Right,' Lily said. Colour had returned to her face, like

she was preparing to reawaken a part of herself that she'd consigned to the grave. 'You're really good at this.'

'I have a brain that knows how to absorb large amounts of information quickly and sort it all out. It's made me really good at my job. But ... maybe not so good at life.'

On Tuesday, the last beach day, I woke up in Mum's guest room to a message from Miranda.

Do you have time for a chat later today?

She'd phrased it as a question, but it wasn't really. I hauled myself into the shower, into a suit and then onto a tram to the city, my stomach swirling the whole time.

I walked slowly across the floor, taking it all in. This place had felt like my home for nearly a decade. All my colleagues, across the many teams I'd been part of, had been my people.

I knew that there was every chance that Alex had turned up to ATG on Monday, all guns blazing, ripping up his contract, broadcasting his visions of vengeance, employment lawyers in tow. If so, this would be my last day in this office.

'Miranda?' I knocked on her office door and she waved me in.

'I'm sure you've been waiting with bated breath, but the partners made their decision yesterday.'

'Yes, of course,' I said. In all the chaos I'd totally forgotten that the promotion meetings were happening this week.

'You got it,' she said, beaming widely. 'The partners were very impressed that you wooed a new client and won more work.'

'So, it's full steam ahead on the new project? And there were no issues on the Alex Lawson contract front?'

'He's going back to Harvard. Apparently, the uni and a whole lot of students were devastated when he left. And all the money he made them when they did the spin-off of his work probably didn't hurt either,' Miranda said.

I tried to keep my face neutral as a wave of relief enveloped me. Partly that he hadn't kicked up an enormous fuss and put my career at risk. But mostly because I knew that he was going to be happy.

'And they don't care that he didn't sign his contract extension?' I asked.

'They can live with this outcome. He's harmless on a campus. They just didn't want his brain at a competitor,' she said. 'Anyway, I wanted to share the good news this morning, before it's officially announced, so you can enjoy the day! So, off you go – celebrate!'

I left the office and went to Siglo, a small rooftop wine bar that overlooked Victorian Parliament, a short walk from the office. I ordered myself a bottle of champagne without even checking the price. Once again, I was sitting on a rooftop, drinking something that made my nose fizz, celebrating. Once again, I was on top of a city. And I'd never felt so flat.

I pulled out my phone and typed out a message to Matt. Then I deleted it. Instead, I opened a new document.

Things I NEED To Do
1. Plan wedding.

Chapter 34

It turned out miracles could happen. The rebuild of our venue finished the day before the wedding and our photographer's eyes had responded incredibly well to laser surgery. Even Belinda seemed chipper.

I don't think I'd ever looked better. My hair had been blown into submission, my skin was glowing with carefully calibrated fake tan and my makeup was flawless.

I did a slow walk through the venue and smiled – all our dreams had come to life. The tables were a riot of pastel-hued flowers, elegant tapers and menus, and place settings lettered with whimsical font. Even the phallic candles matched the dahlias. I walked outside to the courtyard where the ceremony would take place in an hour. A floral arch stood in front of the wall covered in ivy, ice buckets were filled with champagne. It was a perfect summer's day too – not too scorching for tuxedos but not too chilly for strappy dresses.

'Becs.' Stella joined me in the courtyard that soon would be teeming with friends and family. She looked gorgeous in her fuchsia bridesmaid's dress. She'd barely needed any concealer – Alice had slept like a dream since sleep school and Nick was pulling his weight at home. 'We've got a bit of a problem.'

'What's going on?' I asked. Normally, this phrase would have sent my heart racing and my stomach churning, but today I was all out of negative emotions. I knew that whatever happened, it would all be okay.

'Your dad just messaged Nick. He's caught up at work – he doesn't think he'll be able to make it.'

I stared at Stella for a moment.

That's fine, he would have been here if he could, sat on the edge of my tongue.

'Okay. I'm going to go … deal with that,' I said. 'Try not to start without me.'

I ordered an Uber to the hospital. As I clacked through the hospital lobby in my sky-high heels, I realised I didn't exactly fit in – but I guessed a gown was better than a leotard.

By the time I reached Dad's office, I was out of breath and my heels were rubbing.

'Dad, I need you to come with me,' I said as soon as I reached the door. Dad looked up from his laptop. He was in his surgical scrubs and cap. I didn't really care.

'I told Nick that I have to be here,' he said with an exasperated sigh.

'No, you don't,' I said. 'You're not on call. Someone else will look after your patients today.'

'Yes, but,' he began, in the voice I imagined he would have used on me as a toddler – if he'd ever been around when I was a toddler.

'No buts,' I said. 'You missed my dinner times, my bedtimes, my weekends, my holidays, my birthday celebrations, my tell-me-about-your-day excruciating conversations. You missed your marriage. You're not missing Mum's wedding.'

'I feel like your mum's wedding is the one thing I *can* miss,' he said, his eyes flashing beneath his salt and pepper eyebrows.

'No, you can't. Because Nick and I want you there. We … need you there,' I said. 'You gave your life to your work, Dad. But your time is up. The doctors you still consider to be junior are in the prime of their careers — they need you to mentor them, but also to give them space. There were some consultants at my old job—'

'Old job?' Dad said.

I'd resigned a few days after I'd been offered the promotion. Miranda had smiled when I'd told her my plans.

'This job gives me and my family more than it takes,' she'd said. 'But I wasn't sure that would be true for you. And I really hope that it won't be the case for your next chapter.'

'I don't think it will be,' I replied. 'Though your insight would have been helpful before I pursued a promotion single-mindedly.'

Miranda cackled. 'Oh, Bec,' she'd said. 'I didn't get this position by encouraging the people who make my life easier to jump ship! And, more importantly, I think people need to make their own decisions about when it's time to run towards something.'

'Yes, my old job,' I said to Dad. 'We can talk about it another time. My point is, there were consultants at my old firm who'd left the partnership but out of respect had been kept on as "advisors". And they came into the office most days because they had nowhere else to go. They worked so hard that they forgot to have a life.

'Dad, I need you to come to the wedding. It's important to Mum and to me and Nick. Stella, Nick and I are all in Mum's bridal party. You said you'd babysit Evie and Alice. Stella's parents aren't in town. None of their regular babysitters are available. You're it, Dad.'

Dad looked down at his desk for a moment. Did I imagine it or did his eyes rest on my photo frame?

'I'll need to get changed,' he said. I bit my lip so I wouldn't smile. I knew Dad would never say sorry. I wasn't sure that he would ever agree with how I saw his life. But right then, changing out of his scrubs was a start.

An hour later, the sunny courtyard was filled with extended family and friends.

I stood with Lily and Stella, soaking it all in as we each drank an illicit glass of champagne we'd convinced Lucy, who was walking around the venue with the proud energy of a celebrity giving an *Architectural Digest* tour, to sneak us. We'd spent the day together getting ready in matching satin pyjamas in a hotel room I'd booked months ago. We'd done each other's nails and eaten burgers and chips and laughed until the glue on our fake eyelashes had been endangered.

And we'd talked – properly talked. Because at some point, we'd stopped having real conversations. As we'd hit our thirties, we'd all decided that the only answer to the question, 'How are you?' had become, 'Good.' Which was the socially lubricating thing to do in nearly every context, but not with your best friends.

And I knew that things wouldn't always be good, that we were in the stage of life where it all was happening to us hard and fast – the times when things were good would be something to celebrate. We'd need each other, more than ever, for all the other bits.

'Your mum's going to arrive any moment!' Belinda, who'd snuck up on our group silently, interrupted our drink. I felt a flutter of anticipatory nerves in the bottom of my stomach. When I'd emailed Belinda to ask if she would mind doing one small extra piece of officiating, she'd immediately agreed. I liked to think that it was because I'd grown on her, but I think she was just grateful that Mum had prescribed her HRT. 'But before we begin the ceremony, Rebecca asked if I could read out the vows she wrote.'

Lily and Stella looked confused, but Belinda pressed on.

'Lily Li, Stella Evans and Rebecca Evans. We are gathered here today to celebrate over twenty years of friendship and love for one another. You met as girls and helped each other decide what you wanted from your lives ahead. Now you are adults living those lives.'

She looked up from the piece of stiff cardboard she'd been reading from and looked at each of us in turn as she continued to speak.

'And in my experience, it's the next twenty years where you'll need each other even more – it's when you get all the things you wanted, or you don't. When everything looks a bit different from how you thought it would.'

Belinda caught my eye. I hadn't written that line – that had been all her, from the road ahead. I smiled.

'So today I ask you to make these vows, with each other as your witnesses, for the next part of your lives together.

Do you Lily, Stella and Rebecca vow to be there for each other? Do you vow to be open with each other? Do you vow to encourage each other to jump and to be a safe place to fall? If so, please say, "I do."'

I snuck a glance at my best friends, who stood on either side of me, nervous that their faces would be incredulous or sceptical. But Stella looked moved and Lily was blinking, as if trying to furiously fight back tears.

'I do,' we all spoke in unison.

It had taken a bit of work to convince Mum and Hamish to have Matt's and my wedding. Finally Mum had admitted that they would have loved a proper party when they got married, but hadn't wanted to upset everyone.

In the end, it wasn't Nick and me telling Mum to go for it, and Caroline doing the same with Hamish, it was the idea of all the things we'd paid for going to waste that got them across the line. I'd transferred Matt the money for everything he'd spent on the wedding, and Mum didn't want my savings to go to waste.

'Matt wouldn't mind?' she'd asked. I shook my head. This was exactly the kind of Plan B that Matt would think of – he always chose the option that made people happy.

'Well … if it's just money going down the drain,' Mum agreed, her eyes bright with excitement.

I grinned as Mum crutched her way down the aisle. We'd bought her dress together – the brightest thing they sold in Zimmermann, and she'd confessed she'd hated the muted, age-appropriate dress she'd worn to her town hall ceremony with Hamish. Her wedding dress matched her rainbow cast.

Mum caught sight of Hamish, waiting for her at the end of the aisle, and her bright red lips cracked into an enormous smile. She'd never looked happier.

As Mum and Hamish clasped each other's hands, Alice began to wail. I could feel Stella about to move towards her daughter.

'Give it a sec?' I heard Nick whisper to Stella.

'Grandpa. She needs her nappy changed,' Evie said. 'She's done a big poopoo. Can't you smell it? You need to change it.' She looked like an angel in her flower girl dress but spoke with the commanding bark of an army officer.

'Do you know where the nappy bag is?' Dad asked, looking frazzled.

'Yes, I do,' Evie said with a dramatic sigh. 'You're a bit of a silly-billy, Grandpa. I'll show you.'

I had thought Mum couldn't look any happier than she had a few moments earlier, but it turned out she could. She was positively beaming. Alice had just given Mum the best wedding present she could have asked for: Dad was about to change a nappy for the first time in his life.

Belinda stood in front of the floral arch between Mum and Hamish. They were already married, so it wasn't a legal ceremony, but Belinda looked as though she meant business. I stood in between Stella and Caroline. The three of us wore our own dresses but matching diamond earrings, which Mum had given us at the small family rehearsal dinner.

'I had them made with the smallest stones from some old engagement rings I had lying around,' she'd said with a wink in my direction. 'I thought I'd save the bigger stones for the grandkids so they can have jewellery made one day. They might even want to use them for their engagement rings, maybe ...'

'Today, we are gathered here to celebrate the love of Helena and Hamish,' Belinda said.

I drifted off as Belinda pointed out the bathrooms and emergency exits and asked us not to take photos. I surveyed the room. Lily sat a few rows from the front, Aaron next to her, trying to keep Arlo – who thought that sitting was a ridiculous thing to do when he'd just learned to run – under control.

I'd emailed all our wedding guests to let them know that a different couple would be celebrated today, and of course they no longer had to come (along with an effusive apology about the last-minute change of plans). Most had messaged to say they wouldn't come, but of course Lily had still shown up. Her parents had joined us too.

I'd had a chat with them before the ceremony started.

'I hear you saved Lily's business,' Mrs Li said.

'No, actually, she saved herself.'

Mrs Li raised an eyebrow.

'Ask Lily to tell you the story,' I said. 'It's a good one.'

Lily and Aaron had agreed to pivot to an online business. And to shore up their finances, they also decided to sell some of their art. It turned out one of the paintings, which Lily had bought for a hundred dollars after spotting it on the artist's Instagram account, was now worth a gazillion dollars. The artist had become the darling of tech bros and B-list celebrities. Lily agreed to sell her painting for an eye-watering amount. It was a very Lily thing to happen. But I also wondered, was this just life? You made a plan and then things happened, so you changed your plan. The art form you loved lost you money. But the painting you bought with your eye trained by your master's degree subsidised it. In any event, I looked forward to hearing from Lily about her parents' reaction when they found out she'd made more from one painting than Mia made in years of lawyering.

A few rows behind them were Miranda and her husband sitting next to Lucas and Adrian. Lucas, in his usual effervescent style, had texted me: *I never met Matt, but I really like you. Also, free drinks!*

As Belinda read a poem about love (possibly self-authored given the many cat references) I saw Lucas rest his head on Adrian's shoulder. I smiled – another summer had passed and another couple had fallen in love.

I tuned back in to the ceremony for the vows.

'I've learned a lot about love in my lifetime,' Mum began. 'I've learned it can be intoxicating. It can be hopeful. It can be more than you ever hoped …' She turned to Nick and me and smiled. My heart felt like it might explode.

'It can be destructive. It can cause pain. It can feel safe and it can feel scary. It can cause joy and togetherness, like today. And love isn't just romantic love. It's your love for your kids, your grandkids, your friends, your work …' She paused, staring deeply into Hamish's eyes. I could tell the only thing he could see right then was Mum. They were good together, great together. They made each other happy.

I felt like my chest was constricting. I kept smiling because it was Mum's moment, but I couldn't hear anything she was saying. It was as if the DJ Matt and I had picked had turned down the volume on the track of Mum's vows, and flicked it up on another. The only thing I could hear were the vows that I'd written for today, for Matt – all the things I'd felt and never told him.

Nine years ago, I'd attended an academic lecture on love. I'd thought that life was something you could learn rather than experience. I'd believed that love was something dangerous, something that you could break down into concepts, to try to understand, to try to outsmart. As I watched Mum stand in front of a group of people and speak on the topic of love, I knew that love was something you had to feel. The thinking could come, should come, later. But the feeling had to come first.

Once Mum and Hamish were declared husband and wife (again), I threw rose petals and herded groups for photos with the bride and groom.

And then during the inevitable lull that fell between the cocktail hour and the first course, I ordered another Uber. I'd be back for the speeches, before anyone noticed I was missing. But right then, there was someone I needed to see.

Chapter 35

Jane looked a bit shocked to see me standing on her doorstep, and I felt a stab of guilt. This was the day when she was meant to be dressed up in her best raw-silk mother-of-the-groom outfit, surrounded by all her people, graciously accepting compliments about her son and her cake. Instead, she was home in her usual uniform of chinos and a crisp shirt. But she welcomed me warmly.

'I forgot to cancel our honeymoon,' I said.

'You don't normally forget things,' she said, raising an eyebrow.

'I don't,' I agreed. 'I think I didn't cancel it because I didn't want to cancel it. I wanted to spend more time with Matt. The rest of our lives, really. Because I think your son is the best person I've ever met. He's thoughtful and funny and caring. He's a lot like you,' I said. She smiled and I knew that she'd hear me out.

'But it's not just the big stuff, it's the little stuff too. The way he consumes culture like it's oxygen – watching every movie and TV show and listening to every podcast. That he loves good food and wine but isn't a snob about it at all. That he gives everyone the benefit of the doubt, always. He's just … everything about him is good. Even the bad stuff, like his wavering confidence and his inability to say no to an invitation ever and the fact he always turns the heating up too high … is good.

'And I know that there's every chance he's just trying to move on and never wants to see me again. But I also know how much he values your opinion. So, I wondered if you would ask him if … he'd come on our honeymoon? Not to honeymoon, obviously. But just to talk.'

She looked doubtful. 'He's pretty upset,' she said carefully.

'I know,' I said. 'I promise I don't want to hurt him. I just want to have the chance to talk. If he wants to. I'd really like the chance to explain myself and apologise. But I'll understand if he doesn't want to see me.'

'And it *has* to be at a tropical resort?' she asked.

'It doesn't have to be, but it's neutral territory. That's been paid for already,' I said. 'And could you please give him this?' I handed Jane a printout of the vows I'd written for our wedding. I'd been agonising over what to say to Matt. Except I'd realised during Mum and Hamish's ceremony that I'd already put into words everything that I wanted to say to him.

'And I also brought this,' I barrelled on, knowing that once I handed over what I'd brought with me I might lose some goodwill. I'd ducked by Mum's house en route and picked up something I'd had made up a few weeks earlier.

Jane pulled the frame out of the supermarket plastic bag – it was a photo of Matt giving a speech at an industry convention. He was in full flight, spotlights glinting off his hair and glasses, arms outstretched as he spoke to the audience. 'I thought you might want it for above the piano, maybe?'

Jane held the photo between her hands and for a moment, her brow furrowed. Then she finally looked up and smiled.

'I think it would look very nice there,' she said. 'I'll talk to him.'

'So, you've booked the honeymoon suite and a standard room … for two people?' The receptionist in her floral-print uniform looked at me, justifiably confused.

'That's right. Could I please have the key to the standard room?' I asked. 'And could you hang on to the key to the suite for the other person on the booking? I'm not sure if they're going to make it.'

'Of course,' she said, slipping her professional mask back on.

'And just one more thing. Could you leave this note in the room, please?' I asked. I handed over a letter I'd written many, many times over the night before, even though it was only a dinner invitation and a few sentences long.

I spent all afternoon getting ready. I let my hair dry naturally, but I spent ages mucking around with makeup and choosing which light summery dress to wear. In the end I went with a new one in a shade of green that I wasn't sure suited me, but that I loved.

Finally, I left my room and wound my way through the sprawling golf course to the hotel's restaurant. Even though the sun was setting, it was still hot and humid. The air smelled liked the sea – I could hear waves pounding onto the shore in the distance – with a hint of smoke from the cane fires burning in the mountains.

As I reached the threshold of the restaurant, I took a deep breath. If I was going to eat alone, that was okay. I was going to order a drink, just one. And then a main course and maybe dessert.

I was led to the table I'd booked.

'You're the first of your party to arrive,' the waitress informed me. 'Can I get you a drink while you wait?'

'Yes, please. A martini. Oh' – I glanced at the menu – 'and a Tropical Princess.'

As soon as she left, I pulled the book I'd brought out of my bag. I'd left my phone in my room because I didn't want to be distracted by messages from people ostensibly making sure I was okay about the cancelled wedding but really angling for all the juicy details. Or colleagues replying to my farewell email. Or from my family, who were very actively sharing photos from the wedding on our group chat. Or from Dad, who was attempting a new communication style (communicating).

'Oh, that was quick.' I looked up to thank the waitress, but it was Matt. The book had worked too well – I'd been so engrossed that I'd forgotten that I was a nervous wreck.

'Matt. You came!' I said. I stood up so quickly that my chair fell backwards. I'd planned to try to be calm and composed but had failed at the first hurdle.

'Mum told me that if I didn't, I was getting a packet-mix cake for my next birthday,' he said with a small smile.

The waitress appeared next to Matt with a tray as I reset my chair. She placed the pale pink long glass in front of me and the martini in front of Matt's seat. I switched them around as soon as she left.

'Will you sit?' I asked. He hesitated.

'What are you reading?' he asked instead.

'Umm … It's an exam practice book,' I said. 'I'm going to sit the GAMSAT in a few months. See if I can get into grad med. I have to get some extra science credits but—'

'You'll get in,' he said, as he pulled out his chair and sat down. I exhaled. 'You'll be a great doctor.'

'I've quit my job, but don't worry – I'm still going to do some contract consulting work while I'm studying,' I said quickly. 'So I can cover my portion of the rent until we sublet it or the lease ends or whatever.'

'Did you fly all the way up here to talk about our rent?' Matt asked.

'No,' I said. 'I just want to … talk.'

'Okay,' he said. He picked up his drink and took a small sip. 'I like your hair like that.'

I lifted my hands to my head and tucked a stray natural curl behind my ear.

'I love you,' I blurted. Nerves washed over me again as I launched into the speech I'd prepared. 'You were right. I never let myself properly love you. In the beginning I did date you because I thought that the type of love that I could feel for you would be contained and controllable and safe. Except I didn't realise that that was the best type of love.

'You became my best friend. And the person I was most attracted to. And your proposal became the best moment of my life. And you became the fiancé I couldn't live without.

'And I think I realised, maybe on a subconscious level, that I'd done something dangerous – I'd fallen madly in love with the guy I was going to marry. And I got anxious about the absence of anxiety I felt when I was with you. So

I did some extreme mental gymnastics to try to protect my heart. I became obsessed with a family curse that was never anything except a joke. And I let myself get carried away with memories of a relationship with an ex-boyfriend who, by the way, is now on the other side of the world.'

A parcel had arrived at the office, a few days before the date of our wedding, addressed to me and Matt. Inside was a folded piece of A4 paper with a note scrawled across it: *A wedding present for a wedding I hope happens. Alex.* Inside was a pair of porcelain figurines: a wolf with a veil and a dog in a tux.

'I was so scared of the feelings I had for you, so I sabotaged us. I didn't know I was doing it, but I was. And I am so sorry for making you feel like you were the safe choice, or the second choice. Because that's just … not true. You were my only choice – and my scared heart and protective brain made you the dangerous option.

'I've been doing a lot of thinking over the past few weeks and I've realised that the brain can't give you what the heart wants. I don't think I got to decide to fall in love with you. But I think I get to choose *how* I love you.

'And if you let me love you again, I want you to feel chosen, safe and like you're my everything …' I trailed off.

'I love you too,' Matt said. 'It's never been that complicated for me. But the last few weeks have been hell. Breaking up with you, cancelling the wedding – it's been the worst time of my life.'

'I know,' I said. 'And I am so, so sorry that I put you in the position where you had to break up with me.' I pulled a green ring box out of my bag and pushed it towards him. Inside was the ring he'd given me.

'I don't want it back,' he said. 'I gave it to you, it's yours.'

'I'm not giving it back. I'm asking you to not marry me,' I said. He raised a quizzical eyebrow at me.

'Instead, I'm asking you for a second chance to go on a first date. With me. Tonight. And then, if that goes well, maybe we could go on another one tomorrow? And I thought that maybe we could talk about all the things — what we want to do with our lives and how ridiculous our families are and how we'd do a better job raising kids and about our uni days and exes and also about the weather and whether it might rain and what we feel like for dinner and what names we might call our future children.'

He stared at me for a moment. Then the crinkle in his left cheek appeared and before he'd even smiled, my heart felt light for the first time since the wedding had been called off.

'Are we getting entrees and mains?' he finally asked.

'It's a second first date. I think we should go all out,' I said, grinning. 'And there's a cinema at the hotel. I've booked it for after — I mean, we don't have to, just if you want to?'

'That could be perfect for a second first kiss,' he said. He smiled and his dark eyes twinkled at me behind his glasses. And I felt safe, in the best way. And I knew that I would spend my whole life making sure that he felt the same.

Although it was a habit I wanted to break, I couldn't help but cross an item off my mental to-do list: 'Let myself love Matt.'

Acknowledgements

This book is about the head versus the heart, and I've been so lucky to be surrounded by people with both enormous brains and hearts.

Thank you to the team at HarperCollins. Anna Valdinger for giving me my first and second chance and for being the most supportive, brilliant publisher. Rachel Cramp, who is the smartest of smart girls/editors, and also so fun to work with – your editorial comments are the best type of conversation. To Pamela Dunne for such a thoughtful proofread. To Maya Abraham for the gorgeous and fun cover. To Taylah Massingham and Caitlin Toohey for all their marketing and publicity brilliance. And to everyone at HarperCollins who helped to bring this book to life.

To the amazing team at Georgina Capel Associates, Polly Halladay and Simon Shaps. Talking with you about this story has been my favourite work meeting to date.

To Kate O'Donnell for her always insightful feedback and advice.

To all the booksellers, librarians and bookstagrammers who read and promoted *The Love Contract* – I am beyond grateful for your support. With special thanks to Stuart Henshall and Jacqui Furlong.

To Greg Basser and Claire Desmond for their wisdom.

To the Australian writers I've been so lucky to make friends with.

To my generous friends who've answered random questions and listened to me bang on about this story, with special thanks to Millsy Clifford, Alli Parker and Josh Fisher for their feedback.

Part of this story is set in Oxford. Thank you to The Hive – Lucy, India, Jack, Jack, Jack, James, James and Sam – who were Oxford to me (even when my attention should have been on 'Beowulf'). And to Tiffany, Laura and Nick, who took a chance on an Australian girl who'd never read a poem.

Thank you to the Vizard family, whose creativity and energy are an inspiration – Tom and Holly, Mad and Zak, Jim and Immy, Liv and Darcy. And, as always, to the Griffiths family.

To Mum and Dad for always encouraging me to follow my dreams.

To Hugh. And Poppy and Teddy. I love writing happily-ever-afters – I know how wonderful they can be because of you.

And to you, the reader. Watching my kids learn to love books has reinforced how magical escaping into other worlds is. I am so grateful that you chose to spend your time in this one.

About the Author

STEPH VIZARD is an Australian writer and lawyer. After studying literature at Oxford University, she worked in publishing in London. Her debut romantic comedy, The Love Contract, won the 2022 HarperCollins Banjo Prize and has been optioned for a TV series by a major UK production company. She is a connoisseur of salt and vinegar chips and lives with her family in Melbourne.

Can she (pretend to) love her neighbour?

Great Stories Uncovered

Winner
Banjo Prize
for Fiction

The Love Contract

STEPH VIZARD

Discover more romance from Steph Vizard

I didn't know the guy next door. And given he was now my daughter's manny and my fake boyfriend, I needed to find out.

Single mum Zoe had the parenting thing all figured out with little Hazel until a childcare drought derailed her plans to return to work. Enter Will, Zoe's nemesis and frustratingly handsome neighbour. When Will's boss mistakenly assumes Will is Hazel's father and insists he take parental leave, it seems like a simple white lie could get Zoe out of a jam and help Will to make partner at his law firm.

But life with an adorable toddler – and a growing attraction between Will and Zoe – is never as tidy as their agreement's bullet points and dry clauses suggest. As they get deeper into the lie, the lines between truth and fiction blur. But Zoe's hiding a secret and when it comes out, the consequences for all of them could be devastating.

Available to buy now

Stories to fall in love with.

Aria

Thanks for reading!

Want to receive exclusive author content,
news on the latest Aria books and updates
on offers and giveaways?

Follow us on X @AriaFiction and on
Facebook and Instagram @HeadofZeus,
and join our mailing list.